Cece Wainwright's Christmas Wish

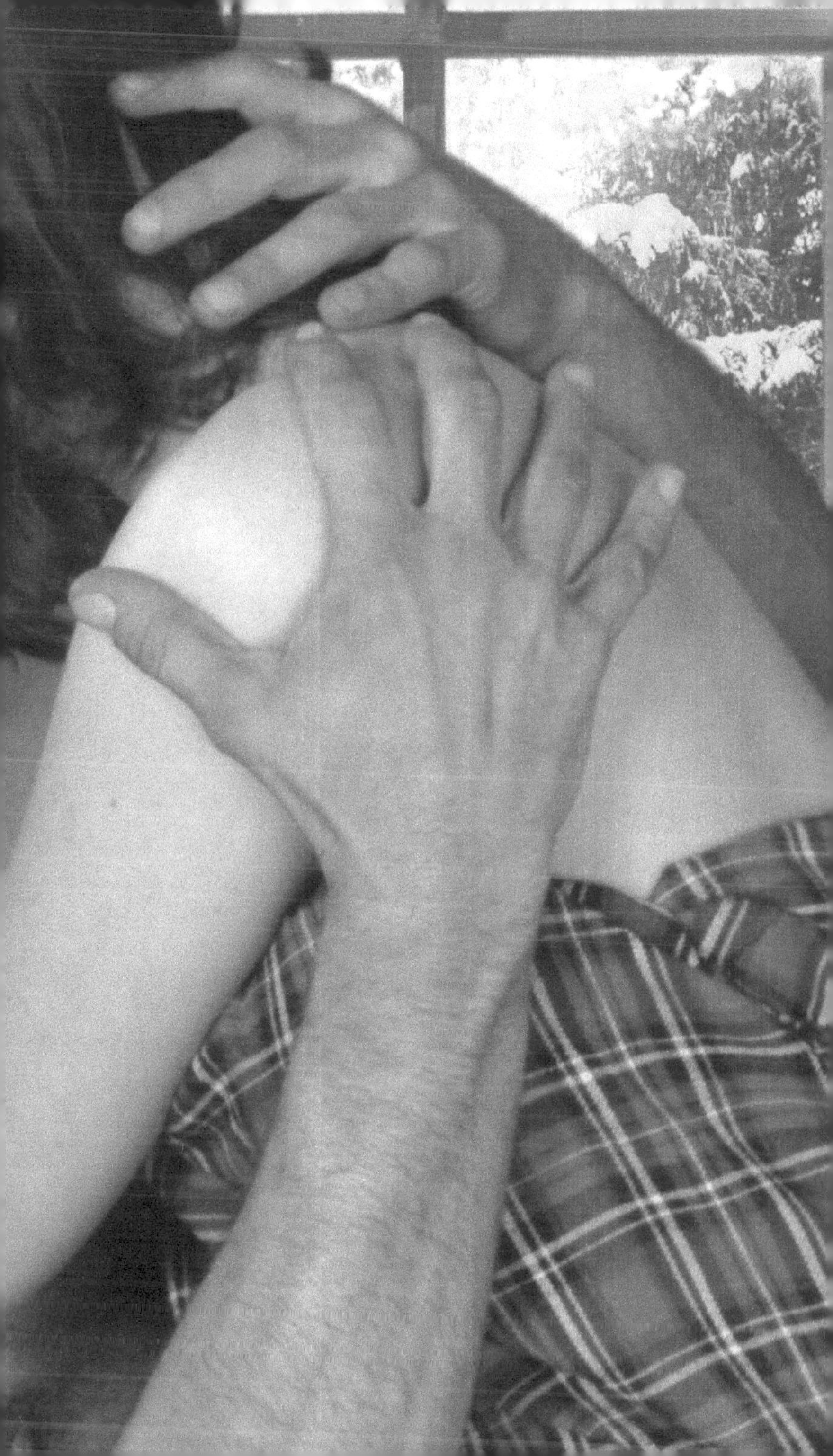

Sometimes we all want to hide in the shadows and watch from the fringes because it feels like it's a reflection of who we are at that time. Don't let the shadows swallow you, let them shape you. Emerging on the other side of the journey makes you stronger, brighter and fiercer. Without your sorrow and your trials, you wouldn't be you and the only way to truly understand and appreciate joy is to feel its absence. I hope you find your joy.

Cece Wainwright's Christmas Wish, by Andrea Jenelle, First edition, 2024.

This is a work of fiction. Names, characters, places, and incidents are products of the author's imagination or are used fictitiously and are not to be construed as real. Any resemblance to actual events, locales, organizations, or persons, living or dead, is entirely coincidental.

Print ISBN: 978-1-962123-35-8

Digital ISBN: 978-1-962123-30-3

Contents

Prologue   1

1. Chapter One   5

2. Chapter Two   25

3. Chapter Three   34

4. Chapter Four   45

5. Chapter Five   54

6. Chapter Six   66

7. Chapter Seven   77

8. Chapter Eight   91

9. Chapter Nine   99

10. Chapter Ten   114

11. Chapter Eleven   122

12. Chapter Twelve   131

13. Chapter Thirteen   145

14. Chapter Fourteen   151

15. Chapter Fifteen   154

16. Chapter Sixteen   165

17. Chapter Seventeen   171

18. Chapter Eighteen   179

19. Chapter Nineteen   189

20. Chapter Twenty   199

21. Chapter Twenty-One   209

22. Chapter Twenty-Two   226

23. Chapter Twenty-Three   236

24. Chapter Twenty-Four   244

25. Chapter Twenty-Five   258

26. Chapter Twenty-Six   274

27. Chapter Twenty-Seven   278

28. Chapter Twenty-Eight   289

29. Chapter Twenty-Nine   303

30. Chapter Thirty   312

31. Epilogue   323

Note to Readers   327

Acknowledgements   330

About the author   332

Prologue

Cumbria, Northwestern England, late Autumn, 1862.

Letter dated July 20, 1853.

Dearest Husband, I must ask, Henry, why have you come up with a new nickname for me? And why liken me to a drab creature like the little brown bird that flits amidst the hedges? Your reasoning escapes me, and I think I should be offended.

CECE HADN'T MEANT TO keep secrets from her sisters. Though she sometimes felt like the glue that held them all together, the one who was always ready with a handkerchief for tears or a cup of tea for confessions, she didn't know how to share her doubts with them. She was the youngest, but had known the most heartbreak. They were so convinced she'd had a fairytale that was cruelly wrenched from her grasp, she didn't know how to be anyone but that tragic heroine. Like Catherine of *Wuthering Heights* or Jane before she found her happy ending with Rochester.

She couldn't bear to tell them the letters had never sounded like Henry to her.

Her sisters all sighed about her grand love story that had ended in tragedy. About the way she'd been swept off her feet in a whirlwind romance, kissed her soldier farewell three weeks later and faithfully corresponded with her beloved until he'd fallen at Balaclava.

Her sisters were especially maudlin when they'd had a little too much whisky.

When liquor was sloshing through their veins they fixated on the pile of letters stacked beside the sewing basket in her room. They'd all read some of the more romantic declarations aloud so many times, they knew them by heart. Just as Cece did.

They lamented that her brave soldier might be gone, but she had lasting, unerring, irrefutable proof of his devotion to keep her warm.

They wouldn't understand her doubts and she didn't want to puncture their grand illusion.

The truth was, Cece had never been entirely convinced the letters were proof of Henry's devotion.

Her first clue was the penmanship. It wasn't atrocious. It was sharp and clean. And Henry's penmanship had been atrocious. Like that of a four-year-old who'd never properly learnt the manner of holding a writing utensil. And that stack of letters had line after line of flawless, concise penmanship.

Those letters had other things too that had never rung true of Henry. They contained little bits of philosophy and poetry smashed in the middle of all those neat stacks of concise words. Like delicious bits of jam.

Henry had been blustering and brave and beautiful. But he'd never been the least bit philosophical or poetic. Every time Cece had broached the subject of Plato or Marcus Aurelius, or even Shakespeare, Henry had gotten an irritated look on his face and distracted her. Usually with kisses.

Cece stared at the bundle of letters secured by the tattered hair ribbon. It had been the first token Henry had given her. He'd said the blue matched her eyes.

There was now another bundle of letters stacked beside it. Secured by a crisp, plaid ribbon. It had arrived that morning and Cece recognized her own handwriting.

The arrival of the letters had unleashed something she'd been pushing down and ignoring. They had been the catalyst for her to acknowledge it was finally time to put aside her black wardrobe.

Henry had died at Balaclava, during the battle made so famous by her favorite poet. That had been a little over eight years ago, in the fall of 1854. The war had ended not quite a year later, in 1855, and the years had crept slowly by as she watched from the wings.

Cece had been green with jealousy over Arie and Fran's newfound happiness. Of the time they'd been granted to spend with their husbands. Both men had served in the war, but come home alive, if not completely sound. Her sisters had told her their husbands had nightmares about the things they'd seen and experienced, and both had returned more scarred and less sound than they'd been before they left for the Crimea. Cece had wanted to shout at least they'd come home. At least Arie and Fran hadn't been stuck in a corner to rot, as if they'd died with their husbands, while their life became smaller every year. She wanted to shout that at least her sisters had the hope of a family of their own. Cece's womb hadn't quickened with child in the three weeks she'd spent with Henry before he left. And he'd died before they'd had the chance to try again.

Chapter One

Cece

Letter dated August 15, 1853

Dearest Little Wren. Why have I decided to call you my little wren? I suspected you'd be outraged when you read it. Oh ye of little faith. Allow me to redeem myself. I've decided you are my little wren because everyone seems to think of wrens as these drab, boring, nondescript brown creatures. You are none of those things – that's not why you remind me of one. You are my little wren because wrens build hearths and homes. They're fierce – like that

bit from Shakespeare you're always quoting at me. They're quietly beautiful, like you.

C ECE KNEW WEARING BLACK said things about her. Told a story everyone who saw her thought they knew in its entirety.

That she would prefer to sit in the corner, a cup of tea in hand instead of punch or ratafia. That she was content to watch everyone else dance and only tapped her foot to help keep the rhythm of the reel.

That she was convinced the best part of her life lay behind her. That she was reconciled to that realization.

That she was full of sorrow, not joy.

As she knelt in front of the chest and laid the bundle of somber clothing inside it, she breathed a sigh of relief.

It was time to let go of the black and tell a different story.

For at least the forty-seventh time since she'd received the stack of letters, Cece ran her fingers over the faded ink. As if she could summon the truth from them.

She'd met Henry at the village fair on the most golden of summer days. A day so bright the sun glinting through the lock of hair draped rakishly over his brow cast a halo over his face.

His laughing blue eyes had met hers, his cheeks covered in pastry and sprinkled in cinnamon, and she'd tumbled head over heels in love.

He'd taken the three pence he'd won in the pie-eating contest and purchased the blue ribbon.

The ribbon was faded now, more of a grayish periwinkle than the brilliant color that had matched his eyes. That he'd said matched hers.

When she thought about her first love now, it was with fondness. Like a kitten she had briefly cuddled in her lap, or the first time Arie had shown her how to bake proper scones. As the years passed and his family shared stories about him, she realized she hadn't really known her husband at all. The tumultuous whirlwind of their courtship, and the brief three weeks they'd spent together before he left with his regiment, seemed like a faraway dream.

She'd been an innocent, and when he pulled her into his arms he'd tasted like fresh-baked apples. He'd quite literally swept her off her feet.

When she'd received the packet, it had jolted her from complacency. Like sitting on a discarded embroidery needle. (This happened quite often in the Wainwright household because her twin sisters Lavinia and Emily were easily distracted and left them lying everywhere.)

She knew what she wanted to do. She wanted to make her way to the remote corner of Scotland the letters had been dispatched from and demand answers. She was convinced this was a rational endeavor, but suspected her sisters wouldn't agree with her.

The faint prick of megrim at her temples meant it was time to seek out tea and abandon her contemplation. The small sitting room in their two-bedroom cottage was where she and her sisters congregated in the evenings.

It was a cold, dreary day and Cece wanted to immediately plop into the overstuffed armchair with the errant spring and contemplate the flames beside her sister. But before she could surrender to that comfort, she needed a bracing cup of tea.

Jess was already ensconced in the sitting room, and the welcome aroma of a strong Darjeeling steamed faintly from the pot beside her. Cece was relieved. Jess was the most deliberative Wainwright sister. She was forever poring over scientific journals and would give Cece's impulsive decision grave consideration.

"Please tell me you haven't emptied the teapot," Cece said as she entered the room.

Jess jerked at her intrusion and sloshed hot tea onto her wrist. It was a very un-Jesslike reaction and Cece wondered why her usually pragmatic sister was so lost in daydreams.

"Why must you creep about like a mouse in want of cheese?" Jess sharply asked.

Jess's irritable outburst was another anomaly. Normally, she was like one of those ships whose sails were seldom ruffled. Cece suspected prying frogs and other slimy, crawly things away from students bent on mischief had made her more stalwart than the rest of the Wainwright sisters.

"Shall I fetch a bit of ice from the cellar?" Cece asked.

Jess sighed and patted her wrist with the edge of the tea towel. "No, I didn't burn myself. You simply startled me from my musings."

"I've been musing too." Cece confided as she poured a cup. She set the saucer over the rim to allow the tea to steep, placed it on the side table and flopped into the lumpy paisley chair that had borne witness to many a Wainwright sister's unburdening. "I need your advice."

Jess's eyes flashed to hers. "My advice?"

"Yes. You know you and Emily are the only Wainwright women within reach who will give me reasonable counsel." She took a deep breath and plunged ahead. "The postman delivered something to me three days ago I never expected to see again."

"Some of Henry's effects? The packet they sent you when he died was so meager. Are you debating whether you should send something to his family?"

"No, not his effects. My letters to him. I thought they'd been lost. But they arrived earlier this week."

"Who sent them?"

"I haven't the slightest idea. But there's a return address. I want to go there and find out who sent them and why."

Jess wrinkled her brow. "Can you not simply post a letter in return and ask those questions?"

Cece shook her head. "I've no guarantee of an answer. The packet wasn't signed and had no accompanying correspondence. That leads me to believe the sender wished to preserve their anonymity. It makes me even more determined to unravel the mystery."

What Cece wouldn't tell her sister was that she needed an adventure as much as she needed answers. Something to occupy her mind besides intricate needlework. Something to reinvigorate her curiosity and zest for life.

Every day, she felt her youth and vitality inexorably slipping away. Like the widow's weeds she'd finally put away a few days ago had left an indelible shadow on her soul. Like all her hope for joy had been buried with her husband.

She gazed at the faded rose wallpaper. According to her eldest sister Arie, the cozy wallpapered parlor had been their mother's pride and joy. It was still cozy, but it had long since lost its luster. It was now a drab, if yet genteel, reminder of the way the fortunes of their family had been cast down by the whims of fate.

"Cece, you must know that such a journey would be quite the undertaking. At least you have plenty of time to plan a trip and find a companion."

Cece pondered how much of her impulsive decision she should reveal as she stirred milk into her cup. "It would be an undertaking. But not necessarily a laborious one. I've always wanted to take the train. And I have some funds I've been saving. I think this is what I was saving them for. I'll be going alone and leaving at the beginning of next week. I'm purchasing my fare tomorrow morning."

"And where exactly will this train be taking you?"

"To Scotland."

"Scotland? All by yourself!?"

"Why not? I'm a widow. I don't need a chaperone or a companion and there is no scandal in it. I'll just don my black again. Like armor."

"I think you're being rash."

"I've never been rash."

Jess raised a brow.

"Yes, fine. But I've only indulged in rash behavior once in my life. We were sweethearts and he was leaving for the Crimea. I wanted to marry him."

"You didn't even have the banns read. You're lucky an exception was made because he was leaving for war."

"And you've never been rash?"

"Once. Very recently. And it's had disastrous consequences."

"Is that why your tea has gone cold?"

"Yes. I'm trying to decide how to rectify the situation."

"Does the situation involve a certain former mine owner who takes entirely too much notice of your school?"

Jess sighed audibly. "Yes. I dared ask him for the return of the microscope."

"And?"

"He'll not return it unless I agree to a completely unsatisfactory proposal." Jess explained with no little amount of consternation.

"Do you feel like discussing this audacious proposal?"

"No. I'm not going to accept it. I'd much rather talk about your situation."

"I feel like my life is at a standstill. Especially since Fran and Arie's marriages."

Jess tapped her chin. "I don't think hieing off to Scotland is the answer. It's a harebrained scheme and you'll likely come to ruin."

"I'm beginning to think coming to ruin might not be such a bad thing. At least it wouldn't be boring."

"You said there was a return address on the packet, but no accompanying explanation?"

"No. I've no inkling why I've just now received them or who sent them."

"Perhaps whoever sent them has good reason to remain anonymous. What if this madcap journey has unsettling results?"

"If that is their wish, they should have provided at least a perfunctory missive. Perhaps then I wouldn't be tempted to seek answers. If they want me to forget about their involvement after I receive an explanation, I'll oblige them."

"I think you should leave well enough alone."

"Why are you so convinced my scheme is ill-conceived?"

Jess gave her an arch look over the rim of her teacup. "Cece, people keep secrets for a reason. Because they want them to remain secrets. And what if this is nothing more than a wild goose chase? Or a hidden scandal you'll wish you'd left buried?"

Cece had secrets of her own she'd kept for years. She was tired of keeping them and she wanted her suspicions either dismissed or confirmed. She cared not which, but it was impossible to move on with her life until she received answers. She needed to know if her husband had held as much affection for her as she had for him. If she'd given her tender young heart in vain. If she was truly his Little Wren. "I feel compelled to go. Even if it turns out to be a wild goose chase."

Jess rose, set her tea on the sideboard, and knelt at Cece's feet. Her gaze was earnest and her clasp on Cece's hands was tight. "We worry for you. You seem so morose of late. Even more inclined to melancholy than when you received the notice of his death. I think revisiting the sorrow of that time will bring you anything but peace."

Cece didn't have the words to explain the depths of her loneliness to her unwed sister. She was worried she would sound ungrateful when she'd at least once had the hope of someone to stroke the gray hairs from her brow. But she was lonely. She grew lonelier with each passing day.

"I need something to break up the monotony I've been mired in the last six months. And I have so many questions about Henry's last days and hours that weren't conveyed in his letters. I've begun to cherish this silly hope that whoever was holding the letters can answer those questions."

And lay to rest her doubts about their authorship.

"If you're so set on this course, we'll not try and dissuade you. But you will take whatever resources we can scrape together and spare."

"As I said, I've saved up some of my coin from the handmade lace I've been providing the dressmaker. I have enough of a nest egg to cover my fare, although I wouldn't turn aside some oatcakes for the journey."

"You'll have so many you'll grow weary of them."

"Just enough for a week's journey."

Jess's face brightened. "I hoped your journey wouldn't curtail your participation in the holiday festivities."

"Are they more robust than they were last year?" Last year's festivities had coincided with one of the coldest Decembers on record. Jess had organized caroling, a student pageant that told the story of the nativity, community dinners and knitting parties and all sorts of other excursions and endeavors designed to ensure no one was chilly or alone.

"We have two sisters wed now, and our first niece. Arie and Thad have invited all of us, including Fran and Mac, to the farm for a feast on Christmas Day. And I have special events planned I'd love to have your assistance with."

"I plan on returning home well in advance of the season. I wouldn't miss it."

"What wouldn't you miss?" Their sister Lavinia entered the room, flopped onto the settee beside Jess, and began wringing water from her skirt.

Cece glared at her sister. "Vin, I mopped the floor yesterday and you're tracking muddy water all over it."

Vin was so entranced by her potions and concoctions she often lost track of what it meant to be considerate of her sisters and their shared space.

Vin grimaced. "I'm sorry. The rain today is terrible and all I could think about on my scurry home was a warm fire and a cup of tea. Please tell me they aren't the same leaves we used yesterday."

"You should have wrung your skirts out by the front door." Jess admonished.

"Don't be cross, Cece. I promise I'll mop up tomorrow after my half-day." She tipped her chin toward them. "Now. Tell me what you were discussing."

Jess wrinkled her brow. "Cece has come to a rather momentous decision."

"She's been immovable from her little nest. Just like the wren Henry used to call her. Whatever decision she's made it must be better than letting the cobwebs and mildew settle around you like a mantle."

Cece crossed her arms. "Cobwebs and mildew? I am offended."

Vin waved a hand and visibly shivered. "You've just recently set aside all those horrid black dresses. You need an infusion of something that will jolt you from complacency, little sister."

"She'll be resurrecting those dresses you despise so immensely." Jess informed her.

Her brash sister flung herself back against the cushions and groaned. "Truly? Why? I was finally able to forget your looming crow-likeness and you're going to adopt it yet again?"

"I am taking a journey by myself, and widow's weeds will protect me from questions and the need for a chaperone."

"A journey? Where? You've never left the parish. Not even after your wedding."

"I received a mysterious packet from Scotland, and I want to find out who sent it and why."

Vin leaned forward with bright eyes. "A mysterious packet? It's like something plucked from one of Gert's lurid novels."

"The letters I wrote Henry, that I thought had been lost, were returned to me."

"Who sent them?" Vin's gaze glowed with insatiable curiosity.

"I don't know. I only have an address on Dunkirk Lane in a small hamlet on the outskirts of Galashiels."

"You're going on an adventure." Vin leaned back and narrowed her gaze. "What if you find something you never expected? I want you to abandon your complacency, but this isn't like you. You're leaping from dead ashes right into the hottest part of the fire."

Cece twisted her hands in her lap. "I can't stay here forever. It feels smaller every day. I feel smaller every day."

"I know you've felt life passing you by. We all have. Ever since Arie and Fran's marriages. They both found wedded bliss against all odds and now we all feel restless. But perhaps you should send a letter of inquiry first?"

"Hah!" Jess exclaimed. "That's the advice I gave her as well."

"You've never been on a coach ride that long. You always became too queasy to go further than the edge of the village. How will you get there?"

Cece blinked at her sister's challenge. "I intend to purchase a railway ticket."

Vin exploded into raucous laughter, clutching her stomach.

Cece knew her sisters expected her to stay close to home, like she always had. But she was ready for something different. "I don't know what you find so amusing."

Vin gave her an impish grin. "We all know you can barely survive a coach ride to church. How do you intend to manage boarding a train?"

"I'll occupy myself with needlepoint and pull the blinds, so I'm not tempted to look out the window. All the advertisements say riding the rail feels like you're not moving at all."

"Cece don't be obtuse. They're advertisements. Of course, they're going to make it sound like the most relaxing experience ever. You'll have to go on an empty stomach and take a flask with you."

"I'm not taking a flask. How will I find my way around if I'm tipsy when I arrive? That's a terrible solution."

Vin sighed. "I was only teasing. I'll brew an infusion of chamomile and ginger to settle your stomach. You should avoid eating though."

"I agree. I'm certain I'll lose the contents of my stomach."

This time all three of them heard the ricochet of the front door in the frame as the wind caught it. "Emily," they chimed in unison.

She strode into the room as if she'd been summoned. "I've spent the day trying to nab the hairpin thief. It's the most frustrating case I've had yet. Please tell me there's still tea in that pot."

The latest rash of petty larceny in the village had begun with the disappearance of Millicent Pettigrew's jeweled hairpins at the last assembly. They were her prized possession and she'd engaged Emily to help her find the culprit.

Emily was dressed in one of their father's old shirts, tucked into a pair of trousers. Her shoulder length hair was stuffed underneath a wide brimmed straw hat she yanked off and placed on the arm of the settee. It wobbled precariously before tumbling to the floor. She'd darkened the divot above her mouth with something. Cece assumed it was meant to be a mustache, but it bore more than a passing resemblance to one of the woolly caterpillars that congregated on the stoop every midsummer.

Cece was glad of the interruption. Emily's latest outlandish disguise would distract her sisters from needling her.

"You look like the boy that prods the cattle through the marketplace."

At least Vin's ridicule wasn't reserved exclusively for Cece.

Emily pulled a voluminous handkerchief from her pocket and swiped it across her upper lip. She frowned at the pristine cloth afterward.

"What did you use, sister? What if you must attend church with that absurd attempt at facsimile?"

Emily shrugged. "So long as this ridiculous disguise nabs the hairpin bandit, I do not care. It's the first case I shall receive remuneration for."

"Leave her alone, Vin. At least she's not abandoning us during the holidays for some madcap, impossible mission."

Emily's eyes widened. "Surely our youngest sister is not the object of your censure?"

Cece was cheerful and well-behaved. She didn't rock boats or thwart expectations. She supposed her sister's astonishment at her sudden rebellion was to be expected.

Fran had felt similarly confined, and she knew she would have had at least one sympathizer if she weren't ensconced in London with her new husband.

She folded her hands in her lap. "Yes, I am the object of Jess and Vin's censure."

Emily narrowed her gaze and Cece quelled the urge to squirm beneath it. Emily's powers of observation were uncanny, and Cece feared what her countenance would reveal. "Are you unhappy, Little Sister?"

Emily's query wasn't meant to be a castigation like Vin's had been. She was curious, and perhaps sympathetic.

"I am content, but I am not happy. Is there a word to describe that state of being in-between that I find myself settling into?"

"None other than discontented." Emily turned to Vin and Jess. "Is she not permitted to question the wheel rut of expectation and duty she has fallen into?"

"Well, it's not that we aren't sympathetic of her situation." Jess spluttered somewhat indignantly.

"No, it's that she has no idea what the world is truly like outside the borders of this village. Letting her go would be like setting a babe free to wander in the woods."

Emily shook her head and crossed her arms. Now her gaze was narrowed in Vin's direction. "A babe in the woods? She's the only one of us besides Arie and Fran who attempted to make a life for herself beyond the walls of this cottage. She's a widow and a woman grown. Not some guileless infant."

"Traveling in a conveyance makes her exceedingly nauseous."

"There are ways to counteract her tendency to empty her stomach. Our urge to shelter her because she's the youngest should not cloud our perspective."

"She knows too little of the world to make such a journey on her own." Jess insisted.

Cece could see Emily's answering glower from across the room.

"You are both patronizing her. We have all raised one another. Because Cece and I are the youngest, you tend to forget that we have crafted the armor to forge our way in this life just as you have."

"Stop comparing your experience to hers." Vin scoffed. "At least you've been to Manchester and London. Cece has never been anywhere."

"And that is precisely the reason she needs this adventure. We should be happy for her and cheering her on instead of persuading her it's against her best interest to go."

Cece hadn't expected solidarity from Emily. "Thank you for rallying to my cause, Emily." She turned to Vin & Jess. "As for the two of you, I'll not allow your misgivings to dissuade me. My course is determined, and I will not be thwarted by your doubts."

"We only seek to protect you." Vin huffed.

"That may well be the case. But I am not the fresh-faced innocent I was when Henry died. I assure you; my sensibilities are no longer delicate. I can muster the courage to endure a solitary train ride – no matter how much it discomforts me."

Jess gave her a thoughtful look. "I agree, you are no longer naïve. But you are determined to set off for parts unknown, to a place with no familiar faces. What happens if you find yourself in some sort of distress?"

"Jess, she's not like the rest of us," Vin said. "Trouble won't find her like it does us."

"It may not find her," Emily agreed. "But what if it does? She needs to have solutions mapped out. Or an escape route."

Cece had grown weary of them speaking of her as if she were sitting in another room. "I'm right here. Stop speaking over my head. I'll make certain I have the coin to secure my return passage."

"You'll need coin for lodging as well. What if your destination turns out to be some hovel? What if an ogre awaits you at the end of your journey? You can't leave that to chance."

Cece hated to admit that her sister's worries had merit. "I shall take every precaution and ensure I have coin for lodging and sustenance upon my arrival."

"We're not discouraging you from your adventure. Not exactly. It's hard for us to remember you're no longer our naïve little sister or a fragile widow. We'll all contribute what we can." Vin assured her.

Cece was relieved. She didn't want these next three weeks of preparation to be fraught with tension. "I'm grateful. And I pledge to return home with my wanderlust satisfied."

Vin gave her a keen look. "I think this urge is far more than wanderlust."

Emily nodded in agreement. "Yes, I think so too. But whatever demon is driving you to this, we'll stand behind you and be here to catch you if you fall."

"Gert is in London for several days meeting with her printer. She's going to get stars in her eyes when you tell her and somehow turn this into the plot for her next lurid novel."

Jess's observation made all of them burst into laughter.

"I can already imagine her glee. When she finds out you're going to Scotland it shall be nothing but talk of governesses and castles and brooding men in kilts," Emily warned.

"I'm not a governess, and I'm fairly certain there are no castles. But I confess I'm hoping to make the acquaintance of a brooding man in a kilt or two."

"You know it's your duty to satisfy our curiosity about what they actually wear beneath those kilts." Vin devilishly pointed out.

"I shall consider it my solemn commendation. Although it may fall into the hovel and ogre territory Jess warned me against."

Vin shrugged and shot them all a wicked smile. "What's cornering an ogre or two in the name of science?"

"I shall endeavor to satisfy your curiosity but promise nothing."

"You'll keep us appraised of your findings via post?" Jess asked.

"I don't plan on residing there longer than a fortnight."

"Plenty of time to advise us of your findings," quipped Emily.

Chapter Two

Malcolm

Letter dated August 27th, 1853

Dearest Husband, Do you remember the blue ribbon you gave me? When I haven't twined it about my curls, I have it tied around my wrist. To remind me of you every moment of my day. To remind me that I'm never truly alone because out there somewhere is a man who loves me and is coming home to me someday soon.

NIGHTS LIKE THIS, FULL of revelry and good spirits, were the hardest.

In the middle of a crowd, Malcolm felt more alone than ever. He'd lost his parents when he was little more than an inquisitive boy, still in short pants. He'd lost his grandfather just before he returned from the Crimea. The laughing faces in the crowd were all people beholden to him because he'd given them a place to belong after the war. They were bound by duty and honor and affection, but not blood. They were grateful to him, but in awe of him. Sometimes the weight of that admiration, and the distance it created, made him feel more like a statue on a pedestal than a man of flesh and bone. Watching the devoted couples, and the children who wended their way along the fringe of the room in a lively game of chase, he keenly felt the absence of the bonds everyone around him seemed to take for granted.

He stared morosely into his amber draught.

When he returned from the Crimea, with his scarred body and bereft heart, he'd seen how his fellow soldiers were treated. Those who had families to return to were barely able to provide for them with missing limbs or shattered nerves. This war had employed weaponry that wrought devastation. The fire from the landmine had left its mark on his back and legs – he'd had to learn to walk again. His left eyelid drooped from the rough patch of scars that pulled the entire side of his face tight and he'd lost the use of his eye. His best friend from childhood had taken one look at him and said he may as well become a curmudgeon because no one could tell if his mouth was smiling.

Duncan's teasing had been in jest, but the words had stung. He'd started wearing a patch to cover the worst of his countenance.

And his plight was better than many of his comrades in arms. He'd brought them and their families here to give them new beginnings.

The farm had been in an appalling state of decay and he'd needed help. He offered the men he'd fought alongside, who couldn't find work in the factories because of their injuries, a home for their families and a stake in the profits from the wool. For the first time in nearly five years, they were finally showing a meager profit. It was a cause for rejoicing.

Some of the wives had arranged a spontaneous ceilidh and were rousting about the dancefloor kicking their heels. Everyone but Malcolm was in high spirits. He was a part of this community. He was the aegis behind its existence. But he couldn't immerse himself in the effervescent joy whirling and skipping all around him.

He'd finally returned the letters. He should be rejoicing about that too. They did him no good because the words only stirred up dreams he needed to leave behind.

He was standing in a corner, his hand curled around a tankard of the latest batch of whisky, when Moira McKendrick flounced down in the chair beside him. "Why are ye not dancin', laird?"

Her cheeks were flushed, likely from the spiked punch as much as from exertion. "The rainy weather wreaks havoc on my joints, Moira. And you know I have always been inept when it comes to reels. Even more so now with my leg."

What he didn't say was his depth perception was atrocious because of the patch, and any carousing across the floor usually left him dizzy and disoriented.

Moira wagged her finger in his face. "Mark me. Companionship is the cure for what ails ye." She pointed to the bevy of single women holding up the opposite wall. "Any one of those lasses would be over the moon if ye asked them to join ye in a reel."

He shrugged. He'd never been much of a dancer, and he was even less inclined now. He suspected he'd look like an awkward, lumbering idiot hauling around a piece of china. None of the lasses moved him to brave that humiliating scenario. The only woman who held that power was one he'd only met through her words and the pillow musings of his former tentmate. One who was completely unaware of his existence or his devotion.

Cecily Wainwright Thompson had haunted him for long enough. His friend had described her down to her littlest finger, and Malcolm was weary of envisioning a freckled face, with eyes like the violets she loved, tipped up for his kiss. He didn't want to replay imaginary conversations about the merits of Shakespeare's sonnets over those of Donne, or anticipate her vivid recounting of the latest Gothic novel she and her sisters had passed around. He didn't want to long for her smiling face, a tray of hot cross buns and warm tea, and a cozy evening by the fire.

"I'm content with my quiet hearth, Moira." A jig with a warm lass would not ease the ache in his leg or grant him the solitude he sought. They either gulped or scampered when they looked at him anyway despite the flushed tittering Moira swore was happening on the other side of the room.

When he'd first seen his visage, he'd driven his fist into the mirror. It showed him a scarred, scowling beast of a man who would send wise women screaming from his bed. A man who no longer knew what it meant to be gentle or soothe a tense moment with flattery or lukewarm platitudes.

Every year that passed, he grew more aware of the armor he'd built around his heart. But there was no one to crack it wide open or remind him the world was full of more than a hard day's work. So every morning he laced up his boots, gulped down tea laced with whisky, and did his duty.

"Laird, we all worry about ye. Ye provide for us, but never see to yerself."

Moira's gaze was clouded with worry, and he wanted to alleviate her concern. He'd grown used to being a solitary creature, and her chiding made him uncomfortable. "Providing for the lot of you brings me happiness. All I need is a roof over my head and porridge at my table with the occasional haggis and dram of whisky."

He needed more than that, but he knew it was futile to wish for it. That ship had sailed with its rigging full of wind and was lost somewhere on the open sea.

She clasped his arm. "I don't know what the Russians did to ye besides leave ye scarred and for dead, but ye deserve more than this half-life ye've convinced yourself is enough."

The left side of his body had been carved by fire when he'd spurred his mount forward to save his friend. His horse had stepped on a buried explosive and his world had upended itself. He'd had to crawl away and drag himself to the grass to roll in the mud. It had smothered the flames, but they'd left their mark on his face, his neck, his shoulder and his ribs. And his leg had never properly healed after his destrier had crushed the bones and trapped it beneath the weight of its body when it fell.

He hadn't felt the pain, he'd gone straight for his mount. Colossus had fared far worse than his master.

Ensuring the friend who carried him through wind and snow and mud had a peaceful rest was an act of mercy. But the act haunted Mal.

His efforts had been for naught, because his friend, the husband of the woman he'd come to love through her letters, had been brought down by enemy fire.

He'd been wandering around the battlefield, blinded by smoke and blood when he'd meandered across enemy lines. The Russian Army had promptly made him a prisoner of war.

War had taught him many things, but the most enduring lesson he'd learned was that the world was cruel and insensitive. That violence and viciousness lived in the hearts of mankind, sometimes softened by moments of light. He was afraid any woman that saw his nakedness in its entirety would shy away from the horror or scream in fright. Or worst of all, curl her lip in disgust.

"'Tis not a half-life, Moira. We have peace here in our little glen. I have a purpose and a family – even if we are nae bound by blood."

Moira wagged a finger. "We are nae bound by blood, but we all love and appreciate all ye've done for us. But ye need a warm hearth and family o' yer own. Dinnae forget I've known ye since ye were a lad and came to stay with your grandda."

"Hearths and families are the dreams of young men, Moira. I am no longer a young man. No woman wants a man who is scarred in body and soul."

"Ye're not yet in yer grave, Mal. Ye're not yet forty, still young enough to find yer solace."

Mal snorted. "Close enough to my fortieth year I needn't skip stones to hit it square."

"The world is leavin' ye behind and there's no one to keep ye company when ye have more than a few strands of white in yer beard. Soon, this peace ye claim is enough will not be enough to soothe whatever wounds ye carry." She laid her hand on his arm again. "Promise me ye'll be open to receive whatever gifts the Lord sees fit to deliver."

"I make no promises, Moira, but I shall strive to keep an open mind."

She gave him a stern look. "See that ye do. Remember, 'tis the season of miracles and ye are far more deservin' than most to receive its bounty."

❖

That night, as he stared into the darkness of the moonless night, Mal thought about Moira's admonition.

When the wind rustled and clacked the branches of the trees and cast ghostly moving shadows across the quiet lane that led to his cottage, he felt the weight of longing.

He didn't know if returning her letters had been the right decision. It had felt right at the time. For him – because he needed to let go of a dream that would never happen. And for her – because she deserved to lay her husband's story to its eternal rest.

The holiday season would soon be upon the village, and with it the abiding hope and goodwill that everyone seemed to exude toward their neighbors. Mal would attend all the fetes, he would bear all the tokens of camaraderie and good wishes and health, but even in all that, surrounded by those who cared for him, he would be alone.

He knocked the ashes from his pipe against the porch column and turned to the door. The sleek gray mouser, Sal, sat patiently at the threshold.

"Aye, ye wee braw glaikit," Mal stooped to caress its head. "Ye'll be my company this cold evening."

When he pushed open the door, the cat twined around his legs, purred, and stretched out in front of the hearth. Shep grumbled under his breath from his pile of blankets. The old sheepdog had a very complicated relationship with the cat.

Mal stripped in front of the banked warmth of the fire, dipping the cloth in the basin and swiping it over all the sweat that had dewed on his skin. He retrieved the liniment from the mantle and smoothed it across his aching muscles. By the end of the day, the tension pulled his scars taut, until they felt like knots beneath his skin, and the salve was the only balm that gave him rest.

Chapter Three

Cece

Letter dated July 27, 1853.

Dearest Wife, Do not mistake me, I love a good journey. But not the kind that tosses up the contents of my stomach and fills my boots with mud.

T HE TRAIN HAD BEEN loud, dirty, and crowded. The ginger hibiscus tea and tin of oatcakes her sisters had insisted she take had staved off the nausea but couldn't erase the smell of so many bodies packed into such a tight space. Cece had been too afraid of emptying the meager contents of her stomach all over one of her fellow passengers to gaze out the window.

Once she stood on the platform in Galashiels, she was well and truly on her own. She felt tumbled about, and a little singed from her journey. She was doubting the wisdom of her impulsive decision. She whirled about when a bleating sound filled the air.

"That'll be the shift change, miss. Down at the mill," a bright-cheeked lad informed her.

"Is the mill anywhere near Dunkirk Lane?" she asked hopefully. Perhaps her quest would be swiftly completed.

"Dunkirk Lane is on the outskirts of town, ma'am. 'Tis not a popular destination. I've heard there's an ogre that lives there, and he doesn't welcome company except tae do with the tweed business."

"I have business there."

"I wish ye luck findin' passage there. Most steer clear of it."

"Can you direct me to someone who can offer direction?"

"The laird does business with most o' the fabric shops up and down Hammer Street. If you go door to door, you may find someone who can guide you there."

"Thank you for your assistance."

He gave her a curt bow and strode away, disappearing into the crowd.

Because she had no idea where Dunkirk Lane was in relation to town, she started asking questions. She determinedly knocked on every shopfront to inquire directions. Each time her request was met with snorts, adamant refusals, and admonitions that she return home as fast as her legs could carry her.

With the swift dissolution of every query her hopes sank further into the bottoms of her shoes.

She'd nearly given up when she knocked on the last door. A wizened, stooped old man answered it. He looked like a forest gnome and his eyes sparkled up at her. "Aren't ye a sight for sore eyes. How can I help ye, miss? Mayhap ye need a new pair of shoes? The pair you're wearin' look ripe for replacement."

Cece realized she was standing in the entrance to a small cobbler's shop and wondered if she had in fact stepped into the fairy tale about the elves and the shoemaker. She knew the condition of her boots was lamentable. But she couldn't afford to replace them. Especially since she didn't know what awaited her at the end of Dunkirk Lane. What if the man she sought slammed the door in her face and sent her packing? She'd need train fare.

"I need directions to the holding at the end of Dunkirk Lane."

"There's naught there but a broody man who bears too much sorrow and carries the weight of the world on his brawny shoulders."

Cece sniffed. "Well that broody man sent me a package and I need answers."

"He's not the sort to bend to the will of a woman. Or a man."

"I'm not asking him to bend. I'm asking for explanations." She gripped the folds of her skirt and earnestly leaned forward. "I need explanations."

He tapped his chin with a gnarled finger and peered at her. "Weel, if you're set upon traipsin' yer way tae what lies at the end o' Dunkirk Lane, ye'll need sturdier footwear. Sit."

"But I do not have the coin..."

He interrupted her with a wagging finger. "I dinnae ask fer yer coin. Sit."

She meekly sat and mused that if he was an elf, who knew what power that glare held?

He started humming under his breath and Cece was shocked to discover she knew the tune. It was one the village costermonger sang constantly and when she'd asked him about it, he'd told her it was courtesy of a cousin that had recently relocated to Spitalfields. Cece had never been to Spitalfields, but she'd heard it wasn't quite reputable because of the gin and the gaming establishments. She wondered if this spry creature had heard *Aw Connut Dry My Heen, Robin* in Spitalfields.

She started humming under her breath because she couldn't help it. Even if the tune didn't originate with a reputable source, its litany lingered in one's head.

"Now lass, I've patched up yer old pair, so ye willnae go barefoot. When I've finished stitching ye a new pair, I'll come round the Lockhart farm."

The man's kindness was like a balm to her soul. "There must be some way I can repay you."

"Och, lass. One good turn deserves anither. If ye do a kindness to anither poor soul in need of it, ye can count your debt paid. Mayhap ye could turn the frown of the laird upside down. Ye'd hae the gratitude o' the entire village."

"The laird?"

"Malcolm Lockhart. He be the only resident at the end o' Dunkirk Lane, though all the cottages round these parts are full now because o' himself. If 'tis where ye're headed, then yer business is wi' him. He sent a letter asking for the farrier to come up this e'en, and ye can ride along in his cart."

—◆—

Fat droplets of rain pelted mercilessly down on Cece and the farrier. Not a downpour, but enough to wreathe their path in a fine mist and make one's clothes uncomfortably damp.

There were sheep everywhere, huddled under trees and against the turnstiles. They dotted the hills like sodden little cloud puffs. Cece's hat and cloak were an abysmal shield against the rain, so she tried to distract herself from the cold rivulets snaking down her neck beneath her bonnet by counting the sheep. She gave up counting them once she reached two hundred.

There were quite possibly more sheep than people in this corner of the world.

The road began to wind through the hills, and became impassable when they encountered a tree wider than their cart blocking the way.

"There's nae help for it, lass. We'll have to walk the last quarter mile."

Cece and her sisters had walked all over Cumbria in the rain because they could ill afford a cart or a horse at one time. But the rain in Cumbria had never been this cold, and the wind didn't feel like a gale determined to blow one completely off course.

She knotted her scarf tighter about her throat, clasped the edges of her cloak in an iron grip, and dismounted from her perch on the bench seat. "Let us make haste before the storm worsens."

"Right ye are. I'll lead the way. 'Tis just over the rise."

Cece wasn't prepared for the sight of the cottage nestled against the gloaming hills. It seemed to spring from the fairy realm with its golden stone, leaning chimney, and bright blue shutters. She halted in wonder. To think this is where her letters had hailed from. This laird could not be so miserable she'd regret her journey. No one who lived in this idyllic place, hemmed in by trees and sheep and hills, could harbor such ill will.

The warning of the cobbler echoed in her head. No one who lived here could possibly be a troll.

"You are certain this is our destination?"

The farrier chuckled. "Aye, lass. 'Tis the only farm at the end of Dunkirk. The laird is expectin' me."

As if Mother Nature sensed the meeting would be an auspicious occasion, she chose that precise moment to open up the heavens. The rain that had been a mere drizzle since early morning suddenly became a downpour. Cece clasped the handles of her bag in one hand, pulled her scarf over her head with the other, and dashed for the cottage door.

She arrived breathless on the threshold, dripping and cold. Her sharp raps against the wooden barrier to warmth met only silence. She rapped again, this time harder and faster.

The door swung open.

"Moira, hold yer wheesht..."

The man towering in the doorway trailed off at the sight of her.

Henry had been like a sapling, easily bent by the wind. In both form and will - full of whims he always indulged.

This man was no sapling. He was like an oak. The breadth of his shoulders was a giant canopy built to shelter you from all harm. It was wide enough to hide songbirds and crickets in the leafy crown.

He was glowering down at her from his towering height. His glare was a warning that she had mere seconds to convince him not to slam the door in her face. She placed her hand on his arm because rain was relentlessly pouring from the brim of her bonnet and puddling on the ground at her feet.

She was cold and weary and exasperated.

She wanted nothing more than a hot cup of tea and a warm fire.

Most of all, she wanted answers. Needed answers.

Had she been Henry's Little Wren? Or was that endearment he'd started every letter with while he'd been stationed an ocean away a falsehood too? Why had this man had her letters in his possession?

She collected herself and stepped under the arm he had braced across the doorway. "Hot tea would not be amiss."

His brow arched in disbelief. "I dinna know ye."

"I believe you do." She stuck out her hand. She refused to curtsey. "I'm Cece Thompson, nee Wainwright. I've come here for answers."

He visibly recoiled as his gaze searched hers.

"Henry's Cece."

His brogue had disappeared. As if it was a product of her imagination. Those two words were sharp enough to cut glass and sounded like a question.

"That's what I've come to find out." She should have been intimidated by his very obvious displeasure. But there was a gray cat twining around his legs and one of his hands was resting atop the head of a sheepdog so old his muzzle was completely white. Cece firmly believed that anyone who kept animals for companions was good at heart. Regardless of appearances to the contrary.

"You showed up here with no warning, when the rain will likely change to snow, because you couldn't let sleeping dogs lie. You'll be on your way back to Cumbria in the morning."

He was glowering again. Her arrival was obviously unexpected and unwelcome. His brows lowered and his arms crossed over his massive chest. And he hadn't bothered to take her hand. She dropped it and braced it on her hip to emphasize her determination. "I will not. I'm not leaving without hearing who you are and how you know my husband. I'll sleep in that barn I just passed if you won't let me shelter here."

He grunted. "I'm Malcolm Lockhart. Some of those in the village insist on calling me Laird. I won't answer to it, so don't bother using it. Your husband shortened my name to Mal because he said it fit my bad temper. I should've known you'd be just as obstinate as he was. Sit."

The avalanche of words rumbled out of him, and she was so transfixed by the hint of brogue that sounded like water over rocks, Cece almost forgot her mission entirely.

He pointed to the rocking chair beside the stone fireplace.

She ignored his terse command and stooped to rub the snout of the dog. "Who are your friends?"

"The cat is Sal, and the dog is Shep. Neither one of them takes kindly to being made over by strangers."

The sheepdog nudged her hand for another caress. Either the dog sensed she was no threat, or Malcolm Lockhart was fibbing.

"Now you'll never have a moment's peace," the man grumbled.

She was convinced he was the behemoth Scot that Henry had mentioned in his letters. The span of his shoulders was as wide as the doorframe, and he was forced to turn sideways so she could enter. When she flicked her gaze to his as she squeezed through, his jaw was tight, and his expression was grim. She swallowed and clutched her valise like it was her only hope of salvation.

Perhaps it was best she followed his instruction. Especially if she wanted tea.

Cece rose to her feet, and moved to inch past him. She sank into the rocking chair as gracefully as possible and set her bag on the floor. As she settled into her perch, she imagined this tower of a man doing the same. His lap occupied by a purring gray cat.

Chapter Four

Malcolm

Letter dated August 22, 1853.

Dearest Husband, Arie came to visit us today. She brought a freshly baked loaf of bread that was still warm from the oven. I snagged the heel and slathered it in the last scoop of black currant jam. I felt like a pirate as I savored every last bite while sitting on the back stoop of the cottage and watching the swallows pinwheel over the fields. I felt guilty afterward for enjoying that simple

pleasure when you're tromping through mud and desolation half a world away.

HER LAST LETTER HAD arrived three weeks after he'd signed the official dispatch of her husband's death. Death notices seemed to be the one bit of correspondence the army was committed to delivering with alacrity.

If he'd answered that last letter, she would have immediately known something was amiss. That her husband hadn't been the one corresponding with her from the battlefront. Instead of answering her final missive, he'd tucked it in his breast pocket and carried it against his heart, for courage and a reminder of what he was fighting for. For cozy hearths and women with quiet beauty and warm hugs.

Her letter had ended up splattered in mud because he'd carried it everywhere, like a talisman. When he held it to his nose and inhaled, he could smell the sulfur from the battlefield mixed with the faint scent of violets. By the time he finally let it go, he'd read it so many times, the creases had worn through it and the corners looked like the sheep dog lolling all over his feet had carried it off.

He'd read it more than the others. Because he'd known it was the last one and he'd be forced to let go of the woman who'd sent it. The woman whose words had made war bearable.

He didn't know why he'd kept her correspondence for so long. The letters were naught more than a reminder of everything he'd lost and would never have by the time he sent them to her. If he was brutally honest with himself, he ironically supposed he'd sent them back in a last effort to save himself from hope. Because on this bleak farm, with the care of so many on his shoulders, and the wolves of hunger and penury pounding on the door, he couldn't afford to hope.

His grandfather had always told him hoping was for fools who lacked industry and common sense. He claimed it led to an early grave because a man was always looking toward the horizon. Rushing toward his death instead of being satisfied with what was right in front of him.

Despite that dire warning, Malcolm hadn't lost hope. Not after the horrors of Balaclava. Not when he returned here to a tumble-down cottage with a sagging roof and a field full of ragged, bleating sheep. Every season he'd cherished the hope that the next one would bring enough food and the right balance of sun and rain. He'd clasped her letters under his pillow every night.

Unable to part with her completely, he'd made a copy of the final letter that he shoved in the drawer of his desk for the day he finally gathered the resolve to send back her correspondence.

Two months ago, he'd sent all of them back to her. Even the last one. The copy he'd painstakingly scratched out was buried deep in the cavern of his cluttered desk drawer. Within reach if he had grave need of the sunshine that seemed to bleed from her words, but out of sight so he wouldn't be tempted to carry it around in his pocket. When he was feeling the cold of the wind in his bones, and the emptiness of his cottage, he pulled it out and read it.

Even though he'd been the one to answer them, those letters hadn't been written for his eyes. Her words weren't meant for him. As much as he longed for it to be otherwise.

And now she was standing on his threshold with eyes like trampled violets and a mutinous look about her. Just the way he'd imagined her. Brimming with passion and defiance and quiet courage. Demanding answers he wasn't ready to give.

He'd just warmed water for tea as a ward against the cold rain. This weather always made his bones ache. At least he could offer her that before sending her on her way. He'd just laid to rest the dream of her, and he wouldn't open those wounds again.

"You cannot sleep here. We'll be hauled in front of the kirk, widow weeds or no."

"As I said, I am perfectly willing to sleep in the barn."

"You'll not sleep in the barn!" He barked.

She shrank back, but then seemed to think better of it, squaring her shoulders. "Fine, I shan't sleep in the barn."

"There's a tiny cottage just behind this one. You'll sleep there."

"So long as I have a warm place to discard my stockings and lay my head, that will be sufficient. Might I have some tea to ease my rest before you banish me from your presence?"

Her voice was soft, but he wasn't deceived. He knew from the letters that she was cloaking her ferocity behind that prim exterior. He half feared that a failure to produce tea would be construed as an invitation for her to sink her little fangs into him instead.

That image should not have been so appealing.

"I have some Assam I've been saving. Have a seat." He gestured toward the stool at the low table.

She sighed like she'd just fallen onto a featherbed heaped with quilts. He felt that sweet huff of breath color the air between them even more acutely than he'd felt the softness of her banked defiance. "Thank goodness you're not the heathen you appear to be."

He raised a brow. "Because I have tea? We Scots are just as civilized as the English across our border. I have a fresh loaf of bread as well. But no jam."

Her stomach rumbled loudly, like the mouser when it spied a fat bit of prey. She flushed and laid her hand against it. "As you can see, I am the one who appears uncivilized. Bread and tea together sound lovely. I have a fondness for jam, but a plain slice of bread will do quite nicely."

He knew she had a fondness for jam. Black currant jam to be exact. When he'd read that letter he'd seen her when he closed his eyes. A drop of sticky jam sliding down the corner of her mouth, her elbows propped on her knees as she stole a moment of solitude. Now that she was here, he could easily imagine that sticky jam sliding over her lips, down her chin, snaking into the bodice primly buttoned over the bosom *he was not going to stare at.* Could easily imagine what it would taste like if he licked it from the salt of her skin.

"'Tis just me, so no proper teapot." He hefted the tin pitcher in his hand and poured the boiling water over the leaves he'd scooped into the chipped cup.

He handed her the cup and the tips of his fingers grazed hers. Their gazes locked.

Her eyes were just as he'd envisioned them. A blue so deep and dark it was like the purple of heather. A man could fall into them.

She dropped her gaze and slid her hand away. He felt the slight tremble and wondered if she felt it in his grasp too.

"Thank you," she murmured as she lifted the cup to her lips, turning it so the chip was facing outward.

He suddenly wished the chip had escaped her notice. He might have had the chance to soothe away her cut lip with his lips and tongue. He wanted to pinch himself to ensure she wasn't a mirage. The spray of freckles across the bridge of her nose and over the tops of her cheekbones wasn't as pronounced as he thought it would be. And he'd always imagined her dark hair falling over her shoulders in waves, not bound up so tightly to the crown of her head.

He was suddenly embarrassed that a chipped teacup and a roughhewn three-legged stool were all he had to offer.

"'Tis naught." He put his hands on his hips and tipped his face toward the ceiling. "What possessed you to seek out this place?"

"I told you." Her voice was sharp. "I wanted answers. And I knew that whatever or whomever I found here would have them. Because this was the return address emblazoned on the packet of letters I received."

"And what makes you believe your questions will be welcome? Or that I'd be willing to give you answers in exchange?"

"I want to know more of my husband. I want to know what it was like for him over there. The things he didn't share in his letters. If they were even his letters. You recognized my name – which means you have some of the answers I seek."

"What if the things I saw and did and experienced during the war haunt me? What if giving you those answers will dredge up things I am striving to forget?"

"I can be patient. And you needn't share anything that brings you pain. I am here because I have suspicions that have been troubling me for eight years, and I want to lay them to rest and get on with my life."

Malcolm drained his teacup and set it on the mantle before turning to her again, his arms crossed over his chest. "You do not strike me as the type of woman who would be timid about getting on with her life. Tell me the truth of why you braved the onset of a Scottish winter storm to come here."

She gave him an incredulous look. "Do not pretend to have divined my intentions or my character on such brief acquaintance. If you truly want to know, I felt stifled. And forgotten."

Loathe as he was to admit it, he didn't know how anyone who met this woman could forget her. "I'm sure you're mistaken. You do not seem forgettable in the least. Quite the opposite, in fact."

She set her teacup down and braced her chin in her hand. "Do you have the slightest inkling what it's like to be a young widow?"

He didn't, but he was sure she was going to enlighten him. "No, I cannae say I do."

She got a faraway look in her violet eyes. "It's like being left behind when everyone else is setting off for grand adventures. It feels like your world is standing still, stuck in memories everyone around you keeps reminding you should be enough to sustain you."

He felt for her plight, but he could not afford to let her stay and indulge whatever flight of fancy had landed her in his doorstep. "That is how it feels to be a former soldier as well."

"We have established that the pair of us are well-acquainted with the ravages of war – although my experience has been much more insular."

"Being a victim of its ravages was clearly not enough. Is this trip meant to be your grand adventure or a way to bury your demons?"

Chapter Five

Cece

Letter dated August 5, 1853.

Dearest Wife, One of my comrades in arms is a mountainous, curmudgeonly Scot with thighs the size of small oaks and shoulders like those of Atlas. He wouldn't stop grumbling when our lieutenant told him he needed to shave his beard and he keeps insisting that haggis is better than the swill we're being served. I am not inclined to believe him. The thought of ingesting sheep intestines makes me shudder. If nothing else, poking fun at him and trying to rouse a smile will prove amusing.

ECE WATCHED THE FIRELIGHT flicker over her host and pondered the question. When she'd set out, finding a grand adventure was her intention. But now she wondered if she wanted more. A place she belonged. A place she was needed.

The wind had begun howling like an ominous banshee beyond the shutters and he wasn't exactly what she'd expected to find when she set out on her mission. Jess had been right to question her ability to make rational decisions.

This taciturn Scot was a giant with a web of scars that started at his hairline and made a path down his jaw and neck. He wore a patch over one eye and though his steps were heavy and lumbering, like he would crash down Jack's imaginary beanstalk and happily squash houses, there was a hitch in them. Cece was certain he was the grumpy Scotsman Henry had described in his second letter. His thighs were hidden by the folds of his kilt but his shoulders were so wide he probably always had to turn sideways when he entered a room so he wouldn't get wedged in the doorframe. The breadth of Atlas indeed.

His hair was tied back in a queue, but she knew it would fall just past the rim of his broad shoulders if she unraveled the leather tie that bound it. The eye that wasn't hidden by the patch was a deep, mossy green. His shirt was open at the strong column of his throat, and she watched with fascination as the bronzed skin of his Adam's apple moved when he gulped down his tea. She shook her head to steer her thoughts back toward the conversation.

"Lass, you've a faraway look."

"To answer your question, this trip will probably be the only adventure I shall ever have. But I need to lay my demons to rest as well. Before you set me on a train to molder my way back to my corner in Cumbria where I'm confined to the pursuits of embroidery and lacemaking."

"I'll not send ye back in this storm. The tracks will be impassable if the ache in my leg is any indication."

"The ache in your leg?"

"Aye. 'Twas injured in the war, and whenever Mother Nature is determined to hurl a blizzard in our direction, it aches."

Blizzards were portentous in Cece's experience. Blizzards brought malady and upheaval and chaos. A blizzard was what had brought Arie and Thad together.

This man looked like he had withstood many a storm that would have eviscerated someone of a gentler caliber. He looked invincible.

"If your aches are telling you the truth, there will be no divesting yourself of me."

He gave her an inscrutable look. "You realize this is a working sheep farm, aye?"

Cece narrowed her gaze. "The approximately thirteen million flecks of wool I saw dotting the countryside were not sufficient indication."

He snorted at her sarcasm. "Well, if the blizzard comes, it's every hand on the till. Including yours to ensure the herd is safe and fed."

"I know nothing of sheep."

"Then you'd best hope my aching leg is telling lies."

Though she knew nothing of sheep or sheep farming, she knew of the ebb and flow of village life and the way calamity and disaster brought all the disparate parts of a community together. She did not want to go back to Cumbria, so she started praying that his aches were predictable. She would immerse herself in a trial by fire if the weather demanded she sojourn here.

"I am hoping for the opposite. 'Twill be an enlightening experience."

"If snow comes, lass, it will bury us for at least a fortnight. You'll be praying for salvation and more in need of warm tea than you were upon your arrival."

"I do not know what gave you the impression I am pampered or malleable." If snow buried them for a fortnight, she'd spend the holidays among strangers. She felt a twinge of guilt at the possibility of breaking her promise to Jess, but she was more tantalized by the prospect than anything. It would truly be an adventure.

"Ye're English."

"As was my husband. A man you called your friend."

"Aye. I was glad to call him my friend in the midst of battle when we defended each other's backs. But he was still English. A Scot can't simply set aside generations of loathing."

"Scottish independence has been laid to rest for over a hundred years."

"Aye, and this village has been struggling ever since. The economy here is finally stable after nearly a century of drought and displacement."

"As I've said, I am not here to disrupt your peace or the pace of life here. I came here because you sent me a packet of letters I'd been missing for over eight years. A packet that should have been returned with my husband's effects. I want to know why you had them in your possession and why you kept them for so long."

He stacked his hands on his hips and frowned. " 'Tis not a tale for this day. Now that you've abandoned yer tea, we'll find Moira. She'll make certain the cottage has peat and bedclothes."

Cece stood, brushing off her skirts. "You can only avoid this conversation for so long."

"And what have we here?" A smiling woman strode through the door and interrupted them. She was a spare woman in her mid-forties with her iron gray hair pinned in a crown of braids around her rosy face.

"This is Mrs. Thompson."

The woman didn't seem the least bit intimidated by his curt, growling response. "Will she bide with us a while?"

A look passed between the two of them that Cece was at a loss to interpret. Almost as if the woman was chiding him.

Her host sighed gustily and crossed his arms over his chest again. "She will bide until the storm has waned."

"Weel, Missus Thompson, ye're in for a right dandy stayathome wi' us."

Cece's brow furrowed in confusion. "A stayathome?"

"Aye. When neither man nor beast sets foot outside except for the necessity of it."

Winter storms in Cumbria could be quite daunting. Surely whatever gale was barreling toward this corner of Scotland would be no worse than what she was accustomed to.

"Please ensure the cottage behind this one is suitably stocked for our guest." Malcolm turned toward Cece. "Madam, Mrs. McKendrick will show you where you'll be sleeping."

He tipped his head in her direction and strode out the door.

Moira must have sensed Cece's dismay, because she crossed the room and laid a hand on her arm. "'Tis his way, and not meant to be a personal affront."

The cottage was nothing more than a tiny shepherd's hut. It would be cozy. There was a small fireplace against one wall, a narrow platform in one corner Cece assumed was meant for a bed, and it seemed warm and dry. Those were the bare creature comforts she was longing for, so it would do quite nicely.

Her guide brushed past her. " 'Tis only a brief lull, the rain will return. Hasten in so we can ensure you're protected against the cold and damp."

"Thank you, Mrs. McKendrick. I'll make the bed and lay the fire so you may return to your other tasks."

The other woman waved a hand in dismissal. "Lass, 'tis no trouble. Ye're a guest and I'd not make you attend to those things yerself. And ye may call me Moira."

Cece smiled tentatively. "Moira, does your village receive many visitors?"

Moira placed the linens on the edge of the bed. "Nay. Only those who want to speak of wool with the laird."

"He insisted he wasn't the laird."

Moira rolled her eyes. "He's laird in aught but the piece of paper granting him the title. Just as his grandda was."

"In aught but the piece of paper?"

"The clan was scattered when the land was turned over to the sheep. But he brought all his former comrades here to give them purpose and honest work. Somethin' a laird would do to take care of his people, ye ken."

"All his former comrades?"

"Aye. 'Tis a community of sorts. We all share in the labor and the profits. The laird said we'll all rise or fall together but we have a fighting chance if we throw in our lots for the common good."

Cece would never have taken Malcolm Lockhart for an idealist if she wasn't being presented with the evidence. "So this is meant to be a utopian community?"

Moira's laughter was boisterous. "Nay, lass. We're not bound together by shared religion. We're an even mix of Protestants and Catholics. We're bound together for survival."

"And it was Mr. Lockhart's idea?"

"He sent letters all over England and Scotland asking the men who were in his regiment to come if they couldn't find work. And he encouraged them to bring those they knew who were in a comparable situation because of their injuries. 'Tis a heap sight better than working in one of those factories like the ones in Manchester."

Cece had read of communities like this one, but she'd never had the chance to observe them on such an intimate level. She was intrigued. "So you receive wages for your work?"

Moira shook her head. "No wages. But all our needs are met. We have plenty of food, never lack peat for our fires, and always have clothes on our backs and medicine when we require it."

"Your laird is a visionary."

"He'd deny it. We see it and know the burden of caring for all of us and making a go of it weighs heavily on him."

"That is why he made it clear this is a working farm. He'll not allow even a guest to remain idle when there are things that need to be done."

"Malcom Lockhart doesn't know how to lay down his burdens or sit idly by a fire twiddling his thumbs. He's always been a man of action with little patience for things he thinks are inconsequential."

"You've known him a long time?"

"Though I'm ten years his senior, he came to live with his grandda when both his parents died of the flux. My father was one of his grandda's bailiffs. I've known him nearly forty years."

"How old was he the first time you met him?"

Cece was insatiably curious about her host, and she doubted he was the kind of man who shared confidences with uninvited strangers.

"He was a wee mite. No more than six summers. All spindly legs and arms and those big green eyes with lashes any girl would be envious of."

Cece hadn't noticed his lashes. The cottage had been too dim, and she'd been trying not give away her fascination.

"He's certainly not wee now. I'd say he's grown out of the gangly stage as well."

Moira nodded firmly. "Aye, he's a right braw lad. But he doesn't see it. Thinks his scars and that patch make him unappealing. He's convinced himself the lasses chase him because they think he has coffers stuffed with gold coin."

His scars made him the opposite of unappealing. His eyepatch made him look like one of the piratic heroes from a penny dreadful.

"Have they not seen his meager household?"

"He lives simply and makes sacrifices for the good of the community. He has coin to spare, but he'll not spend it on a woman whose affections he cannae be sure of."

"I do not blame him for his caution. But is he not lonely?"

Moira chortled. "He'll never admit it."

"Men and their pride. Even surrounded by my sisters, I am often lonely. For someone to build my dreams with. For the house full of giggling and running feet my husband's death cheated me of."

Her companion's eyes grew misty and she laid a gentle hand on Cece's elbow. "I did not realize ye were a widow, lass."

"I am just out of mourning. Henry served in the Crimea with your laird."

"Is that why ye have come to our little hamlet? Because ye wanted stories about how he fared over there?"

"I will stay for the stories, but they are not what brought me here." Cece blurted out in a rush.

"Then how did ye find us? The laird clearly wasn't expectin' ye, but seemed resigned to yer presence."

"As I mentioned, my late husband served with your laird in the Crimea."

Moira eyed her carefully. "So ye came because ye wanted to know more of yer husband's time on the battlefield?"

Cece sighed. "That's part of it. But I came for explanations as well. My husband and I enjoyed a lively correspondence and I had thought my letters to him lost until they were delivered in the parcel post two months ago. They were posted from this place – and I suspect your laird is the one who sent them. I want to know how he came to have them and why he kept them for so long. The war ended over seven years ago, and Henry's been gone since Balaclava, eight years past."

Moira's look was assessing. "He returned from the war greatly changed. Nothing like the boy or man I once knew."

"How has he changed?"

"He's like a stray dog ye ken? Who flinches and snarls at anyone new and goes off to gnaw on his bone in private. I think he's afraid to let anyone truly see him. Except for those of us that knew him before."

"He is rather intimidating."

"He's become a big, brooding oaf and I've told him so. He was a lad full of sunshine and constant laughter before he left. Now he nurses his damned tankard of whisky and sulks in the corner."

Cece couldn't imagine that stern mouth curved in a smile. Or what kind of rusty laughter would emerge from it if he was ever so moved.

"I'll leave ye to unpack yer valise. I'll bring ye porridge and toast in the mornin'."

Moira left with a wave and quietly shut the door behind her.

Cece sank onto the bed and flopped backward. The excitement she'd been tamping down fizzed in her veins and bubbled over. It felt like she was finally taking her life back from the shadows.

Chapter Six

Malcolm

Letter dated February 10, 1854.

Dearest Husband, The wind is howling outside the cottage as I write this. As you know, there is nothing I hate worse than the coldness of the stone floor beneath my feet in the morning. When there is a patina of ice on the surface of the wash basin, I struggle to remember the virtue of Marcus Aurelius's sentiment, "When you arise in the morning, think of what a pre-

cious privilege it is to be alive – to breathe, to think, to enjoy, to love."

THE CLATTER AND BANG of the door against the wall woke Malcolm from the first decent sleep he'd had in months. Whoever had disturbed him was going to rue the day they were born.

Before he had the chance to berate his interruption, she stormed into his sleeping room. Shep's ears perked up from his corner, and Sal's claws grazed his bare chest as she leapt off the bed and prowled toward the intruder.

"The cottage you so graciously banished me to has a roof that leaks like a sieve. I'm colder and wetter than I was when I arrived and I've run out of buckets." She was glowering at him, her hands braced on her hips. "You've been derelict in your duty as my host."

Mal slept in the altogether, and he wasn't keen on revealing the state of his undress to the harpy glaring down at him from the foot of his bed. Especially since her glittering eyes and flushed cheeks had a rousing effect on certain parts of his anatomy. He clutched the plaid to his waist, grateful for its scant cover.

The accusation in her words sank in and he returned her glare. "Derelict in my duty, Mrs. Thompson?"

Was she astute enough to realize she'd overstepped? Her insinuation angered him.

"Yes. Derelict in your duty. Where am I to sleep, Mr. Lockhart?"

"I'd remind you, Mrs. Thompson, that you are an un-invited guest."

"I'm well aware of how unwelcome I am. But I cannot sleep in that leaking cottage. I'll end up confined to the bed with bronchial catarrh."

"Fine, Mrs. Thompson. You'll sleep here. I'll make a pallet in the loft."

She vehemently shook her head. "There's no cause to patronize me, Mr. Lockhart. I'll not displace you from your bed. I'll sleep in the loft."

"I'm not patronizing you, I'm pacifying you. I would argue with you, but I know it would be futile." He grabbed his eyepatch from the bedside table and slipped it on. "Let me gather some things. Wait in there by the fire."

"I never would have guessed you sleep naked as the day you were born, Mr. Lockhart." She cocked her head to the side and grinned impishly. "You don't sleep in a nightshirt and the fact I'm standing here is making you uncomfort-able."

"Lass, ye don't know the half of it. Let me make myself decent."

She flounced out of the room, the flannel of her night-gown swirling about her ankles.

When she disappeared, Mal turned his attention to the part of his anatomy now standing at full attention. He'd been dreaming of the slide of sheets over skin, and violet eyes raised to his. Of soft moans and the wet, warm welcome once he was clasped inside a woman's body. He needed to think of icy rain trickling down his collar, and the pimpled arse of the skinny parson he'd glimpsed urinating into the hedges at the edge of the cemetery.

He closed his eyes and willed his arousal to subside enough it would escape her notice. She could never know how the very thought of her had haunted his dreams for almost a decade. She'd never let him forget it.

"If you intend to keep to your word and turn me into a sheep farmer on the morrow, I'd like to find some rest."

Her snappishness was a welcome intrusion. It was the exact remedy for his issue, and his cock finally relaxed.

Her sarcastic quips had been amusing when they were part of her letters. They were not amusing now. They were like stinging nettles that burrowed beneath the skin.

"Hold your wheesht, woman!" He barked.

He snatched the quilts from the cupboard and took a deep breath.

When he entered the room, she was staring up at the ladder with her hands on her hips. "I'll climb and you can toss them up to me. I don't think I can manage an armload."

"I'll follow you."

"Your assistance is unnecessary. I am perfectly capable of managing by myself."

He told himself he was following her up the ladder because he was worried for her safety. She could slip and topple. Twist an ankle or break her neck. He reasoned that he could steady her if necessary.

He gritted his teeth as she started her ascent and closed his eyes. He was not going to ogle the curve of her bottom.

He started climbing behind her and was surprised at how quickly she clambered up the rungs, as nimble as the mouser that had just carved its mark into his chest.

When he stepped from the last rung and into the loft, the space shrank. He had to bow his head so he wouldn't bang it against the rafters.

He sensed her exasperation when she whirled to face him. "I told you I could manage. And now you can't even rise to your full height. You cannot possibly be comfortable."

Malcolm wasn't going to give her the satisfaction of admitting she was right. "It's fine."

"I know you're lying, but I won't argue."

"A wise choice." He thrust the blankets toward her. "Here make up the bed you insisted on taking."

She opened her arms to catch them, but the fabric billowed over her face and obscured her vision. She lost her footing and fell forward. In a flurry of curses Mal tried to brace himself and at least ensure she had a soft landing. Somehow, he lost his footing as well.

They ended up sprawled together, his body pressing her into the straw ticking of the mattress.

He was bare beneath his kilt and his cock, spurred by her scent and the cradle of her thighs, decided it was the perfect moment for a resurrection.

The woman pinned beneath him started squirming and that made his cock more enthusiastic. Ignoring the way she affected him was impossible.

Her eyes grew round, as he thickened and rose against her and he knew if her hands were free instead of trapped beneath his body they would flutter to her mouth to cover an outraged gasp.

She began to wriggle in earnest, and he laid his forehead against her shoulder and stifled a groan.

"Stop moving, woman. Or I shall embarrass us both even further."

"You are not an animal, sir. Control your base urges."

Her prim response shouldn't have goaded him even further. But there was something about the shrewishness of it that made him want to silence her with a kiss. "I am not going to ravage you, but I will spend nonetheless if you do not hold still."

"Remove yourself." She'd managed to extract one of her hands and ball it into a fist. She thumped it against his side.

"I am endeavoring to do so, madam."

He couldn't stand unless he wanted to end up con-cussed, so Mal inched his knees around her thighs so he could scoot away.

Every slide of his skin against hers was like a nail in a coffin. He was so close to spilling his seed it was demoralizing. He felt like an untried schoolboy.

"I'm going to assume you've gone some time without female companionship and any woman would have had that effect on you. Moira said you've been a recluse since you returned from the Crimea."

Mal scowled. "'Twas not her place to speak of me with you."

"I asked. Because you were not forthcoming during our introduction."

"What else did Moira say?"

"She said you'd rather nurse your whisky than dance."

"That preference is not so strange. I don't want to waste my energy in idle chatter. Whisky makes a much less aggravating companion."

He wasn't going to share the extent of his injuries and why he now found it difficult to keep pace. Especially in a reel.

"I'll not remark on how sad and churlish I find that observation."

He'd finally managed to extricate himself and sat back heavily on the floor. "As I'm certain the meddling besom told you, I am not as fond of social gatherings as I once was. Why would you ask her about me or my inclinations?"

She slid further away, as if she were afraid of imminent impalement. Or leprosy.

"I'm curious. And as I've told you, I came here for answers."

"I've given you all the answers I have to give. All the wiles at your disposal will not pry forth more than I've already told you."

She crossed her arms and raised a brow. He tried to ignore the way her new pose accentuated the curve of her bosom beneath the gown.

"I think you underestimate my wiles."

This time he couldn't mask his obvious surprise. "Do you truly believe seducing me will work?"

"Seducing you? Those are not the sort of wiles I was referring to. I intend to weaken your resolve with freshly baked scones."

He mimicked her by crossing his own arms and raising one of his brows. "What if I told you Mrs. McKendrick keeps me well-supplied in scones?"

"I'd say that you haven't tasted mine. Don't disparage or refuse something you've yet to savor."

If she only knew how it was taking every ounce of his willpower not to pin her to the mattress and savor to his heart's content.

"In truth, her scones have a marked resemblance to hardtack. In both taste and consistency."

"Even more reason not to dismiss my scones out of hand."

"Are scones the only thing you have worth bartering, Mrs. Thompson?"

"We've established I will never win a shearing contest. But I've been told I have a fair singing voice."

His friend had never mentioned this. Was she fibbing or had her husband truly not known her? "If your repertoire extends beyond bawdy tavern songs it will be most welcome. Especially if we find ourselves isolated by the blizzard."

"What happens when winter is so merciless?"

"We make do, Mrs. Thompson. As we always have. The gardens this year were bountiful and there are bushels of root vegetables put aside in our cellars. I hope you have a fondness for potatoes and turnips."

She wrinkled her nose. "Potatoes yes, turnips no. But I will eat whatever is set before me. There were lean years after our mother died, and I'll not turn away nourishment."

Yet another facet of her he wanted to dig into. She'd carried her loneliness for as long as he had. "I lost my parents when I was six summers."

She smiled gently. "Moira told me as much. She said you are much changed from the boy you were then."

"Do not pity me, Mrs. Thompson. My grandfather gave me what he could, and I never doubted his love."

She stepped forward and laid her hand across his knuckles. Her expression was earnest and he braced himself to recoil from her kindness.

"It is still hard to lose one's parents. And please call stop calling me Mrs. Thompson."

"Aye, 'tis hard." Their gazes locked and the moment stretched between them like a tightrope.

He glanced away first and rocked back on his heels. "We must maintain propriety. I cannot call you by your first name."

Her laughter tinkled merrily between them. "Propriety? I am standing here in my nightclothes and am intimately aware that everything they say about what Scotsmen wear beneath their kilts is true. Exercising it now would be like shutting the gate after the horses have run away."

He flushed. He'd hoped she'd be too delicate to mention his inconvenience. "As you said, it was only a natural reaction after my celibate state."

"Please call me Cece. I haven't felt like Mrs. Thompson in a very long time."

"You are a widow and you should go by the name you are known by until you remarry."

Her mouth quirked up sardonically. "Until I remarry? I'm considered well and truly on the shelf. I do not believe marriage is in my cards, Mr. Lockhart."

Why was she opposed to marriage? Had her union with Henry been unhappy? Or worse, a mistake? Her letters had sustained an entire regiment. "You have an aversion to matrimony?"

"Not precisely. But this is the first time I've ever left my village. This journey has opened my eyes to possibility and the realization that I have never stretched my wings. Remarrying would cut short my voyage of self-discovery."

"And this journey will be cut short if you marry."

Cece snorted. "In my experience most men believe a woman's aspirations should reflect their own."

"I am not most men." He sketched a curt bow. "I will leave you to your rest."

As he laid back in his bed and stared at the ceiling, Mal resolved that he would ensure she became intimately acquainted with the tasks that would be most loathsome to a gently raised Englishwoman. She was too much temptation and the easiest way to overcome the threat she posed was to neutralize it. If she was disgusted by farm life and the things he asked her to do, perhaps she would return all the sooner, or seek out lodgings in Galashiels.

Chapter Seven

Cece

Letter dated July 31, 1854

Dearest Little Wren, There are rumors a large contingent of the French army will be arriving soon to supplement our forces. I expect heavy fighting in the months to come. My fellow soldiers and I who have read Shakespeare have been discussing the eerie similarities between Henry V and the situation we find ourselves in. This quote especially, rings true for all of us, "Once more unto the breach, dear friends, once

more; Or close the wall up with our English dead." Forgive my grim musings, darling. I find myself clasping your letters beneath my pillow and close to my heart.

CECE HAD MADE A discovery when he's been braced above her. His eye had glimmered with the same heat she'd seen in Henry's before he tugged her between the stalls and kissed her like a man who was drowning. When Malcolm Lockhart's gaze had flickered, she'd tasted the memory of that sugary, cinnamon first kiss.

The big, brooding Scot hadn't kissed her. But her lips tingled as if he had.

She knew he'd wanted to kiss her. His lack of under-garments beneath the kilt had left no doubt of her effect on him.

She wanted to rub the back of her hand against her lips. To erase the memory of her first kiss and her desire for the next one from a man she was certain barely tolerated her. No matter if his reaction to their proximity had given the impression he wanted to brand her body with his own.

The heat in his gaze had made everything inside her ignite.

Suddenly, she was warm-blooded again. Cece hadn't even acknowledged to herself how cold she'd been since Henry died. Like a frozen, immobile, icicle of a statue.

This stern man, whose work-roughened hands had curled around the base of the teacup he'd thrust in her direction, was like the first trickle of sunlight dancing across the arctic tundra of her soul.

When he'd looked at her just now with a gaze full of banked heat and promise, she'd felt awake and inquisitive. Like the world held promise once again. Like she was once again the effervescent girl who'd blossomed into a woman so long ago. A woman whose wants and needs had been shoved beneath a mantle of sorrow and doubt.

She plumped the pillow beneath her head and mused that this adventure was already turning out to be more than she'd expected. There were no gloomy castles or wailing ghosts, but she could now answer the question her sisters had posed about what Scotsmen wore beneath their kilts.

Sleep was going to be elusive. She'd already counted a few bloody hundred sheep, so that clearly wasn't the solution. Mentally composing her first letter to her sisters might do the trick. She had the answer, after all, to their question.

Dear Vin, she would write first, *it is an irrefutable fact that there is nothing but what was bestowed at birth beneath a kilt. I can see your eager expression in my mind's eye and I know you're demanding to know how I proved the veracity of this rumor in less than a day. I shall tell that tale in person, because I want to witness your glee when you hear the details of my adventure.*

Cece would address Jess in a separate paragraph. *Dear Jess,* she'd continue, *there is a terrible winter storm marching inexorably toward this little pocket of Scotland. Your scientist's heart would be examining the capricious cloud patterns and predicting the direction of the wind. The only proof I have that it is on its way is the assurance from my host that his war wounds only ache like this when we are on the precipice of a long, cold, miserable snowfall.*

Emily would be eager to hear about the mystery itself. *Dear Emily, she'd begin, I still don't have the answers I sought. I realize only a day has passed, but I have the sense that my host is hiding something. I plan to ferret out his secrets. Perhaps he'll betray his confidences whilst he instructs me in the proper care and feeding of sheep.*

I can hear all of you exclaiming about the sheep. I tell you true that I have never seen so many of the woolly creatures in one spot. Like earthborn clouds of fluff dotting every field and hillside. I don't know that I would describe the scene as bucolic. It is a trifle daunting to consider the fact there are more sheep than humans in this corner of the world.

I make their acquaintance on the morrow.

Perhaps the part about the sheep had been effective. Cece's eyelids grew heavy and she smiled as she imagined vexing her host on the morrow.

The rattle of the door on its hinges woke her up. Cece looked around blearily, trying to make sense of her surroundings.

"I hear you stirring. Up and about, duty waits for no one."

With a pleasant jolt she remembered where exactly she'd landed. The brusque command of her host skated across her nape, just as his words had last night.

Cece stretched her toes toward the rafters. "Tea would not be amiss," she called down.

" 'Tis not a boarding house."

She smiled at the gruff irritation lacing his tone. "No, but I know you have tea because you provided it yesterday. And if you expect me to express enthusiasm for whatever lessons you're handing out today, I require tea."

"Your lessons today will be on lambing."

Lambing? Cece's pulse raced in alarm and anticipation. She swiftly braided her hair and rushed down the ladder. "I'll be responsible for helping you deliver a lamb?"

"Aye. Once you've donned the garments I laid over there."

She glanced in the direction he was pointing. He'd procured her gown from yesterday. It was laying over the back of the chair. The mud was absent from the hem and she wondered if he'd been the one to brush it off or if it had been Moira. There was also a gleaming copper tub that hadn't been there yesterday.

"I have older, more suitable clothing."

"The rain turned to snow last night. You'll have to trudge through it to retrieve them."

She glanced down at her slippers in consternation. She'd been so incensed and miserable last night she'd left her boots by the door when she'd decided to demand more comfortable accommodation. "I don't know if I can manage that without becoming soaked through."

He braced his hands on his hips and gave her a long-suffering look. As if she was the most agitating creature on the face of the planet. "Drink your tea and I'll carry you."

Her mouth dropped open. "C-c-carry me?" She stammered.

One of those beguiling, condescending brows rose in response. "Aye, lass. Carry you. If you catch cold, I'll have to tolerate your presence far longer. And I don't want the possibility of your demise on my conscience."

Cece wanted to squirm beneath his flinty gaze. And sputter with indignation. "Tolerate my presence? I am not a termagant."

"You have upended my routine, Mrs. Thompson, and are therefore intolerable."

The sheer arrogance and assuredness of that statement prompted an urge to stomp on his instep. She tamped it down. "From what I've observed, you need to have your routine upended."

"You haven't known me long enough to observe anything. Do not presume things on such a brief acquaintance, Mrs. Thompson."

Every time he said her married name it was like the jab of a well-aimed needle. She'd been pinned beneath him on a mattress for pity's sake. He'd shared confidences with her last night. Did those moonlit confessions mean nothing? They'd progressed beyond mere acquaintances, even if it had only been a day. "You may call me Cecily. Or Cece."

"I'm not sure such familiarity is wise."

Familiarity? After she had the answer to her sisters' question? He was being ridiculous. "I assume you're referring to the effect it will have on my reputation. If the effect doesn't concern me, why should it concern you?"

He heaved a great sigh and turned back to the kettle now steaming on the stove. If his sighs were any indication, he found her exasperating in the extreme. "Your letters were not an accurate representation of how maddening you are."

"I'm not maddening. I simply think such formality is uncalled for. Especially considering you tumbled me into a straw mattress last night."

He turned about somewhat clumsily, as if she'd shocked him. "Here."

He thrust the steeping tea into her hand.

She'd most certainly embarrassed him. The red streaks creeping up his neck and into his cheeks were evidence her blunt observation had disconcerted him.

Cece wanted to revel in the upset to his stoicism. She curled her hand around the cup and gave him her most winsome smile. "Thank you for taking care of me."

"You are not receiving special treatment. I would provide as much for any guest who found themselves beneath my roof."

She decided teasing him would be an amusing way to consume her tea. "You offer to carry all your guests?" She pointed to the tub in the corner. "And lug metal bathtubs through the snow for them?"

He lifted his own cup to his mouth and glared at her over the rim. "You know I do not."

"Then I thank you for your special treatment."

"Aargh," he muttered and turned away from her.

She studied the tense line of his shoulders, the tapered waist nipped in by the tucked folds of his linen shirt, and the taut curve of backside beneath his kilt. Whether or not he believed it, he was truly a mountain any woman in her right mind wouldn't balk at scaling.

"I only meant to tease you."

He sighed yet again. Honestly, with all those laborious exhalations of air on her behalf, how did he have any air left to draw into his lungs?

"I am unaccustomed to teasing. Mrs. McKendrick is the only one brave enough to chance my displeasure."

"Well, I am very accustomed to teasing. It is the natural outcome of growing up with six sisters and an inescapable part of my nature. Surely you know this if you are acquainted with my letters?"

He turned to face her again. "Your letters didn't capture how mischievous you are."

Oh, she liked being called mischievous. She wondered if he thought her a saucy minx and couldn't help imagining him calling her exactly that in a gravelly, exasperated growl. That delightful possibility made her toes tingle.

"I'm not mischievous, Mr. Lockhart. I merely know my own mind and am unafraid of speaking it. And I believe life is too brief to spend the time we're granted complaining instead of laughing."

"I've found the brevity of life demands the opposite consideration, Mrs. Thompson. The time we are given shouldn't be spent on frivolity."

His grim expression made Cece wonder who'd defecated in his porridge. "You could do with more than a bit of laughter, Mr. Lockhart. You truly are the dour stick-in-the-mud Henry suspected you were."

"As Mrs. Mckendrick is irritatingly fond of reminding me. But now is not the time to indulge. The storm has just begun and we have work to do. It takes all sorts to make up the world, Mrs. Thompson, and I am perfectly willing to shoulder the responsibility for those who do not find themselves up to the task."

Was he calling her idle? "I'll have you know, Mr. Lockhart, that you shouldn't make assumptions about my commitment to industry. My sisters and I have been fending for ourselves nearly our entire lives. I may not have the advantage of your years, but I have been wielding a needle since I was little more than five summers."

"Your ire amuses me, Mrs. Thompson. I was neither assuming nor challenging you. I was simply making a point. By the by, just how many years do you think I have?"

Cece sniffed and crossed her arms. "If you intended no insult, you should moderate your tone. I'd hazard you are in the twilight of your life." Cece privately thought he was in the prime of his life, but she didn't think he deserved to know the scope of her admiration.

He strode toward her and the air filled with the same tension that had flared between them last night. "Tell me, Mrs. Thompson, did it feel like I'm in the twilight of my life? Though I have the occasional aches and pains, there are other parts of my body that would disagree with your assessment."

He stood so close she could see the rise and fall of his chest, and the thread of silver in the hairs that curled just above his collar. She had the absurd urge to straighten his collar so she could accurately determine the texture of those hairs.

As the meaning of his words sank in, she twisted her free hand in the folds of her nightrobe and clutched her empty teacup as if it was a rope pulling her away from imminent drowning.

"I am not here to engage in scandalous behavior, Mr. Lockhart, despite the impropriety of my unannounced arrival."

"As you've warned me, Mrs. Thompson, I'll neither assume nor guess at your intentions or motives. I would simply remind you that I am a man and will respond accordingly when you cast aspersions on my capabilities."

Cece rolled her eyes. "Men and their obsessions with their cocks."

She slapped her free hand over her mouth when she realized she'd spoken aloud.

Her host merely gave her the nearest approximation of a smile she'd yet seen. "Indeed."

He glanced at her empty cup, which now dangled at her side. "If you've finished your tea, I'll convey you to your cottage."

Cece felt her cheeks suffuse with color. She swallowed the sudden dryness in her throat that should have been assuaged by the tea. "I'm finished."

The croak she heard in her voice made her wince.

He reached between them and unfolded her fingers from the clasp on the handle. His arm stretched behind her to place it on the shelf and she grew light-headed.

He dangled a bright plaid scarf in front of her. It was big enough to swaddle her. Obviously designed for men of his proportions.

"You need to wrap this around yourself."

"It's the size of a bedsheet. Where would I even begin?"

"I'd not thought you helpless, but we don't have the time for long-winded explanations."

He looped it around her shoulders and pulled her near. This close, she could see that flecks of brown, the color of peat and cherry wood, broke up the uncanny green of his iris.

"Arms up, lass."

She lifted them without protest, a peculiar weakness in her limbs. Like he'd mesmerized her.

He crossed the ends at her neck, his knuckles brushing against her skin like a trickle of fire. One of his hands landed on her hip as he turned her so he could wind the cloth around her body. He was wrapping her like one of the mummies she'd seen in the pictures of the Exhibition Fran had sent them from London. By the time he tucked the end of the plaid in a fold at her waist she felt like a trussed sausage.

When he was finished, he pulled the hood he'd fashioned over her head. Before she even had the chance to blink he stooped down and slid his arms beneath her legs and around her waist.

"Arms around my neck," he roughly instructed.

Cece closed her eyes and obeyed. She was cradled against his chest, and the position made her aware of several things at once.

The texture of those hairs against her cheek was like the finest silk. Not coarse at all.

The skin beneath his shirt was warm. Like one of the pans she and her sisters put beneath the covers on the coldest of nights.

He needed a shave and a trim. His beard fell to well below his chin, and there was several days scruff on his upper cheeks.

His mouth beneath his mustache was shaped like the most sinfully tempting pillow. The loft had been too dim last night for a sufficient appreciation of its kissability.

She hadn't conjured his smell from her imagination. It was just how she imagined heather and misty mountains would smell.

He'd become still as a statue beneath her perusal. "Are you finished cataloging me so we can be on our way?"

"I wasn't cataloging you." She protested. "I was merely adjusting my hold."

He snorted. He clearly didn't believe her. "If you say so. I felt your scrutiny. Am I not gentlemanly enough to suit your tastes?"

She couldn't very well tell him she suspected he suited her tastes perfectly – despite his unkempt, rat's nest of a beard. She had a soft spot for pirates, rogues and marauders, and preferred them to gentlemen. Henry had been somewhat of a rapscallion, and she knew it was why she'd tumbled into love so quickly. "I'll not bother addressing that ridiculous question. If you were privy to my correspondence, you are well aware I don't expect you to be a gentleman. At least not in that sense."

He peered down at her. "And what sense is that?"

"In the sense of appearance. However, I do expect you to conduct yourself with decorum."

Chapter Eight

Malcolm

Letter dated March 9, 1854.

Dearest Husband, I've set aside the pile of socks that need darning to write you this letter. I was grateful for the excuse to abandon them for the evening. It's my least favorite chore but my sisters insist my stitches are the neatest. I have a sneaking suspicion they drop so many of theirs because they don't like this chore either. Gertrude is waxing poetic in the corner about her latest plot twist. Somehow the heroine's

carriage wheel has loosened and rolled away off the side of the cliff. It sounds as if the resident of the ruined castle is going to miraculously save her. All of the twists and turns are a bit hard to follow, but my sister insists this is the type of story everyone in London is clamoring for. We all hope she's correct and her scribbling will soon find a publisher.

MALCOLM WAS CONVINCED THE object of his long-term pining was daft. Thus far, neither one of them had acted decorously. At least not in the restrained way he'd been led to believe was a prerequisite for polite society.

He shifted his stance because the weight of her nestled against him, even when she was swaddled like a babe, was enough to ignite his senses. "I don't know about decorum, but I'll treat you with respect. Even when you don't return the favor."

"I have been respectful since the moment I arrived. I resent your allusion to the contrary."

If she were standing in front of him, she'd be huffing and puffing like a wee dragon. Instead, she turned stiff as a board in his embrace. He'd been teasing her – in his own awkward way. Moira was constantly telling him that his sense of humor was too dry for anyone to understand. His guest's reaction proved she was telling the truth.

"I was teasing you, lass. Your arrival may have been unexpected, but I understand why you're here. I would likely have done the same had I been in your position."

"And what position do you think I'm in, Mr. Lockhart?"

"You're a bit at my mercy, aren't you, Mrs. Thompson? Because you need answers and stories only I can provide."

She was at his mercy in other ways too, because of the storm. Because of the vulnerability of her social station. Because she was a woman alone and that status could be damning in certain situations. Whether or not she wore widow's weeds. He was reminding her of her situation, that she was there on his forbearance.

Her jaw flexed, as if she was biting back a sharp retort. "I suppose I am." Her admission was rueful as she twirled her finger in the loose laces of his shirt. "Funnily enough, I trust you not to take advantage of it."

She was asking him to treat her gently. To let her down easily if he was unwilling to part with the confidences she sought. "I won't. I may be scarred and crabbit, but I'm not a monster."

Her brow wrinkled in confusion. "Is crabbit Scots for acting like a lion with a thorn in its paw? Or a bear being chased by bees because he stole their honey?"

"'Tis exactly what it means. I may roar, but my bark is far worse than my bite. And I have an adverse reaction to bee sting. I'll not be chasing them."

"I suppose I shall find out the extent of your crabbit-headedness when you begin my lessons with the sheep today."

"Aye. We've wasted too much time already. One of the ewes is on the brink of delivery."

"If you were so impatient to begin you should have woken me earlier. And we're still not quite ready. You're not wearing any head covering. And your legs are bare."

"My blood runs hot, lass. And I've a thick skin. I'm accustomed to the cold."

"Hmmm," she murmured and snuggled closer. "You are very warm."

Mal took a deep breath. Her snuggling, and the rapid puffs of her breath against his throat, was heating more than his blood.

They were only seven steps from the door, and he counted every single one to distract him from her soft sighs and incessant squirming. If her objective was to vex him almost beyond endurance, she was succeeding.

He shut the door firmly behind them to ward off the cold that was sure to seep into every nook and cranny, and hefted her higher for the short trek to her lodgings.

The snow gently pelted them. It fluttered over her hair and cheeks, spangling the dark strands and dropping silvery, lacy kisses over the crests and planes of her up-raised face. She'd abandoned the nestle of her chin against his breastbone, and had lifted away enough to peer up at him with an indecipherable expression.

"What has beguiled you, Mrs. Thompson?" Mal gruffly asked.

"You are a conundrum, Mr. Lockhart."

Mal didn't care to examine that statement. He was grateful their arrival at the door interrupted any further commentary.

He pushed it open. The fire in the hearth was nothing but ash, and their breaths were visible in the frigid room as he gritted his teeth and set her down. Since he'd already nearly embarrassed himself when she was in such proximity, he took care to lower her without brushing her body against his.

"I assure you, madam, there is no mystery about my person." He told her as he began unwrapping the scarf. When he reached her waist, she placed her hands over his. Insistent that she could manage the rest of her extrication.

"I would hazard you are the only person who thinks so." She stepped away and gave him a curt nod. "No matter. I am here for answers and I will receive them."

She crossed the room and bent over her valise, extracting a bundle of clothing.

"You are in for a considerable disappointment, Mrs. Thompson if you think to unearth some grave or lurid plot like those in your sister's novels."

She whirled about at his pronouncement and her eyes widened. "Do you read those novels, Mr. Lockhart? Such an endeavor seems quite out of character for you."

"As we've discussed, Mrs. Thompson, I do not have time for frivolity."

"I think my sister Gertrude would make you quite the parody in one of her stories."

Malcolm crossed his arms. "And where would she obtain such insight into my character, Mrs. Thompson? Such intimate detail about my life could only spring from those who have made my acquaintance."

She flushed and dipped her head to study the seams of the clothing bundled in her arms. "My letters," she mumbled.

A flash of annoyance, like the sound of gold nuggets ricocheting off the edge of a tin miner's pan, sizzled down Mal's spine. "I am well appraised of your prolific letter writing tendencies. You will ensure that your sister does not use me as fodder for her next novel."

She lifted her head, eyes blazing. "I would never purposefully malign you. Surely you know enough of my character to think better of me than that. You should also know that I only relate events and people as I see them, and

I have no control over the creative inspiration or license of my sister."

"Malign me? I would hope not. I may not be a ray of sunshine, Mrs. Thompson, but I do not deserve a character assassination."

She straightened her spine, set her chin at a prominent angle, and threw back her shoulders. "I agree, Mr. Lockhart. You do not. Now, as I have no desire to have you cart me back in the same manner you carried me here, I thank you to turn around so I may dress."

Mal dipped his head in acknowledgment and pivoted, giving her his back.

He couldn't hear her divesting her nightgown. But he imagined the flutter of it hitting the floor and the gleam of her limbs in the soft morning light. He closed his eyes and clenched his jaw. This obsession was becoming damned inconvenient.

He imagined her chemise floating over her head and caressing every hollow and curve of her body as the fabric settled around her and brushed against her upper thighs. He imagined her sliding her pantaloons over those luscious hips, her nimble fingers drawing the waistband tight and nipping it about her trim waist. He imagined her briskly fastening the hooks down the front of her half-corset and securing a ruffled petticoat over the whole of it.

"You may turn back around."

He slowly did so, willing his raging imagination and raging cock to calm down. She would be fully encapsulated in all that voluminous fabric. Not at all tempting.

She was wearing a sober skirt and blouse of dark navy. When he squinted, he saw it was a calico sprinkled with tiny white sprigs of an indeterminate flower. A crisp white apron dangled over her wrist and she was securing the final button at her collar.

The length of her arms was covered. She was not displaying even a hint of skin below her neck. There was no reason for her delectability other than the fact he recalled the very particular weight of her in his arms and could still feel her breath against his skin.

She efficiently twisted the apron strings into a bow at the base of her spine. "As soon as I retrieve my cloak, I shall be ready for our lessons."

She walked past him, her shoulder scraping against his. He felt that fleeting contact even through the layers of clothing they wore. This was becoming more inconvenient by the moment.

She filched her outerwear from the hook by the door and stuck her arms through it. She pulled the hood over her head and turned back to him. "I am ready."

Chapter Nine

Malcolm

Letter dated May 10, 1854.

Dearest husband, I've just spent a delightful afternoon with my elder sister Arie and her new husband. Their fields are full of ewes and lambs and when you look over the fence all you see is a green meadow speckled with fluffy white clouds. We've finally heard from Fran. She's been accepted into Nightingale's ranks and is leaving the front for Scutari. I often wonder if I should have followed in her footsteps, even though I

don't possess her training. I would be nearer to you, and have a better understanding of what you're going through.

S HE'D TRUDGED BEHIND HIM, valiantly sticking to the trail made by his boots. When they reached the paddock she swept past him, oblivious to the effects of the snow she sank into as she forged ahead. Her feet would be icicles. "Mind you avoid covering your boots completely. I don't have time to keep your toes from turning black and falling off if your antics cause frostbite."

He would take care of her, but he would blame himself if she came to harm.

She squinted at him over her shoulder. "We have snow in Cumbria, Mr. Lockhart. I'm wearing thick wool socks I knitted myself." She hoisted herself up on the railing and slung an arm around the post. "I've never in my life seen so many sheep. I gave up on counting them all on my journey here."

The wonder in her voice made him smile when he never smiled. Not like this. Because her comment about the sheep was exactly the sort of whimsical revelation she'd shared in her letters. He covered the quirk of his mouth with a brusque swipe because she couldn't know she possessed this particular ability. It would be another arrow she'd stow in her arsenal and brandish at will. "My homecoming was chasing them down. They were scattered far and wide across the entire county."

"How did they get loose?"

"My grandda had a better sense of them when he had all his faculties, but the neighbors say when his mind became muddled he lost track of where he'd left them."

"Their wee black faces are so endearing. They're not like any of the other sheep I saw during my train ride." She wiggled her fingers in their direction. They ignored her.

"Grandda was one of the only farmers who didn't replace our native herd with Cheviots. After the last bad winter we had, everyone else saw him as wise instead of stubborn."

"Why did they think he was stubborn?"

"Because he stuck to his old crofter ways. What the other landowners didn't see is that our terrain is rugged and Blackface sheep fare better when the weather becomes treacherous. They're good at foraging and don't need our intervention to survive. The ewes are fierce protectors of the lambs and will brave predators and storms."

"If they usually fend for themselves, why have you brought all of them into the main corral?"

"This weather makes for a perilous onset of life. The lambs born into it have a greater chance of survival, and the ewes as well if there are any complications, if they are in the paddock. And we'll need to lightly shear them to ensure they don't get caught in the gorse and bramble once we set them loose for the winter."

She leaned against the top fence rail. "They're much larger than they appeared from my vantage point in the lane."

Her shoulders were hunched forward, and a sidelong glance at her profile showed him she was biting her lip.

He moved into place beside her, his arms dangling alongside hers.

"You needn't be afraid. I know the horns can be intimidating, but they're mild mannered and like to be scratched behind the ears."

"I don't want to raise their ire. I'm accustomed to dogs eager for my attention and cats content to sit in my lap or groom themselves by the fire."

Malcolm's laughter rumbled between them. "Sheep are not unlike large dogs."

"You'll instruct me?"

Oh, the ways he wanted to instruct her. But she was speaking of sheep, not bedsport.

"I will. Just as my grandda instructed me."

The memory of the morning he'd shorn his first sheep sparked just then.

He'd been missing his parents. His father's low whistle and his mother's soft lullaby. The way he'd fall asleep nestled between them. Riding on his da's shoulders for a madcap circuit down the lane. The loss of them had been sudden and devastating.

It wasn't his grandda's way to coddle a man's sensibilities. Or those of a boy. Mal figured that stoicism had been instilled in him at an early age and it was why he was so gruff and blunt – he'd had that example of tough love. His grandda had sensed his sorrow but hadn't commented on it or tried to erase it. He'd brought him to the paddock and introduced him to the newest lamb. It's wet muzzle and soft coat had healed something inside him. He'd taught him how to bear the sorrow and make it a part of him. "Remember lad, those we love are never truly gone. They're here, just like the rise and set of the sun. Reminding us to hold the memories close but take the path forward." The old man's hand had landed heavily in his shoulder, like an anchor.

He hadn't known of his grandfather's passing until he stepped onto the platform at Galashiels and was greeted by the somber vicar. He'd been mere hours late. Yet another opportunity to say farewell that had been stolen from him.

Her hand closed on top of his. He'd gripped the wood so forcefully at the onslaught of memories, a splinter embedded itself in his palm. He winced at her touch.

"I apologize if my questions have stirred painful memories. My sisters often chastise me for asking inappropriately mortifying and agonizing things."

Mal sighed. "Your question wasn't agonizing. It just stirred regrets I don't enjoy dwelling on."

Her expression was abashed. "I didn't intend to disrupt your ghosts. Please forgive me."

"My grandfather and I didn't part amicably. I was eager to make amends."

"Why didn't you?"

"His burial was the first task that awaited me on my return." Mal grimly replied.

Her hand tightened on his. "On the heels of all the carnage you'd just witnessed on the battlefield, I'm sure it was quite the terrible blow."

Mal swallowed the tightness in his throat. "He died believing I was still angry. I couldn't apologize for my rebellion or the awful things I said. I couldn't say goodbye."

She turned toward the frolicking lambs. "My mother died when I was barely three summers. I don't remember much about her. She scented her clothes chest with lavender sachets, and I used to fall asleep cuddled in her arms and wreathed in that perfume."

She was contemplative, and though it wasn't in Mal's nature to share his remorse, her tender acceptance urged him to let go of some of his burdens. "I carry so much loss here." He thumped his fist against his heart. "My parents. My regiment. My grandfather. Letting people in means accepting the truth that someday you will have to let them go."

Her eyes clouded at his admission, and she stroked his knuckles with the pad of her thumb. "Yes. There's such hollowness to it. One becomes used to carrying it around, and forgets the pang of it. Until it ambushes you from nowhere. It's easy to imagine what you would have said in those last moments if they weren't stolen from you."

"You're thinking about Henry."

She nodded beside him. "I wonder what I would have said to him. Our marriage was not the product of a long acquaintance. I was caught up in his whirlwind, giddy with possibility. You were close – you know what his energy was like. He was a lightning rod. He wakened something in me and I felt so mature, getting married."

"How old were you?"

"I was almost eighteen and foolishly thought myself invincible."

So she was a fresh twenty-seven or thereabouts to his thirty-nine. "You were barely out of the nursery, but not foolish. Love is never foolish, no matter how untethered it makes you seem."

She lightly punched him in the shoulder. "I had been out of the nursery for quite some time. But since I was the youngest, my sisters tended to indulge me. I wish they hadn't. I was wholly unprepared for the harsh reality of widowhood."

Mal was acquainted with several war widows. Had even welcomed them into his bed at one time to ease their loneliness and his. But he wouldn't pretend to know the distinctions of her situation. "Your husband died valiantly. He charged ahead of the rest of us. I know he wanted to return to you and raise a family."

"We struggled to put food on the table and clothes on our backs after our mother died. Our father drowned his grief in ale and the business suffered until he remarried. He treated his daughters like objects to be bought and sold. I thought I would finally have the chance to provide the safe haven for my family I didn't experience. I know you're not ready to speak of it, but when you are, I have so many questions. About what he wanted when he came home to me. If he spoke of me in his last moments."

Her gaze was guileless, and though it was clear she would bide her time until he was ready to speak, he decided that sharing at least one memory would answer some of her questions.

"Did you ever wonder at your husband's faithfulness?"

She twisted her head to the side and then faced forward again. There was a faint blush in her cheeks. "Yes," she quietly admitted.

"You needn't have worried about that. He was fonder of horses and cards. And pastry when we could find it. He developed a mild addiction to baklava. He insisted all women but you were more trouble than they were worth. He nattered on about your sweetness and how he was ready for the infernal war to end so he could watch your belly round with child."

She smiled. "Thank you. I'd hoped he was as ready to hasten our babes into the world as I was. I imagine it was very lonely, marching from one battle to another and I'm happy it was only my memory that kept him warm."

Mal snorted. "'Twas more waiting than marching. The battles were short and often confusing. Men and horses wheeling about beneath the veil of smoke, the screaming of soldiers and the thunder of cannons landing all around you. We spent most of our time standing back in a state of heightened awareness, polishing our rifles in anticipation of the next engagement."

"I cannot imagine the toll such uncertainty would take on one's nerves."

Her hand covered his again and he had the irrational urge to shake it off and downplay the vulnerability she sensed.

"Some men in the regiment deserted because they couldn't bear it. It was hard to watch them hunted down and shot for treason. All of us had the urge to abandon our posts, but if we had someone to return home to, we didn't want to take the chance the journey across the sea would be in a pine box."

"We all read the papers. And my sister Frances was a nurse at Scutari. She said the conditions were atrocious before the arrival of Nightingale."

"She's right. More men perished from disease than wounds they received in battle."

"How did you return unscathed?"

Mal's gaze bore into her profile. "Unscathed? Have you not guessed the extent of my scars?"

"But you have made a sanctuary of sorts here, from what Moira has told me. You kept your health aside from your injury. Your mind seems whole."

He expelled a rough breath in protest. "I have nightmares. Like nearly every soldier. One cannot experience that singular melee and tragedy without it invading his sleep. And I'm certain all of us suffered from malnutrition. I'm grateful that one of our comrades was an amateur apothecary and always managed to scrounge up some sort of greenery to ward off scurvy. But there were other threats. Finding clean water that wasn't up or downstream from the camp's privies. The spread of cholera."

"Fran and her husband Mac don't speak of it much. I know it's because they witnessed and experienced terrible things. I know it's truly a miracle you're standing here."

"I still don't know why I was spared. I had less to return to than others. No family. No wife, No bairns."

"You were spared for a purpose, never doubt it. I believe we all have a role to play, and perhaps this was yours. To give others who couldn't manage to stand on their own a soft place to fall."

"Perhaps. And perhaps it was to teach a stubborn English lass how to oversee a lambing and properly shear a sheep."

She shot him an incredulous look. "As if you've given the lass a choice. It was either the sheep or the blizzard."

"Do you truly believe I would have turned you away?"

"When we met, I wasn't certain. Even after a day's acquaintance I'm still not certain. I don't know the extent of your beneficence. You're quite intimidating, you know."

"I'm aware. I've been scaring timid woodland creatures and the faint of heart since I sprouted up a half a dozen inches the summer before I turned fourteen."

"It's not your size that's intimidating, Mr. Lockhart. It's your scowl."

"I don't scowl, Mrs. Thompson. I simply disapprove of chicanery, frippery and shenanigans."

"Chicanery, frippery and shenanigans are what make the world a lighter place. One should indulge in them whenever the opportunity presents itself."

"When the days' work is done. If it is ever done. Which brings us back to our first lesson. Come." He tugged her behind him until they stood in front of one of the stalls.

One of the ewes was lying in the straw, her sides heaving, her head bowed.

"Is it happening soon?"

She sounded anxious and Mal immediately wanted to reassure her. "It is. But she'll be fine. This is Hilda's ninth time."

Mal watched in astonishment as Cece dropped to her knees beside the ewe, heedless of whatever excretions might be hiding in the straw. "Such a strong mother," she cooed and stroked Hilda from her forehead to the tip of her velvety muzzle.

Hilda's sides heaved, and Mal saw the tip of one hoof emerge. The irony struck him – his sheep was just as susceptible to this woman's soothing touch as he was.

He lowered himself to his haunches. "Come on, old girl," he coaxed as he gently ran his hand over her flanks.

"I know you can do it, Hildy," Cece urged.

The way she'd just shortened the ewe's name and made it sound like an endearment...it made him feel like his friend's widow belonged here. In Dunkirk, in this barn. That the feelings he'd nourished for nearly a decade were justified. Because she was clearly special and had the capacity to charm and cajole any and all creatures. Human or otherwise.

Hilda's grunt signaled a concerted effort and the lamb's hind legs emerged. Mal pulled them slowly, until the pelvis was fully visible, then switched the angle toward the ground behind the ewe.

"Make certain he has a soft landing," Mal instructed.

She crouched by his side and gently lowered the lamb to the straw. When she went to stroke its head, Mal fiercely shook his head. "No. If we handle it too much around the face, the mother may reject it."

Her eyes fluttered wide in alarm and she slid back, holding her hands in the air.

Mal shook his head again – this time in irritation. "Christ, woman, I wasn't chastising you. Just warning you what could happen if we aren't careful."

She shot him a look of annoyance in return. "I know you weren't. I'm not so lily-livered as that. I was simply letting you know I understood."

"Come, then. We need to get her to accept her new offspring and make sure she expels the afterbirth."

She knelt in the straw again. "What do you need me to do?"

"Coax her to turn around and acknowledge the lamb."

Cece moved to the ewe's head and began uttering what sounded like nonsense in a low tone. No matter what her mumbling sounded like to Mal, the ewe seemed to like it. She nudged Cece's hand and her answering smile was so bright it made something in his chest thump erratically. He'd been certain this whole experience would sour her impression of him and the farm and send her scurrying home. Instead, it seemed to invigorate her. Perhaps she was like the sister who'd served with Nightingale at Scutari.

Once the lamb was taking its first feeding, and they were watching the bucolic scene together, he turned to her. "You did well, lass. Far better than I expected you to."

She took his hand in her own and he flinched.

Of course the woman was too observant not to notice. "Did you hurt yourself?"

He tried to loosen her grasp. "Merely a splinter in my palm. I've had worse."

"Let me extract it before it causes an infection or digs itself even deeper."

She lifted his hand and turned it toward the light streaming in from the open door. "I'll need to use my teeth to grasp it," she informed him and set her mouth to his palm before he could protest.

Her teeth were like tiny needles, but he felt the brush of her mouth in his groin, and when it swelled from the contact, he was glad of the folds of his kilt.

Her ministrations only lasted a handful of moments and she dropped his hand and spat the offending wood onto the ground. "All done," she cheerily informed him.

He couldn't look away from her mouth. Her plump bottom lip beckoned him. Her eyes swirled like pools of spring heather and her cheeks were flushed. He moved toward her -as if she'd pulled him closer like a puppet master jerking his strings.

He dipped his head and she sighed.

Her sigh jolted him from his daft confusion and he retreated as if struck by lightning. He sketched a bow. "I thank you again for your assistance, Mrs. Thompson," he said as he turned on his heel.

He could feel her gaze like a lance burning into his shoulders, but he refused to turn around.

Chapter Ten

Cece

Letter dated December 21, 1853.

Dearest Little Wren, One of the things I miss the most is the regular dependability of water. There never seems to be enough time for a proper bath and the army has a penchant for situating privies too close to streams. I never thought of myself as fastidious until the smell of my own dried sweat and that of my comrades nearly gave me the vapors.

THREE DAYS AFTER THE lambing, Cece woke to loud caterwauling. When she listened more closely, she recognized a bawdy tavern song that made her cheeks red with secondhand embarrassment. The voice was female, and she assumed it was Moira.

She wondered how late she'd slept this morning. She'd fallen into bed exhausted after a day learning dyeing and spinning under Moira's tutelage.

Her shawl was hanging on the hook and she wrapped it around her shoulders before exiting the room. She was glad of the additional coverage when she opened the door-because her host was sprawled on the bench. His hair was mussed, and he threw his head back as he laughed.

His gaze brightened when he saw her. "We'll have another lesson today, Mrs. Thompson."

Cece crossed to the bench and sat down as gracefully as she could. "What will it be this time?"

"The laird has organized the fall shearing, and many hands make short work," Moira explained from behind her.

"The whole community of Dunkirk will be at the paddocks today, so you'll meet them." Mal informed her.

"Don't terrify the lass, Laird," Moira admonished before addressing Cece. "Mrs. Thompson, we're all aware of your visit, and everyone is eager to make yer acquaintance."

"Even though I'm an Englishwoman?" Cece teasingly asked.

"I told them ye don't put on airs and ye're here to help. That ye're a widow and they should treat ye with respect. Though I suspect some of the lads will fill yer ears with compliments."

Moira's assurance surprised Cece – she sensed the woman had her thumb on the pulse of the entire farm, and gaining her approval was quite the coup de grace.

"You'll let me know if anyone you meet today behaves inappropriately or makes you feel uncomfortable or un-welcome."

Mal's tone was stern, and though Cece was grateful for his protection, she almost worried for the fate of anyone who dared upset her.

"I'll let you know if I'm made to feel any of those things."

He acknowledged her agreement with a curt nod. "Good."

The tension that had risen between them after the lambing, when she was certain he'd been on the verge of kissing her, hovered between them again. It was so palpable she could almost taste it.

"The laird told me ye helped deliver one of the lambs. Ye didn't mention it at the spinning wheel yesterday."

Cece shook her head vigorously at Moira's words, as if she could dispel the trance like she'd empty water from her ears.

"Ye didn't?"

Cece's usually taciturn host had a knack for disconcerting her. Especially since she'd felt what he hid beneath his kilt. Moira had misinterpreted Cece's shaking head, and Cece remembered what Emily had once told her about body language. That someone's intent could be construed from it and it was an almost infallible indication of guilt. "Yes, but I didn't do much. I just helped ensure the ewe accepted the new arrival."

Moira grunted. "That's the tricky part. I was told ye did well."

Cece felt the color rise in her cheeks again at Moira's approval. It would seem her enigmatic host had been praising her. When he'd strode off after a curt farewell, she'd assumed she'd done something to offend him.

If her assistance had resulted in begrudging praise, perhaps his annoyance hadn't stemmed from her actions. In for a penny, in for a pound she reminded herself and took a deep breath. "You praised my efforts?"

"You did well. You weren't squeamish in the least. I'd thought you'd complain about the way cleaning up the birthing would soil your skirts. Like all the other sheltered Englishwomen I've met," he gruffly told her.

Cece laughed outright. His brow lowered and she wondered if her amusement irritated him. Or her tendency to prove false all his notions of how she should behave. "I told you, Laird. Heathsted is a far cry from London. I grew up in the country and if you're as familiar with my letters as you claim to be, you'd know a lambing is not going to send me screaming in the opposite direction."

"You didn't complain about any of it."

He sounded flummoxed and a trifle grim. Surely he'd actually needed her help.

"Were you trying to convince me to board the train at the earliest opportunity? Or to find lodgings in Galashiels?" She asked suspiciously.

He crossed his arms over his chest and glared.

"That's exactly the outcome you desired!" She exclaimed in disbelief. The revelation he'd been trying to get rid of her was a painful one.

His scowling countenance was surly enough to make milk curdle in the pail. "You have no business staying here. I harbor no secrets and you should accept that your husband died as a hero who was exceedingly fond of his wife."

"As I've already pointed out, Laird, I'm not going anywhere until I find the answers I seek."

Moira's gaze had been flitting back and forth between them with growing delight. "The two of ye are at an impasse. I suggest ye work out yer differences with the shearin'. After one sweaty afternoon and a mug of ale, ye'll be in much greater accord."

"Ale ensures everyone is in accord, Moira," Mal sarcastically observed.

Moira snorted. "Unless there's too much of it and the fists begin to fly because of imagined insults and benighted pride."

"I will ensure the night doesn't end in a brawl. No matter how many barrels of ale are consumed."

His pronouncement was directed at Cece. As if he was assuring her he would see to her safety if a melee came to pass.

She squirmed in discomfort. Sometimes being the focus of his singular attention made her feel like one of the hermit crabs she'd read about and she wanted to burrow into the sand to avoid it. She cleared her throat. "If it's done steeping, I'll have some tea, Moira."

"Aye, lass. That's yer cup on the table. This lummox told me he needed coffee this morn. He should count himself lucky that my man had some stashed in a tin." She grimaced. "Nasty stuff."

"My major in Calcutta was fond of telling us drinking coffee would put hair on our chests and make our balls drop."

Cece's jaw fell open. She wasn't sure he was teasing until she saw his mouth curve up in the barest smile. A quirk so minute it was almost unnoticeable.

"Malcolm Alistair Lockhart, ye're incorrigible," Moira cackled.

She turned to Cece, "Ye must excuse his lack o' manners, no doubt he's tryin' to shock ye."

Cece smiled. "It's not the words themselves that shock me so much as the messenger. I was under the mistaken impression his sense of humor was virtually nonexistent."

Moira tossed her head back at that and chortled. When she finally caught her breath, she wagged a finger in Malcolm's direction. "Never say this lass can't give as good as she gets. She has ye figured out."

She waved Cece toward the bench. "Have a seat, lass." The fresh scone Moira handed her smelled of cinnamon and vanilla. Cece held it to her nose before dipping it in the tea. The texture of the scone did not match it's enticing scent. Even the saturation of the tea did nothing to soften the brick she held in her hand. The brick she feared would chip her tooth if she bit into it.

She glanced up and Mal's laughing eyes conveyed he knew exactly what she was thinking and was aware of her plight. She narrowed her gaze and dunked the scone again as Moira nattered on. Some crumbs fell into her mug, and she decided it was safe to consume it.

She closed her eyes when the warmth of the spice hit her tongue. It was sharp and comforting at the same time. When her eyes flickered open again, she caught the glint of something very like hunger in the laird's gaze before he hurriedly glanced away.

"I'll meet you in the paddocks," he tersely ordered and rose to his feet.

After he'd made his exit, Moira turned to Cece with a speculative expression. "I've never seen him so easily perturbed by a woman."

Cece smiled wryly. "I'm simply not of the ilk he'd made me out to be. I confound him."

Moira tipped her head. "Ye may confound him, but ye fascinate him as well."

The fascination was mutual, but she shoved hers into a vault. She was certain it was one-sided. He was simply grateful for the comfort her letters to Henry had provided.

Chapter Eleven

Mal

Letter dated June 17th, 1854.

Dearest Husband, Have you ever felt like a stranger amongst family? As if you're on the verge of jumping out of your skin, casting them off and running away? None of my sisters will let me dwell on the desperation and sadness I feel. I don't know how to express to them that I need the space to feel all the things I'm feeling- even if they aren't feelings that are easily digestible for others.

WHEN SHE STEPPED INTO the paddocks, all the boisterous laughter abruptly stopped. Every single person gathered for the shearing turned their attention to her, the hushed awareness inescapable. They were waiting on a cue from Mal.

He beckoned her closer and when she obliged, he took her hand. He felt the leap of her pulse, but ascribed it to nerves in the face of so many strangers.

"Friends, this is Mrs. Thompson. She's joining us for a time and wants to learn all she can while she's here."

"Is she English?" One of the men asked, just before a long stream of tobacco narrowly missed Cece's shoe.

She tilted her chin in the man's direction, her expression flinty. "I am English. But that shouldn't be a barrier to learning how you manage things on this holding."

One of the younger lasses, Hazel MacPherson, stepped forward and curtseyed. "We're happy to welcome any guest of our laird."

Malcolm's guest gave him a pointed look. As if she was telling him at least someone was happy to welcome her. "I thank all of you for your hospitality," she said with a curtsey befitting a queen.

"I'm Liam MacTavish and I'll be happy to show ye the way of it, Mrs. Thompson," one of the farmers eagerly offered.

Mal shot a glare at his cousin for his affability. Duncan's younger brother was single and flirtatious. He was letting him know in no uncertain terms that the only one who'd be giving Mrs. Thompson instruction was him. Mal grimly acknowledged that the knot in his chest at the thought of someone else standing so close to her was jealousy.

He extracted the hand shearer he'd stashed in his satchel and said, "I'll be the one showing our guest how it's done and this is what we'll be using."

She came to his side and frowned down at the tool resting in the palm of his hand. "It looks unwieldy."

"You'll become competent if not proficient. An accomplished shearer can finish five sheep in an hour."

MacTavish thrust out his chest, and Mal knew a boast was coming. "I'm up to ten in an hour. Are ye sure ye don't want me to teach her. Laird?"

Mal's answering glower must have conveyed how he felt about the proposition because the man visibly deflated and gave him a respectful nod.

"Come, Mrs. Thompson. We'll begun with the gentlest of the lot." She followed him to the corner, where the oldest ewe was munching on a shank of hay.

"Don't you have to ensure they're immobilized for the shearing process?"

"I'll make sure the ewe is still during today's attempts."

He approached Molly. He knew her by the spot of white to the left of her nostril and the fact she didn't bother to acknowledge Shep's barking and prancing around her feet.

"Molly's our oldest and most docile ewe. We'll begin with her. You'll need to sit on this stool." He and the rest of the men had brought them out of the shearing shed that morning. The threat of snow had lifted and there were at least a hundred ewes with coats thick enough to require shearing if they were loosed on the heath.

She gingerly sat down. He crouched behind her, his hands enfolding hers, aware of the surreptitious glances being cast in their direction. He twisted her hands around the clippers. "Make certain you have a firm grip before you start cutting."

She bit her lip, and he felt her fingers tighten in his clasp.

Despite the frigid air, it was hot, sweaty work, and they were both mopping their faces with their sleeves by the time they'd finished shearing seven of the sheep.

There was only one ewe left, and MacTavish was swiftly depleting her of her coat. Those who'd already finished had already bagged up the wool for carding.

"We'll deliver the bags to the carding shed," Hazel informed him.

Mal nodded gratefully. "I want to thank all of you for your hard work today. It means the herd will be safer on the heath and we'll have extra wool to trade."

The crowd of tenants whooped and a couple threw their hats in the air.

"Will you have a drink with us at the tavern, Laird? You can bring the lass. She deserves a pint as well."

Mal wiped off the shears and dropped them back in the satchel at his waist. His leg was paining him and he ground his knuckles against the knot of scar tissue on his outer thigh.

He glanced over at Cece and noted she was as bedraggled from the shearing as she'd been from the mud and rain on the day she'd appeared on his doorstep.

She was mutinous and savage and determined, not the creature of grace and light he'd imagined while penning those letters.

She wasn't afraid to challenge him, and now he knew she got a glint in her eyes that had more iron than a forge when she was determined to get her way.

Belonging to this woman would rip him to shreds and make him anew. That knowledge scared him more than the charge at Balaclava. And he still wanted to kiss her. More than he'd ever wanted anything in his life.

He knew she would be like spun glass in his arms, molten and sparkling. He knew she would absorb him like the dark waters of the loch, until he was drowning and completely a creature of her making. He shook his head to clear it of the traitorous consuming thoughts and realized he hadn't answered MacTavish's question.

"Perhaps another time, MacTavish."

"Thank you for the offer, Mr. MacTavish, but I'd much rather have tea than ale." Cece spoke up as she tipped her head back and rolled her shoulders.

She wasn't used to this kind of work – what had Mal been thinking? He shook his head to dispel his musings. The remorse hit him like a fist to the gut.

They watched the crowd of laborers depart in a wave of laughter and high spirits.

"I'm sorry, lass. I shouldn't have manipulated you into doing this."

Her eyes flickered open, even as she pressed her fingers against her temples. "You didn't manipulate me, Mr. Lockhart. I am a grown woman and perfectly capable of refusing your demands."

The thought of taming that brazen streak, of seeing those eyes half-lidded and drunk on sex, made him quake where he stood. "I manipulated you. You're not accustomed to work like this and you'll be sore later and regret not standing up to me."

Her hands went to her hips, and he tried to ignore the way it stretched the material taut across them. Showing him how perfectly the curve of his hands would fit there. How easy it would be to latch onto that bounty and tug her against him.

"Mr. Lockhart, is shearing something everyone in your community does?"

"Aye. We all must set our hand to it."

"The women and children included?" She waved her hand to encompass all the sheep that had been wrestled with by the women, their husbands and their children.

Mal grimaced because he saw where she was going with this. He should have kept his mouth shut because of course he knew that the road to hell was paved with good intentions. "Aye," he cautiously agreed.

She stepped forward, jabbing her finger into the center of his chest. "Then why should you coddle me? I'm not afraid of dirt or hard work."

"You're a guest and I overstepped." He stubbornly insisted.

"You didn't overstep, and I'm an unwelcome guest you're stuck with indefinitely."

He stepped forward then, so close they were almost brushing against each other. He needed to reassure her that though she may have been unexpected, she was welcome. Most of the people in Mal's life were either afraid of him or in awe of him. She'd been reminding him he was just a man. She didn't tiptoe in his wake like she was navigating a path of broken glass. She wasn't afraid to fence him with her words or chastise him for being churlish.

He raised his arm, slowly, giving her the chance to back away. Her face hardened and her eyes blazed and he could tell she was bracing herself.

"Little Wren, you belonged to all of us, you know." He didn't know where the words came from, but they were true. She *had* belonged to all of them. Every single man in the regiment had looked forward to her letters. And he'd been her confessor of sorts and the architect of that sly humor.

His palm slid up the side of her neck and cupped her jaw. A soft sigh escaped her lips and she leaned into his touch.

"That was his name for me. I suppose you read it in the letters."

"Aye. I heard it from his lips. When he read aloud the correspondence the two of you shared."

The lie sat like stone on the tip of his tongue, coating it in venom and remorse. He swallowed the poison and salved his conscience with a resolution to tell her the truth. Soon. Eventually.

"Then you are well aware I never quite understood why he chose such an innocuous endearment."

"You may not have understood his reasoning for such an unconventional choice, but all of us did. Your letters..." He stroked the hair from her brow and cleared his throat. "You cannot know what your letters meant."

"I suspect they meant more than I dared to hope. But I cannot know what they meant, not truly, unless you tell me."

He dropped his head. "Everything." His reply was guttural, something between a rasp and a growl, and her eyes flickered in response. "Everything. They meant everything."

"Everything?"

He could hear her breathless anticipation.

"Everything, Little Wren. Hope for each day. The strength to carry on. The dream of you and what you represented. Hearth and home. Abundant love."

"You dreamt of me? Before you even knew me?"

He caught her hand and raised it to his lips, brushing a kiss across her knuckles. "I knew you. The woman you are snuck between your words, imbued them with your spirit. Your light and your humor and your sweetness. Even the sharp bite of your sarcasm."

Chapter Twelve

Cece

Letter dated October 11, 1854.

Dearest, Sweetest Little Wren. I prayed last night. We received word we're headed for a battle that may be a great reckoning. We know our regiment will be a line of first defense, but details have been scarce and somewhat garbled. I think I would trade anything right now, even the immortal soul that may soon be imperiled, for one more glimpse of your violet eyes and the cherry red of your lips swollen from my kisses.

Pray for me too, dearest wife. That I may come home safely.

CECE WOULD CARRY THE feel of those rough satin lips against her skin for the rest of her days. And the look he'd given her. She'd wanted to lift her hand to his face in return, to brush soft kisses across his scarred knuckles.

She thought he might haul her even closer, bracket her face with those broad palms and blunt fingers. So she could feel the hard calluses against her cheeks when he set his mouth on hers.

He did none of those things. He dropped her hand, straightened his shoulders and retreated. Something shuttered in the jade green of his gaze, and it became more brown than green again. She wondered if his other eye was still that beautiful color, if he'd ever let down his guard enough to show her what lay beneath the patch.

She gave herself a mental shake to put her jumbled thoughts to rights. "I'm usually not the sarcastic one, you know. My sisters tell me I'm the only Wainwright with more honey than vinegar in my veins."

His mouth quirked to one side, lifting the corner with the scar so she could see the hint of a dimple. "I've yet to see evidence of this honey you're purported to have."

Cece shrugged and threw him an impish grin. "You seem to bring out a different aspect of my character."

He regarded her thoughtfully, his hand stroking his beard. "Or mayhap 'tis who you truly are, and you only let everyone else see tiny bits and pieces of it."

He was far too insightful. Cece knew everyone believed her to be the Wainwright sister made of spun sugar and light. She was the sister who met sorrow with sunshine and always sang the loudest. The unavoidable truth was that she didn't want to taint everyone else with her doubts and regrets. She wore a mask so that wouldn't happen. It had taken less than a week for him to delve beneath her armor and expose her for the charlatan she was. "Mayhap."

He leaned forward again, and she clenched her fists so she wouldn't rise to her toes and meet him. He shook his head and cupped his nape, tipping his head toward the sky. "The worst of the next storm will hold off for several days. Would you like to accompany me into the village for supplies?"

"Supplies?"

"Aye. Flour and beans. Tea. Oats for Jed." Since his horse would be carrying the two of them through the blistering weather, the least he could do was reward him with oats.

"I'd like to purchase some fabric. And my boots may be finished."

"Your boots?"

"The cobbler on Marbury Lane insisted on gifting me new ones. He said the price was doing a good deed in return." Cece flushed at the memory. The dapper shoe-maker had said making this man smile would be pay-ment enough. She wanted to make him smile. A real, full smile that tilted those kissable lips beneath his mus-tache.

"Ah, Jem. He's my grandfather's age."

"He was very spry."

Malcolm's mouth quirked up. The barest hint of a smile. "He is indeed. And canny. I'm surprised he didn't require some devil's bargain in return."

She could feel her cheeks burning again. "Just a good deed for someone else."

He cocked his head to one side. "You escaped easily. He must have been captivated."

She took a deep breath because she didn't know what his reaction would be to the proposal she was about to make. "You should make an effort to be presentable. I think mice could make a nest in your beard."

"Lass, shaving my beard won't make me presentable. It'll put my scars on full display. Which means getting rid of it will make me monstrous and brutish."

His words landed like a bludgeon between them.

She wanted to cup the stern line of his jaw. She want-ed to alleviate the buried hurt she saw in his hard gaze. Who had called him monstrous?

Yes, he was huge and scarred and intimidating.

But he wasn't in the least monstrous. Or brutish.

He was like the lion in the fable who only roared because of the thorn in its paw.

"I can wield the razor, if you'd like." She braced herself for his refusal.

The unblemished corner of his mouth curled into a rueful half-smile. "Should I fear your retribution? You may punish me for insisting you retire last night as weary and caked in dirt as the rest of us."

Cece shrugged nonchalantly. "I might have sought retribution. Until I spied the tin bathing tub tucked into a corner in front of the hearth this morning. I was quite surprised by your departure from your normally inhospitable behavior."

He snorted. " 'Twas as much for myself as for you. I didn't care to hear you muttering and complaining."

"I think you were compelled by kindness, but I know you are determined to eschew that aspect of your personality. In truth, I believe you are plagued by the same level of uncertainty you have subjected me to."

"Your determination to dissect my motives is amusing, but I will subject myself to your ministrations all the same. Come, let us return to the cottage. There is aught else to do here and Moira will have prepared our evening meal."

Moira met them at the door. "I wondered where the two of ye had gone off tae. There's mutton stew on the stove."

"There was a hole in the roof of the cottage, so I'm making my bed in the loft," Cece blurted.

"Are ye now?" Moira smirked. "That's an unexpected turn of events." She turned her speculative gaze on Mal. "And the laird isn't always keen for surprises or things that dinnae go his way." She pulled her shawl off the hook and wound it about her shoulders and head. "I'm off to care for the bairns." She saluted them and turned on her heel, taking off with a brisk stride, the snow flying in her wake like dust as she doggedly plowed through it.

"She lives nearby?"

"Aye, three cottages down. Her bairns are her five strapping sons. And her husband Farley when he doesn't listen to her."

"I'd wager they all listen to her if they know what's good for them." Cece observed.

"There's the sarcasm I've missed."

"I've been trying to put my best foot forward, Mr. Lockhart."

"This has been your best foot? Argumentative and rebellious? A trifle belligerent? Rousing a man from his sleep in the dead of night like a banshee?"

Cece was going to tell him exactly where she wanted to put her foot, for better or worse, when she saw the twinkle in his eye. "Yes, my best foot. I shall even set the table if you'd like to get cleaned up first."

"I'll not gainsay you."

By the time he returned, she'd swept the hearth free of the mud and snow they'd tracked in and ladled the soup into the two clay tureens she'd found on the mantle. The wooden spoons were lying beside them.

His hair was damp, and he'd donned a clean shirt and trousers. The mossy, misty smell was stronger, and she knew he'd taken what Arie called a Swiss dot bath. She called it that after the muslin dress their mother had left hanging in the wardrobe. Swiping a soapy rag over the bits most likely to offend. Dabbing them until there was time for a proper dunking.

He finished his first bowl before she'd barely touched hers, tipping it up to get the last dregs. She'd had to grip the edge of the table so she wouldn't leap across it when he licked a stray droplet from his mustache. When he'd finished his second bowl, he tipped his chair back.

She daintily wiped the corners of her mouth with the sleeve of her gown. She'd searched high and low for a linen napkin or tablecloth and finally concluded it was probably something a rough and tumble sheep farmer didn't consider essential.

"You may do your worst, Mrs. Thompson." He gestured in the direction of the shelf behind him. "You'll find the razor and the scissors in a box on the mantle and the strop is hanging by the door."

She clutched her skirts and lifted her chin. This was her chance to finally see what he was hiding behind his nest of a beard.

She gathered the bowls and spoons and set them in the dry sink to scour once the shaving business was done.

He was quiet while she sharpened the razor and filled the basin. "Do you have any soap?"

"Aye. There's a shaving stick in the cupboard above the sink."

She carried the basin, the towel and the implements to the table, laid them down and stretched on her toes to retrieve the soap.

When she held it to her nose it smelled of lavender and bergamot, and when she waved it in the air she caught a hint of lemon as well.

It was already difficult to focus when he walked into the cottage with his hair slicked back from his nightly dip in the loch. He always smelled of rainwater and spring, clean and sharp. When she'd asked him why he braved the frigid water so frequently, he'd assured her she didn't want the stink of his sweat in the close confines of their living quarters.

She'd bitten her tongue so she wouldn't blurt out that she adored the smell of his sweat. She imagined an afternoon spent herding or shearing, or setting fence posts, plastered his shirt to his skin. She knew he always smelled heady and real and she was tempted to lick the trickle of perspiration from the hollow of his throat. She kept those intense, overwhelming impressions to herself.

The cool water of the basin was the perfect counterpoint to the heat that suddenly suffused her cheeks. She held her hands there for a moment and closed her eyes. When she'd sufficiently bolstered her resolve, she turned toward him.

He'd draped a plaid around his neck and his head was tipped back. His Adam's apple bobbed in his throat as he swallowed. "Are you just going to stand there and watch me, Mrs. Thompson?"

"How do you know I'm watching you?" Cece had only shaved Henry a handful of times. Years ago. Her hand was trembling. Why had she insisted on doing this? Why had she even brought it to his attention?

"I can feel it. You're looming over me like a vulture, and I'd wager you're having second thoughts."

"I'm going to clip your beard first." Wielding the scissors wasn't as daunting as wielding the razor.

The wayward hairs sticking out like corkscrews snagged her attention first. When she stepped back to survey her progress, she realized the trimming part of the task wasn't as susceptible to error as the shaving part would be.

She snipped and assessed, snipped and assessed. Until his beard was closely cropped to the contours of his jaw and chin and his sideburns once again had a discernible shape.

The next part was the one she was dreading the most. What if her hand slipped and she cut his throat? Is this what it felt like on the eve of a battle?

Working the soap to a lather in the basin and counting her breaths was calming. It would be fine. She would be fine.

His jaw felt bristly beneath her palm when she angled his face for better access. She inhaled and exhaled one last time before settling into a rhythm. Scrape. Brush. Rinse. Scrape. Brush. Rinse.

Her hand slid to his cheek, along his sideburns threading into his hair before his eye opened. She untangled her fingers because a demon had possessed her. Her thumb grazed his earlobe and longing suddenly bloomed between them.

He inhaled and she gasped. All the air was suddenly sucked from the room and lodged like a bonfire in the pit of her stomach.

Cece took a deep breath and reminded herself she was holding a razor.

Her hands could not tremble when she tackled the stray hairs that trailed down his neck.

"I'm not quite finished." Her voice sounded gusty and breathless.

He closed his eye again. It was a surrender of sorts. He was telling her he trusted her, and she didn't know what to do with that admission. She felt as if she'd known him even longer than she'd known Henry. In the span of less than a week. The train ride had clearly addled her mind as well as her stomach.

The last bit of beard was defying her attempts to tame it, and she had to adjust the angle of the blade. Her body was suspended above him as she bent her elbow. When he swallowed, she felt the flex of his throat against the hand holding him in place.

She stepped away with a sigh of relief when she was finished.

The scars were more prominent now, but they didn't detract from the stark, asymmetrical beauty of his face. The ridges carved by the fire were etched into the skin of his upper cheek, and trailed down his jaw and neck.

"I can feel the weight of your stare, Mrs. Thompson. I told you I was even more monstrous beneath the beard."

He was back to calling her Mrs. Thompson. Obliterating the intimacy that had risen between them. "If you can call me Little Wren, you can deign to call me Cece. And you're not monstrous. They're battle scars. Anyone who believes them monstrous doesn't deserve the sacrifice you made on their behalf."

He opened one blazing green eye and pinned her with it. Her heart fluttered in her chest like the fly quaking before the spider. Instead of flailing away, she stood her ground. "If I start calling you Cece you're going to think that gives you the right to call me Mal. It's an invitation to anarchy."

She was certain he was teasing her, but his expression revealed nothing. Not even a hint of amusement. She lifted a shoulder. "Being called an anarchist isn't the worst insult I can imagine, Mal."

He was teasing. A smile flickered at the edges of those supple, tempting lips until he couldn't hold it back. "If they'd sent you to the Crimea, you'd have charmed the Russians into abandoning their claims."

Earning that grin felt like a victory. Cece wanted to shout or pump her fist in the air.

He stood and gave her a curt bow. "Thank you. I feel as if my humanity has been restored. I'll finish bathing in the loch and when I return we'll set the tub up for you."

She watched him walk away and debated following him. Was the certainty she'd gain about the state of his kilt worth the risk of being caught?

Cece had decided to follow him. She was crouched behind a boulder and a clump of gorse.

She didn't know how he withstood the sharp bite of winter in the air, but she was grateful for his stoicism. The snow had finally stopped, but the roads were impassable for carriages and there was a thin layer of ice over the water. He'd obviously cracked it with his hand or his dirk, because he was standing in the middle of an oasis.

While she wondered at his mental stability, she was grateful for his fortitude. She'd been wondering what he hid beneath his kilt. He'd been careful to avoid any intimate contact since that first night.

Now she knew beyond the shadow of a doubt what he hid behind his plaid, and the image was burnt into her retina. Like she'd looked on an eclipse without shielding her eyes. His thighs were indeed as thick as tree trunks. Lightly furred with dark blond like the path that trailed across his sculpted chest and down, down, down to the long length of cock that was now in repose between his legs. She'd heard that exposure to the cold shriveled a man's member, but she saw no evidence of such an effect. She wanted to run her fingers over every inch of him – to map the two sides of angel and beast. The scarred half of his body was turned away from her, but she knew it was beautiful too.

Her first missive to her sisters would confirm she had first-hand knowledge of the proclivities of Scotsmen. At least regarding their undergarments. From this distance it appeared his appendage stood at half-mast. A closer examination was warranted, but she didn't want to chance discovery and mutual mortification.

Though if his whispered epithets that first evening had been any indication, he would not shy away from describing the effect she had on his body.

She knew she should seek cover other than the scraggly bush she'd hastily ducked behind. At least her cloak was dark and wouldn't be like a beacon announcing her espionage. Her muscles had frozen in place and she stretched her toes and flexed her wrists. She'd flee once he ducked beneath the water again. Someone was granting the wishes of women with no sense of self-preservation, because he bent forward. She couldn't look away, and she knew she was running out of time to make a dignified escape.

Cece crept away on hands and knees until she was out of sight enough to avoid detection. And then she fled for the cottage like the hounds of hell were in hot pursuit.

She made sure she was seated at the rough table when he returned, a pile of mending in her lap.

As soon as he entered the cottage, the space became smaller. His presence seemed to absorb every spare inch, and the scent of his soap filled her nostrils. Her cheeks burned at the memory of him scraping that tiny sliver over his skin.

Chapter Thirteen

Malcolm

Letter dated October 13, 1854.

Dearest Husband, Gert brought home a copy of Tennyson's Collection of Poems from the library. There's one poem I've read so many times it's emblazoned on my mind. I've memorized it in its entirety. Emily teased that I was going to request they set me on a bier and cast me out to sea with my long hair unbound and floating behind me like a dark cloud when I died. I know there are things you don't want to speak of. I

know death is all around you. But death is all around me too, Henry. The death of hope. The death of my youth. The death of my dreams. The way Tennyson portrayed the Lady was like looking at my own reflection. I am half-sick of the shadows, just as she was. Please come home to me soon.

MAL WAS TRUE TO his word. He lugged five buckets of snow inside and let the fire melt and warm them before he poured them into the tub. When he handed her some of the lavender soap he'd bought ages ago because the scent had calmed him, her eyes lit up. She rose to her tiptoes and leaned forward, like she was going to kiss him in thanks. Mal awkwardly stepped back to avoid her embrace and she turned bright red.

"I'm sorry," she mumbled. "I only meant to thank you for the bath."

"I'll leave you to it," he told her with a bow and swiftly scrambled up the ladder to the loft. So the splash of the water and her soft sighs would be muted. So he could ignore the images of wet skin, and dark, inky damp hair like a veil of midnight silk drifting over her shoulders. He needed to escape before he made any more blunders. He knew he'd be staring at the ceiling for hours, trying not to think about the way the firelight would cast half her body in shadow, or what the arch of her arm would look like when she curled it to scrub her back. He wondered about the sheen of the water in her hair, and if it would smell like lavender too. With a pang in his chest, he recalled her letter about the Lady of Shallot. After the confidences shared during her shearing lesson, he knew the sorrow she carried in her heart matched the depths of his own.

He stripped to his usual sleeping costume of bare skin and thought back to the satiny feel of her skin when he'd taken her hand. The pads of her fingers had been as callused as his, and he knew it was because her needlework was how she made her way in the world. Widow's pensions, though finally standardized by the Crown, were paltry and required the women who received them to supplement the income to survive.

Though his friend's widow looked as delicate as the violets her eyes had been compared to, she was a woman who would brace her hands on her hips and scream into the headwinds of a hurricane instead of cowering before it. By her own admission, she'd accepted her widowhood, though she was far from inured to it. There'd been a handful of moments today when he'd nearly lost his resolve and kissed her senseless. When he'd been on the verge of confessing her words had held all the broken parts of him together amidst the wreckage of war.

He scrubbed his hand across his face. Their departure to the village would be delayed until the weather cooperated, and there were just enough tea leaves remaining for a single pot. The snow was still too deep for the cart, the farm trek still invisible beneath the white mantle, so their eventual departure would be doubled up on the back of his plow horse.

He thought he'd seen the flash of her skirt behind one of the leafless gorse bushes from the corner of his eye. It amused him that she'd been spying. when the weather had broken enough for a dip in the loch. He idly wondered if he should bring it up. If she'd admit her clandestine activities or blush and stammer and avoid his gaze.

⸺◆⸺

When he came in from the morning feeding, she was singing. It was an old folksong that made his heart ache because it was about a soldier and the girl who watched him march away to war. A girl who waited by the fire for his return. The poignancy in her voice filled Mal's own heart with longing. *He wanted that soldier to be him. That girl to be her.* He'd dreamt of her standing in his cottage just like this, a dash of flour on her cheek, sweaty tendrils of hair drooping against her neck.

She shot him a bright glance over her shoulder when she heard the door. "I'm making scones with the last of the flour and some butter Moira brought over."

Mal's stomach rumbled and he cleared his throat to disguise the sound. "You didn't have to do that."

She laughed, and he wanted to catch it in his hands.

"It was part of our bargain, remember? My scones for the shepherd lessons?"

He shook his head and smiled in acknowledgment. "I was teasing," he said as he strode toward her. "You're my guest and you've already helped more than you know."

Hilda's labor and delivery had been seamless. Once the afterbirth had been expelled, they'd left the new arrival asleep in the byre with its mother. Her soothing tone and gentle touch had been a balm to both of them. Just as they were to him.

She'd taken to shearing as if she were born to it and had said nothing about the blisters he'd noted on the sides of her thumbs. She'd acquired them from her tense grip on the shearing comb.

"I'd love another bath, if you wouldn't mind lugging in more buckets of snow."

She returned her focus to the bowl, and Mal thought she might be hiding a smile.

He wondered if her whole face was glowing, like it had been when he handed her the soap and she'd stretched up on her toes to bestow the kiss he'd avoided. He relived the moment he'd stepped away and retreated to the loft.

"I don't mind obtaining them for you," he assured her. Mayhap this time he would have the courage to stay in the same room. "Moira offered the use of her bathing screen if you'd like me to retrieve that as well."

She turned to him with a bemused smile, not bothering to hide her consternation. "I have no need of the screen unless the thought of me naked makes you uncomfortable, Laird. You may retrieve it if it will preserve your modesty," she glibly informed him.

In truth, Mal didn't want the screen to hide the curve of her back from his hungry gaze. He'd had vivid daydreams of combing the snarls out of her damp hair as she sat in his lap, of brushing the locks of it across her breasts before he bent his head and suckled her. He'd imagined wrapping his hands in the dark, stormy mass as she laid her head on his shoulder and rode his cock.

Chapter Fourteen

Cece

Letter dated June 17th, 1854.

Dearest Little Wren, We walked through a field of wildflowers today and they reminded me of you. I imagined laying you down in them and the way the petals would caress your cheek and fall softly on your skin. I imagined examining each one until I could pronounce without a shade of uncertainty which hue was the closest match to your eyes.

T HE OTHER EVENING, HIS actions had mortified Cece. When he'd lurched abruptly back after he gave her the soap, she'd felt like the veriest fool. As if she were a leper. She'd only meant to give him a peck on the cheek in thanks. When she expressed her desire for another bath this morning and he willingly went outside to lug the buckets in, despite the way she could tell his leg pained him, she decided that this time she wasn't going to allow his retreat.

She felt him hovering in the doorway and some devil possessed her. She twisted her hair and settled it over her shoulder, baring her neck and the length of her spine. Then Cece leaned forward and provocatively asked, "May I trouble you to wash my back, laird?"

He drew closer, his footsteps echoing as the space between them became mere inches. Gooseflesh broke out all over the exposed parts of her body, and she could feel the devil that spurred her mischief cackling on her shoulder.

"Do you know what you're asking me to do, Mrs. Thompson?"

She dipped her chin to hide the smile. *She did know.* And now he was using formal address to establish boundaries. To make it seem as if he'd never been on the verge of kissing her senseless, no matter what she'd seen in his eyes when he told her she was his hope and strength. "Yes, Mr. Lockhart, I know exactly what I'm asking."

She thought she heard him murmur something about hell and good intentions before she felt his breath against her nape. One lean, weathered hand reached around her and retrieved the cloth she'd laid on the side of the tub. She closed her eyes at the sound of him lathering the soap as the honey lavender scent rose around them.

His warmth was layered behind the rough fabric when he stroked the length of her spine. It was like a lick of fire across her skin, the perfect contrast to the cooling water. Cece drew up her knees and rested the side of her face against them.

He drew a shuddering breath that sounded like a muted roar and laid the cloth back down. "I cannae do this," he gritted into her ear, the brogue in his voice heavy.

She knew her ploy had worked, that he was just as disconcerted by the encounter as she was.

He brushed against her as he stood.

"I'll see to the animals, Mrs. Thompson. Enjoy the rest of your bath."

His retreat this time hadn't been as panicked, but Cece sensed he held himself tightly leashed. She wanted to see him unleashed – that tight control nothing more than tattered threads.

She smiled and hummed as she soaped the rest of her body and wrung out her hair.

Chapter Fifteen

Mal

Letter dated August 12th, 1853.

Dearest Husband, I've decided I shall forgive you for the nickname. Your explanation persuaded me. I will suffer being compared to a drab little brown creature because it means I am your home and hearth. I will build a cozy nest for you here and welcome you home with open arms.

S HE'D HARDLY MET HIS eyes in the last few days, and when she did, her cheeks turned bright pink. As if she knew the reaction her taunting had provoked. As if she knew the number of times he'd taken himself in hand and imagined a different ending to her bath. As if she was aware of the weight of the tension between them.

He rubbed his eye and groaned in frustration. The mere possibility of her spying on him at his ablutions made him restless. As if he was standing on the edge of a daunting abyss he'd struggled his entire life to avoid.

The numbers in the ledger were blurring together and he rubbed his eye beneath the monocle again to bring them into focus. The older he became, the more difficult he found the completion of this task. He knew he could ask Duncan to keep the books – he trusted him. But the tidy column had a way of soothing him and he was loathe to turn over this part of the business.

"Would you like some tea?" She was suddenly hovering in the doorway - as if he'd conjured her.

He let the monocle fall and tipped the chair back. He would like some tea, but they hadn't enough of it left. And he feared it would keep him awake. "I've heard drinking it this late is not conducive to peaceful slumber."

She slipped into the room and arranged her skirts to perch on the corner of his desk. "Does sleep elude you?" She asked, her face bright with curiosity.

"Aye," he nodded as he rubbed his eye again.

Her expression was sympathetic. "I am sorry sleep eludes you. Ofttimes my mind is too busy for it as well." She grinned mischievously. "May I tell you a funny story?"

He abandoned all hope of balancing the accounts this night. She was determined to thwart him. He'd missed their easy banter, and he welcomed its return and the absence of skittishness she'd displayed the last few days. "By all means."

"I used to count sheep. It always helped lull me into a peaceful slumber. That was before I started counting your sheep and was overwhelmed by their sheer number and magnitude."

There were more sheep than people in the hamlet. Especially on this farm. His guffaw of laughter startled them both. He laughed because she was right. He suspected she was startled because she'd never heard his laughter.

She tipped her head back, her hand on her heart. Her eyes sparkled so much he could see the twinkle. Even without the monocle.

"Was that laughter? From the dour, grumpy laird?"

Mal slowly righted the chair. The thud of it hitting the floor echoed between them.

She leapt to her feet with an alarmed expression and backed away.

"Perhaps I've pushed you too far?" She ventured with a squeak.

He rose in one smooth motion, clasped his hands behind his back so he wouldn't be tempted to do things he shouldn't, and strode toward her.

"I'm not dour. Or grumpy. I simply have no tolerance for people who waste my time. However, since I cannot find the fortitude to focus tonight, I am open to distraction."

Her mouth quirked up in a naughty smile. "Do I waste your time, Malcolm Lockhart? Because I indulge in what you consider frivolity and chicanery?"

Trying to decipher her contradictions was giving him a headache. He needed to cauterize this growing familiarity at the root. He closed his eyes again. "That's only a small part of it, Mrs. Thompson. I find you particularly exasperating. For many reasons."

The wry smile stayed there, curling her mouth like an infuriating question mark.

"Would you care to enumerate them, Mr. Lockhart?"

"Are you prepared for such an accounting? Do you think your delicate sensibilities can withstand it?"

She snorted. "My delicate sensibilities? Delicate is one thing I most assuredly am not. Life has starved all the delicacy from my soul."

"I do not know you well, Mrs. Thompson. But what I do know of you tells me that you are rash, reckless and impulsive. These are qualities that will land you in boiling water when you least expect it."

"You are the first to ever accuse me of having such quali-ties. But go on, I'm all agog to hear about the other aspects of my person that offend you."

"You are entirely too saucy and pretty for a grieving widow."

"Entirely too saucy and pretty? I've only recently set aside my somber weeds. I am heartened to hear at least one man believes I haven't left the flush of youth behind me. Is there anything else about me that drives you mad?"

"Five things aren't sufficient? Seven if you count your tendencies for frivolity and chicanery?"

She shrugged. Her insouciance made him want to pin her against him and kiss her senseless. To silence the rebel-lious streak she was wielding like a battle ax to push him over the edge.

"I'm sure you can think of more than seven things if you set your mind to it."

She was challenging him. The gleam was back in her eyes, and they were dancing with mirth. She was enjoying their sparring far too much.

He banished his conscience somewhere he'd find it later and edged her against the bookshelf along the back wall. When he braced his arms on either side of her head and leaned in, she gasped. The teasing look she'd had in her eyes disappeared.

"Your confidence seems to have waned, Mrs. Thomp-son," he murmured.

Her eyes flitted over his lips, and the tips of her breasts brushed his cotton shirt as she took a shaky breath. "It takes more than a shallow insult to injure my pride, Mr. Lockhart," she archly informed him.

The sheer audacious magnificence of her was enough to bring him to his knees. Where he'd gladly worship her for days - if not weeks.

She was begging to be kissed. But kissing her would be a mistake. There'd be no going back.

One of her hands feathered across his shoulder, the slightest graze. His jaw clenched in reaction to that light caress because it felt like she'd stroked the entire length of his spine. Or his cock. He moved his hips away so she wouldn't be aware of the way she affected him.

Her boldness already had him out of sorts. He didn't dare add fuel to the fire.

"I like the look of this on you." She raised the monocle to his eye and held it there, the back of her hand barely touching his cheek.

This close, he could make out the sweep of each dark lash against her cheek.

"The green of your gaze mesmerizes me," her voice quavered.

She shouldn't be mesmerized by him. Couldn't be mesmerized by him. He told himself his life had been one of contentment before her arrival. That he'd wanted for nothing and no one. Even as he knew he was lying to himself.

He was bitter enough to admit there'd been a single shard of hope left when he'd returned her letters. It was still burning in his lungs like an ember. He needed to stamp it out before it destroyed him.

He should have known that sending back the letters would lead to a moment exactly like this.

A moment where she clearly wanted him. A moment full of promise and redemption. He shoved the hope away. "I am a man consumed by shadows."

Her eyes softened at his gruff admission and now he was the one whose breath came short. She stroked her fingers over his jaw, across the line of his lips. He bit the inside of his cheek so she wouldn't feel how her gentleness made him tremble.

"The shadows won't swallow you. Even though you tell yourself you are half-sick of them. *The Lady of Shallott* is my favorite poem – probably because of that line. It's a very apt description of the half-life I've been living. I know what the shadows are – I struggle against their hold every day."

He saw his own inner turmoil reflected in her gaze before she glanced away.

He remembered that letter because it was the last one she'd sent. She'd catalogued all the reasons that particular poem fascinated her.

He'd read it so many times he'd memorized it. Cherished it so much a copy was hidden in the drawer of the desk behind them. It had spoken to all the things he wanted to run away from. All the things he wanted to run toward.

"I understand why you want to be swallowed," she continued, her voice much quieter, her gaze introspective. "Trust me, I know all too well what that feels like. It's hard to be stoic and pretend the pain away. But that's what we're expected to do. So we do what's expected of us and ignore how it slowly breaks us. It's like watching tiny fragments of yourself disappear beneath the power of a flood you don't have the strength to fight."

She bravely lifted her chin and swiped away a tear.

Even though it went against his better instincts, he raised a hand to her face. When she leant her cheek into his palm he closed his eyes and gathered her close.

He clasped her tightly, because he felt unmoored and undone. Her arms crept around his back and she clasped him just as tightly, her fingers winding into the fabric of his shirt like she was looking for a safe place to anchor in the storm.

He felt the slight quake of her shoulders and knew she was holding back the release of emotion she needed. "You may cry on my shoulder, Little Wren."

His words broke the dam. The muffled sob against his shirtfront brought tears to his eyes as well. He rocked her back and forth, crooning softly in her ear and rubbing circles in the space between her shoulder blades.

This was the last thing he'd wanted. To see the fragile, blooming heart that was still healing behind her brave façade. Not because he was repulsed by it.

Just the opposite. Her tragedy spoke to his. He longed to tell her all his secrets. Even the ones that would destroy this tenuous trust. He bit his tongue to stop the confession from pouring out. Bit it until he tasted blood.

When the hazardous weather ended, she'd be on her way. Stepping onto a platform and waving farewell until he was nothing but a fleck in the distance and a fleeting memory. A fond reminder of her singular adventure.

"Let's have that tea, shall we?" He'd finish off the last of it to escape the nameless thing this moment was making him feel.

She nodded against his chest and dropped her arms, stepping away. "Forgive me my loss of control."

Her embarrassment made him want to soothe her again. To rock her in his arms and sing her to sleep until her eyes were no longer red and swollen and that heartbreaking quiver in her voice was extinguished. "There is nothing to forgive." He sketched a bow. "Now, come. I'll steep the last bit of Oolong. And you may take this with you and read it until it woos you to sleep."

He slid his hand along the shelf until he found his worn copy of Tennyson's *Collection of Poems*. Because he believed it would make him feel closer to her, it had been the first book he'd purchased when he returned home.

When he handed it to her and she tipped the spine toward the light to make out the title, he held his breath. He hoped she wouldn't puzzle out how much that letter had meant to him and why. He'd just laid all his cards on the table and it was far from a royal flush.

The gaze she turned on him was full of tears again.

"I am sorry," he apologized. "I thought to bring you comfort, not add to your misery. I'll return it to its place on the shelves."

She shook her head. "No, you will not. I can scarcely believe you knew the poem. Or that you have what is obviously a much beloved, and often read, copy in your personal collection. Reading it again will bring me more comfort than you know. I never knew how Henry felt about that quote because I didn't receive an answer. Now I know he shared it with his friends. That brings me solace."

Her gratitude made him uncomfortable. It was the least he could do and a small price to pay for his deceit. When he'd read the letter aloud to Henry, his friend had rolled his eyes and said, "You and my wife would gild the world with words if you could."

Henry had never been adept at reading or letter writing. Mal had started out simply transcribing his friend's thoughts, but when the letters began to arrive with frightening regularity Henry had confessed the reason for his reticence in answering them. He told Mal words always jumbled together on the page and he had a difficult time making them out. He said his learned father had berated him for the shortcoming and he'd joined the army because soldiering was a career of action more suited to his capabilities.

He winged his arm toward her. "Come, let us drink tea."

"May I bring Sal to bed with me tonight?" She tentatively asked.

The skinny gray mouser usually curled up on the pillows above Mal's head. The purring drove him mad, but he didn't have the heart to banish the cat he'd rescued as a kitten to the barn. "Yes. Her incessant purring makes me restless."

Shep would be more settled as well if the cat found another perch. His sheepdog tossed and turned and whined from his pile of blankets in the corner whenever the cat pranced across the coverlet or decided to knead its paws against Mal's chest.

Chapter Sixteen

Mal

Letter dated April 3, 1854.

Dearest Husband, I've finally managed to convince Emily I can get a much better price at the market than Lavinia. Lavinia gets too distracted flirting with the butcher's son, and always gives in too easily. I like haggling with the stall owners – especially the costermonger. I always manage to secure us more beans and cabbage and stretch them into almost a week's worth of meals.

IS DECISION-MAKING ABILITIES WERE impaired. Or despite the absence of his cantankerous cat in the bed last night, he still hadn't slept restfully. Perhaps both. That was the only rational explanation for his assumption he could survive this.

Why had he been so foolish as to think he could suffer through a shared horseback ride without wanting to ravish her?

Every jostle of their bodies, every creak of the saddle beneath them, every shift of her shoulders against his chest that released the effervescent scent of violets that seemed to permeate her skin, it was all driving him mad.

It was only the thought of the reception he'd receive that settled his nerves.

She'd see the truth others saw. Why he wasn't something she should fancy or want.

This would be his first trip into the village since his return. For six years he'd been sequestered on the farm. Duncan was his man of business and handled all the transactions with the wool merchants and tweed factories. Mal was perfectly content handling the care of the herd and maintaining the financial records. He'd always had a head for numbers, and he liked the quiet order of them marching in rows and columns down a page.

The entire journey home from the Crimea had been characterized by whispers and looks of revulsion from strangers. His scars had been fresh then, and they were horrid enough to cause one of two reactions. People either stared in morbid fascination or visibly recoiled from the sight of him. He'd belligerently eschewed a patch over his eye then. He'd since learned his lesson.

The milky cast of his eye made people uneasy, and he wore the patch now to spare himself, and them, any discomfort. He was also secretly fond of the piratical, mysterious air it lent him.

The wounds had healed and the scars had faded, but the ravages of war still mapped his body and his heart. He still towered over nearly everyone he met, like a great looming shadow. He'd been certain his size and scarred countenance would send everyone they encountered scurrying to the other side of the street. Especially the children.

While he'd caught several peoples' gazes skating over his features before they hurriedly glanced in the opposite direction, none of that scrutiny had been delivered by children. It was anticlimactic.

The first stop they'd made was to retrieve her new pair of boots from the cobbler. Mal had greeted Jem Ozymandias Crum with a nod. The man had been supplying Mal's shoes since he was a lad. "Laird," he'd said when they entered and winked.

Mal hadn't known what the wink meant and was even more confused when the man turned to Cece and said. "I see ye've made good on yer bargain, lass. I knew if anyone could have that effect on him 'twould be you."

Cece had laughed brightly, a mysterious blush painting her cheeks. "I wouldn't count it as a success quite yet, Mr. Crum. It's only been the once I could coax it from him."

The cobbler had patted her hand. "The first o' many, tae be sure, lass."

Mal had a sneaking suspicion the bargain had concerned him, but neither of them confirmed it. They'd gone blithely about the business of her final fitting as if he weren't standing there.

When he and Cece made their way to the market square from the cobbler's, it was surprisingly busy. Despite the snow on the ground and the chill in the air. He supposed that was because of the holiday season. His companion spent far too long lingering at a stall that sold perfumed soap. She inspected every single cake until she finally settled on one that smelled of honey and violets and one she insisted was made just for him. She effortlessly drew him into the conversation with the purveyor, and neither of them seemed to be deterred by his gruff, one-word responses.

That's when the children had noticed him. The boldest of the pack had stared at him for a long while before saying, "Ye don't truly look like the picture of the ogre in my wee sister's book o' fairytales. I'll tell her Ma was wrong."

Was that what they said of him? That he was a hideous ogre? The boy's nonchalant observation had disconcerted him.

They'd taken shelter under the eaves to escape the brisk wind gusting down the alley and his arms were full of parcels. Things she'd insisted were needed for holiday festivities since the weather would soon be descending upon them in earnest and swatches of fabric she'd told him her sisters would appreciate. She'd somehow convinced him to barter a skein of wool for a ham. She'd offered to throw in a bobbin of handmade lace to decorate the wedding dress of the farmer's eldest daughter and he knew grumbling about the transaction was futile. He'd ended up with sackfuls of apples and strawberries filched from some nob's conservatory.

His skin was prickling, and though they might not think him an ogre, he and his guest were the subject of intense scrutiny and the source of the chatter swirling through the market square. "We need to be on our way, Mrs. Thompson. The storm will overtake us."

She pointed at the dry goods sign swinging in the wind. "That's the last stop. Once I get the packet of needles I require, we can depart. But first ..." She stepped closer, her hand moving to his freshly shaven jaw. She cupped his cheek, splaying her fingers over the silver web of scars and rough patches of skin. "You were certain the children would run when they saw you. But they didn't run. And I'm not going to run either. No matter how much you bellow or scowl. Underneath your scars you're still a man. Not a monster. We all see it. When will you see it as well?"

She turned on her heel and left him standing in the middle of the dusty lane.

She walked away with a fiercely tilted chin and a straight back.

His face burned where she'd touched it. Her softly spoken parting salvo hung in the air, hovering in the wake of the crisp sweep of her skirts.

Those hovering words lodged in his throat and made it scratchy with emotion.

She'd just cracked him in half. More swiftly and efficiently than the war that had changed the course of his life. The rupture had begun the first time she made him smile. The fissure widened when she finally teased him into laughter. This proof of her unconditional acceptance was the final nudge. He would never again have the fortitude to retreat into the armor he'd built against softness and affection. All his resolve was shredded beyond recognition.

When she re-emerged from the building with the packet of needles and a jaunty smile, he simply resigned himself to heartbreak.

Chapter Seventeen

Cece

Letter Dated May 20, 1854.

Dearest Little Wren, I fell asleep tonight imagining the way that black currant jam would stain your lips. And wondering if ripe strawberries would do the same.

CECE WAS TRYING TO remember Vin's receipt for strawberry compote. She'd baked a small oatcake and was looking forward to having sweets once again. And surprising her dour laird. He could do with some cheering up and some sweets.

The strawberries weren't as plump and ripe as the ones she and her sisters had picked over the summer, but they still tempted her. Surely one stolen strawberry wouldn't make a difference in how the compote turned out. Cece had been craving them since the season ended in June, and she couldn't wait any longer.

She decided it was worth the risk the berries wouldn't stretch as far, rinsed them in the basin and popped one into her mouth. She moaned when the juice burst on her tongue with all the sunshine goodness of summer.

There was a clatter behind her back, and she sighed. Couldn't a woman have this one simple pleasure to herself without being interrupted?

The cat had been following her about since they returned and had already lain two fat mice at her feet. It had done so with prim ceremony, meowing piteously to snare her attention and then nudging the carcass toward her when she'd stooped to pat its head in praise. She'd gulped and swallowed her revulsion because she knew the value of a good mouser. If she seemed unappreciative, who knew what would happen?

Shep seemed affronted at the fact she'd allowed Sal to sleep on her bed last night. He'd been under her feet all evening, his liquid eyes simultaneously censorious and pleading.

When she whirled around, she realized neither Sal nor Shep had made the noise. She'd been certain Sal was knocking things over in yet another bid for attention, or imperiously demanding a saucerful of milk. The possibility had also existed that Shep's overeager tail had once again wrought havoc.

Neither animal was the culprit.

Mal stood in the doorway and a shovel lay on the floor at his feet. As if he'd unintentionally dropped it.

His green eye was blazing at her from the threshold, and his mouth was parted. Even from a distance she could see the white of his knuckles where they clutched the bunched fabric of his kilt.

"That sound you just made...is it the same one you make when you eat bread with black currant jam?"

His voice sounded like a door with rusty hinges - the growl on the tail end of it so deep his words were barely intelligible.

She schooled her expression to one of nonchalance and tipped her head aside to study him. "I'm astonished you remember my fondness for it. I only mentioned it in a few of my letters. What of it?" She was relieved her voice sounded steady – because her knees were not.

"I remember every word you wrote. I told you your letters sustained us all. And it wasn't a mere few letters. It was ten. 'Twas obviously a favorite." He looked ready to pounce. Like a feverish lion.

"Would you like a taste as well?"

He didn't answer, just shook his head slowly back and forth. Either chiding her or trying to get his bearings. Cece couldn't tell which.

She palmed a berry in her hand and approached him like she would a wolf with its paw caught in a trap.

Cautiously.

Warily.

He kicked the shovel away and it spun across the floor, finally coming to rest against one of the table legs. It was a reaction of such repressed impatience her knees went weak again.

When the tips of her boots were nearly touching his, she stretched her arm between them. He took it in his own and touched her cheek. She felt the swipe of his knuckles against her upper cheek.

"Flour," he explained as he flicked away the powder.

Then he lifted the wrist he'd seized and brought her hand to his mouth.

There was a brush of rough satin that made her quiver from head to toe as he stole the berry from its berth. His mouth nipped her fingertips, his tongue grazing them as he lapped the juices from her hand and wrist and arm.

Seconds could have passed. Or moments. Even days. And Cece would have stood enthralled.

When he finally dropped her wrist, the juice trickled down his newly shaven chin.

He closed his eye and an expression of sheer ecstasy suffused his face.

When his eye flickered open, the hot jade flame of it licked over every inch of her. He swiped his chin and tangled his hand in hers.

"Just like you, Little Wren. Plump, sweet and begging to be creamed."

His observation was serrated and rough, and her body responded to the want in it. He lifted her hand to his mouth again and she was too stricken and breathless to protest when he licked the rest of the juice from her knuckles.

The gaslight illuminated the nearly invisible golden stubble that gilded his cheeks. His whiskers scraped against her skin as he slipped his tongue in the crevice between her thumb and forefinger.

This was far more intimate and dangerous than the almost kiss in the barn or being caged against the bookshelf last night. Cece felt like she was teetering on the edge of something and the slightest push in the wrong direction would send her careening into oblivion. She should snatch her hand away and run as far away as she could. But she rarely did what she should.

"Such familiarity," she chided. "I wonder if I should punish you for your audacity."

"As if you could, Little Wren. You don't possess the fortitude." His mouth curled in a half smirk and he looked supremely satisfied. "Surely you're aware that I almost caught you."

She gulped against the panic. Caught her? She'd made her spying as inconspicuous as possible. She'd tiptoed away from her clandestine post to avoid detection and been assiduously determined to remain still as a statue during her observation. Perhaps she shouldn't have baited him. "Caught me?" She innocently asked as she held her breath.

He smiled faintly and shook his head again. Most certainly chiding her. "Yes, caught you," he repeated and tugged her closer. "I'd not thought to find a peeping tom hiding behind those letters."

"I'm always the model of propriety. I know nothing about such things." She was both mortified by his awareness and held captive by it.

His grip tightened and his mouth quirked again. "Lies, Little Wren. I'd warrant you're not above asking for what you want. Being tempted and tempting."

"I'm not a liar. If I've tempted you, or been tempted, it wasn't intentional."

His thumb stroked the vein on the underside of her wrist.

Slowly.

Steadily.

His jade green eye gleamed with an unholy light. Like a pirate intent on sacking a ship he saw on the horizon.

"You can't fool me. I feel the flutter of your pulse. Seductress. Little villainous deceitful wren."

She tried to wrest herself away. "I'm none of those things." She wasn't. He didn't know what she thought about when she laid her head down on the straw mattress every night.

She'd only looked at him. She'd yet to touch him. Not the way she wanted to, anyway. She wasn't lying or deceitful. She was just keeping those thoughts to herself. Because they would only complicate things between them and because, despite his reassurances to the contrary after the sheep shearing, she was convinced he was barely tolerating her presence.

"I know you don't want me here. I know I remind you of things you want to forget."

His laugh was brittle. "I may not want you here, but you're impossible to ignore. At least a hundred times a day I ask myself why I didn't put you right back on the train – weather be damned. I've been fighting the way you twist me up inside since the moment we met. You're everything I dreamt you would be. And more. And that's why I can barely tolerate you, Cece."

It was the first time he'd used her given name without it sounding like blasphemy. Or an insult.

He was unexpected too. And she grew weary of feeling as if she were the only one thrown off kilter. She jerked away, crossed her arms and shot him an evil grin. "What do you mean you dreamt of me? Because I was your nightmare incarnate?"

"You were the exact opposite."

She narrowed her gaze. "The exact opposite? If I am the exact opposite, why are you barely tolerating me?"

He ran his hand over his stubbled chin. "You make me want things I can't afford to want. Just like you did then. Every time he read aloud one of your letters I felt the envy curdle in my soul. That he had you and I had nothing but an old man who'd gladly play the bagpipes at my funeral and a farm on the brink of financial collapse."

"There was no one to write you letters?"

"Even before I became a monster, I wasn't fond of conversation or company. I've always been more comfortable with my own counsel."

Cece frowned. "How many times must I tell you? You're not a monster. And if you've always been such a reclusive beast, why were you so ensorcelled by my letters?"

"I explained why you bewitched me."

His reply was practically a snarl.

"Bewitched you? You wouldn't know a hex if it hit you broadside, Malcolm Lockhart. How exactly did I bewitch you? Don't tell me you brought yourself to completion with the assistance of my letters."

Chapter Eighteen

Mal

Letter dated September 27, 1854.

Dearest Husband, Is this marital bliss? With an ocean between us? I miss the solid warmth of you all around me in our bed. I miss the delightful things you taught me there, and the way conjugal bliss made me feel. Sated and as if a thousand pinpricks of light were going to burst from my skin.

MAL BOWED HIS HEAD and clenched his teeth. His body was straining toward hers and he was incapable of speech. Rendered into both clay and stone by her boldness. He laughed harshly. There'd been one letter in which she referred to the marriage bed. He'd dutifully read it to Henry and wished the sentiment had been meant for him. That she was missing his warmth and the delightful things they'd gotten up to betwixt the sheets. Her words tore the confession from him. "Frigged myself raw imagining your voice and your touch." All his irrational fury was stripped down to those words.

He was angry because she'd affected him then. Just as she affected him now. A thorn in his side he didn't need and couldn't afford to extricate. Even the thorny parts of her were wrapped around him. Had been since her first letter.

"Show me."

That soft, implacable command echoed between them – reminding him how the loneliness of war and its destruction had fragmented him. Until his letters to her had become a vessel for all that hope and fear. He kept his gaze on hers as he lifted the folds of his kilt and tucked it into his belt.

When his fist brushed against the ruddy, already glistening head of his cock it nearly brought him to his knees. She licked her lips, and that delicate flick of pink drove him higher. He tightened his grip, helpless against the evidence of her fascination. He'd never frigged himself in front of a woman, and even as he wondered why he hadn't, he was glad she was the first to see the raw edge of his passion.

"Is this what ye wanted to see, lass?" He was so undone, he couldn't keep the ragged burr of his childhood from his voice.

"My time with my husband was short and we were young. We usually barely managed to get one another's clothes off. There was no time to share things like this – to fully indulge my curiosity. I've never seen a man's cock in broad daylight." Her tone was matter of fact, but he heard the quickening of her breath.

Had she been told wants like this should be held close? "Why me? We may as well be strangers." He was afraid to hear her answer, but he couldn't keep the question at bay.

She shrugged, but he wasn't fooled.

"I'll not continue if ye don't tell me why."

"There is something between us. Part of me feels as if I've always known you. And I think you're just as lonely as I am. I don't think of you as a stranger."

He heard what she didn't say. That she didn't fear rejection from him, that she wasn't afraid to demand he satisfy her curiosity because she trusted him to give her a taste of power she'd never been allowed.

He'd not take her gift for granted. Her surrender made him want to do more than slay her dragons. The boy had called him an ogre and he wanted to act like one in truth – to keep her in his lair forever.

Her fingers twitched against her skirts and he knew she wanted to set her hands atop his. He abandoned the last shred of shame. He had done exactly this when he thought of her. Henry had waxed poetic enough that he'd dreamt of pert breasts topped with cherry nipples soft as satin and a sweet cunny that would swallow him whole.

He'd yet to see any of the parts of her he'd dreamt of, but that didn't prevent him from pretending his fist was her tight channel, and the harsh sound of their shared breaths in the empty room was the two of them on the verge of tumbling off the edge of the world.

"I did this, leannan." He murmured as he stroked himself from root to crown. "I did this while I dreamt of taking your nipples in my mouth. Of biting and suckling while you wriggled beneath me. Of bringing you ecstasy with my head buried between your thighs, looking for El Dorado and paradise and finding it when I tasted you on my tongue."

She moved her hand toward the buttons that marched up and down the front of her dress. He stifled a groan. *Would she do it?* She toyed with the edges of her bodice, as if she were shy, the deep blue of her gaze flickering beneath her lids. He could see the evidence of her arousal. Could almost smell it. A shy woman would not have demanded a demonstration. Or teased him with a coy look like that from beneath her lashes.

"What would you like me to do?" She asked as she fluttered her lashes again.

What he asked of her in return wouldn't be enough, but it would ease the emptiness she'd leave in her wake. "Show me. Just as I'm showing you."

He held his breath while those nimble fingers slowly extracted every one of the buttons and peeled aside the plackets of her blouse.

She wore a thin chemise and half stays. Her nipples were dark against the thin cotton, and he needed to know the color and texture. If they were like cherries – or strawberries – ripe velvet against his tongue and under his hands.

"The straps, lass." He pleaded with a tattered whisper.

She fingered one of them, sliding it back and forth over one creamy shoulder. "What about the straps, laird?"

"I'm not a laird."

She knew he hated being called that, and it was just another way for her to be defiant.

"A laird is someone others look to for care." She tugged the strap taut and he wanted to protest. She'd leave marks on the pinkened ivory of her skin. "I suspect you have been doing just that your entire life. Always mindful of what you say and do. Always thinking of others before you think of yourself and putting their needs before your own. I know you learned how to be this way from your grandfather. That is what makes a man a laird – it is a title of respect that is earned, not inherited. Laird."

From her lips, it sounded like an endearment instead of the chains of responsibility he didn't want. She was teasing him while she spoke the truth. Telling him that was how she thought of him – as a man who took care of things. And people. *His grandfather had taught him to be this way.* To put aside his desires for the greater good. To carry the burdens of others because, like all the Lockhart men, his shoulders were sturdy enough to bear them. It was a legacy of sorts, and he thought the old man who'd raised him would be proud of what he'd built.

"I do what needs to be done, Wren, I'm just a man." Nothing had compelled him to sign with the East India Company. Nothing had compelled him to leave this farm for the heat and spice of Calcutta. Nothing had prepared him for what he'd see either. Or what he'd have to do to survive. He'd been young and brash and stupid. So certain the world beyond the borders of the farm held adventure he'd not find tending sheep. That world was full of deeds that haunted his dreams.

She smiled and pushed one of the straps to her elbow. It dragged down the side of the undergarment, drawing it tight across the center of one breast.

"Mal Lockhart, you are not just a man. That is like comparing a hill to a mountain. You are a laird."

He could imagine her whispering the title in his ear when she was astride him. He wanted her to see only that part of him. To find him worthy of the words that had poured from her soul and onto the paper. "I don't deserve your torment, leannan. I'm being obedient. Lower the straps."

"Let me tell you a secret, my laird. I enjoy tormenting you almost more than anything else in the world. I can tell when I've driven you to the very brink of your iron control. Your nostrils flare – just as they're doing now. And your eye turns an even darker shade of green. Like the pines instead of spring leaves."

"Lass, I'm begging you. Show me some mercy."

"Mercy? Is that what you want me to show you? Truly? I thought you wanted me to show you something else entirely."

"Saucy minx," he growled.

"Oooh, I like it when you call me that. Perhaps I'm not ready to reveal my secrets." She giggled and the resulting shiver of her body sent one of the straps sliding to just above her elbow.

The state of the chemise was now promisingly precarious.

He just needed to make her laugh again. He couldn't tell her a joke. She thought his jokes were pathetic. Her eyes had lit up when he called her a saucy wench, perhaps therein lay persuasion.

"Reveal your secrets, temptress. Show me the way I'm showing you," he gave himself a determined tug for good measure. "Let me see you pluck those gorgeous nipples that are playing peekaboo right now."

Her laugh was husky this time. She pushed the other strap to her elbow and wriggled.

Her breasts bobbed free, the nipples already little pebbles. They were the color of dark cherries and he immediately wanted to taste them. To see if they were as tart and sweet as they looked. She reached up with both hands and cupped them. Like she was offering them to him on a platter.

"Fook, woman. You'll be the death of me." He swiped the bead of pre-cum over the ridges of his arousal. "Use your thumbs. Like this." He swiped his thumb over the tip of his cock again to demonstrate.

She watched him through half-lidded eyes as she mimicked the movement of his thumb across the tips of her breasts.

He wanted to taste her, but she hadn't issued an invitation. He wanted her to taste him, wondered if that slice of heaven was in the cards or if it would stay in his dreams.

She tweaked one nipple, tugging it to a belligerent, mouthwatering point, tempting him. And then she set her boot on the bench and began to raise her skirts.

When the delicate lace at the edge of her stockings came into view, the scarlet of the plain woolen hose cupping and accentuating the curve of her calf above the sturdy boot, he started cursing. "You're the bloody devil's spawn."

She grinned wickedly and inched the skirt higher, revealing the bright blue ribbon of her garter. He'd expected something as sedate as the plain ruffled cotton of her petticoat and the utilitarian structure of her corset. He wanted to pull the ends of that ribbon all the way through with his teeth. He wanted to see it bound around her wrists as she knelt in front of him.

She loosened the ribbon and slowly rolled the stocking down. When it was wrinkled about her ankle, she lifted her foot and removed it. The sight of her half-clothed body and swaying breasts was too enticing.

He groaned when she shook her tousled hair about her shoulders.

"Are you overcome, laird?"

"Aye."

Her gaze on him was so intense it was nearly rabid. In direct contrast to the languid circle of one hand about her breast and the slide of the other one under her skirts.

"I am undone, lass."

His release roared from the pit of his stomach, and he emptied himself into the clutch of his fist. It left him so dazed and weak-kneed he stumbled to the wall, his hand still around his cock.

Her delighted laughter tinkled in the air between them as he sank to the floor and stretched his legs. He closed his eyes and willed himself to stop trembling.

"I want to watch you wipe your release with this." She removed her petticoat, so she stood in her knickers and chemise, and tossed it in his direction.

Malcolm flushed. He'd never had such a strangely intimate request from a lover in the aftermath. "I'm accustomed to using my kilt."

She raised her brow and put one hand on her hip. "I told you what I want to see. I think you owe me at least that much."

Christ, her sauciness was going to ruin him for all future women.

He saw that he'd put her on a pedestal that didn't even encompass half her sum. She was smart and competent and witty and warm. But she was a minx and a termagant too. In the best of ways.

This woman was his perfect storm and Mal realized he'd spend his life frigging himself to the thought of her.

Chapter Nineteen

Cece

Letter dated February 19th, 1854.

Dearest Little Wren, One of the officers told me his great uncle is translating the poetry of a famous Persian mathematician into English. I asked one of the Ottoman cavalrymen about it because my curiosity was piqued. He recited his favorite and then translated it for me. I know how inordinately fond of verse you are, so I'm including it here: "Ah! My Beloved, fill the Cup that clears today of past regrets and future fears

– Tomorrow? Why tomorrow I may be Myself with yesterday's seven thousand years." It's a melancholy piece that reminded me of my own fleeting humanity. I long for the day I once again hold you in my arms, so we may drink deeply of the Cup together. Your loving husband, Henry

CECE DIDN'T KNOW WHAT had possessed her. She couldn't believe he'd acquiesced to her demands. She squeezed her thighs together because his head was tipped back, and she could see the voluptuous, sinful sweep of those dark gold lashes from here, and he was still clasping his cock. He'd wrapped her petticoat around one hand, and something feral and primal inside her needed him to use it as she'd instructed.

The world beyond the stone cottage was the heavy quiet of winter settling down for a long nap. The eerie howling wind simply whistled at the windowpanes and the fire crackled merrily in the hearth, warming the room and creating a pool of golden light. It caressed the scarred half of his face, gliding over the planes and hollows so he resembled a satyr. Or a fallen seraph.

"I believe I shall find that hothouse and buy up all the strawberries they have," she told him in a teasing tone.

His eyes slid open, still hazy with release. "'Twasn't the strawberries."

"No," she grinned. "It was because the strawberries made you think of other sweet, juicy things."

"Was Henry already a soldier?"

"Why?"

"I can't imagine any man in his right mind walking away from you. Not unless he was facing a court martial for disobeying orders if he remained at your side."

She slipped the last button into its hole and sighed. "Yes. I don't know what flight of fancy possessed me to throw in my lot with a man whose duty called him elsewhere. I think I was swept away by the romance of it all."

"Like Lydia Bennett."

Cece burst into laughter. Her dour Scotsman was full of surprises. "Yes, exactly like that. Although he didn't have to be coerced to the altar like Wickham. I can't believe you've read *Pride and Prejudice*!"

He shrugged, the tips of his ears pinkening with embarrassment. "I'd much rather read a novel than the dry treatises on husbandry I must peruse. Let me guess. His regiment was stationed near your home and you and your sisters went to see what all the fanfare was about."

"Not so neatly summed up as all that. I'm surprised he didn't tell you how we met."

"There wasn't much conversation of the way things began. Just a lot of bemoaning his absence from your side."

"Henry was very fond of pastry."

Mal laughed for the second time in less than twenty-four hours. "He would seek out the stalls at every opportunity."

"Henry was so fond of pastry he styled himself an amateur pie-eating champion. He'd just won the contest at our village fair and when he spied me in the crowd he convinced me he deserved a victory kiss."

"Quite bold of him."

"Very. But 'twas only on the cheek." She blushed. "At least the first one."

"Henry was a man who didn't waste time pursuing the things he wanted. Like cake. And kisses."

"I don't think you're that sort of man either, Malcolm Lockhart. Not when it's something you truly want."

"But I have a tighter rein on my control, Mrs. Thompson. Therein lies the difference between your late husband and I. When I finally indulge in something, as I just did, it's because the dam has broken and I am helpless to rebuild it."

"When you say your dam has broken, Mr. Lockhart, what does such a disaster entail?"

He tucked himself back beneath his kilt, eased to his feet, and strode toward her. Cece held her breath until he was standing so near she could see the rise and fall of his chest.

"It means, Little Wren, that my walls are down. That you have successfully broken through all my defenses like the marauder you are."

"I think my walls have crumbled as well," she admitted. "And my resolve."

"Then we are in accord. My resolve is nothing more than a heap of debris."

"I did not come to Scotland to begin a liaison. Although I'm told by my sisters it's my prerogative as a bereaved widow to find comfort where I can."

He lifted his hand and tipped her chin up, his thumb stroking her bottom lip. "Are you a bereaved widow? Are you still grieving? If you are, this will go no further. I'll not take advantage of you."

"It has been eight years. There's still heartache. But it's the heartache of young love thwarted and silenced before it had the chance to bloom. Henry was the love of my youth. The bright dream borne of my wish before the Yule log every year. I will always miss the loss of that dream. A corner of my heart will always love him because he chose me out of a crowd."

"Because he was the first one to touch these lips as I am doing now."

His eye was dark jade again. Pinning her in place.

"Yes. He was the first one and the only one."

"Do not tell me things like that, Little Wren. Things that make me want to claim these lips for my own."

The pad of his thumb was rough where it pressed into the middle of her bottom lip. Like the maker's mark from a forge, branding her.

"There is nothing to claim, Mal. I will always belong first to myself."

"Perhaps I want you to claim me instead."

His thumb slipped to her chin and exerted subtle pressure. She responded, tilting into his touch when his long fingers slid over her jaw.

She'd seen more of this man than she had of her husband. She should be scandalized by her own actions. She wasn't. She could barely breathe for the excitement coursing through her. This wasn't the sort of adventure she'd been seeking, but she thought it might be the one she needed.

"Are you finally going to kiss me?"

"Against my better judgment," he murmured as he set his lips on hers.

He let his mouth rest just there. Barely touching. Nothing like the way she'd imagined his kiss would be. She clutched the corded muscle of his forearms and rose to her toes, demanding he do more.

He groaned into the space between them, and she felt the vibration against her lips and against her chest where it met his own.

"Please make that noise again," she commanded as she set her palm against the hollow of his throat.

He obeyed her. Either because he wanted to oblige her or because he was overcome and unable to resist. This time she felt the vibration against her fingertips and all the other places they were touching.

"You're still not kissing me, Malcolm Lockhart. Not the way you want to. Not the way I want you to. Let go."

Cece had once been caught in a whirlpool after she and her sisters had gone swimming in the wake of a summer storm. Arie and Vin had crouched on the bank with an outstretched branch, and she'd hauled herself to shore, shaken and exhausted. Malcolm Lockhart's kiss made her feel like she was being sucked down into that whirlpool again.

His lips were firm and supple, the raised imprint of his scar roughly textured beneath her tongue. He wound his hands into her hair, threading his fingers through it until it hung loose around her shoulders. He lifted his head and gathered the tendrils, closing his eyes and letting them brush against his mouth.

"Ye'll destroy me, lass."

His eye was dark and his body was hard where it pressed against hers. But there was sadness in his gaze. His words were too somber and they sounded like resignation, not praise.

Cece covered his hand with her own and brought it to her mouth. She fluttered kisses over his scarred knuckles before she cradled him against her cheek. "I have seen the way you punish yourself. You are not hideous or horrid. You are a testament to survival."

His lips dropped to hers again, and this time there was no hesitation or gentleness. He didn't hold her as if he were afraid of breaking her. He held her as if his life depended on it.

The brush of his tongue against hers when it slipped into her mouth was like an arrow straight to the heart that had withered and hardened when she lost Henry. His callused palm abraded her cheek like rough velvet when he placed his hand on her cheek, his fingers spearing into her hair and curling around her ear. His touch felt like both surrender and benediction.

He slipped his other hand from her waist to her back, lingering at the divot between her spine and arse before he branded her there too. Even through the cover of her skirt, she could feel the imprint of each of his fingers, as if they were clasping her bare skin to raise her to him. She was pinned against him, the steely length of his arousal unmistakable against her stomach. Henry had needed more time to recover between their bouts of lovemaking.

She could smell the musk of his release, the one she'd brought him to. Salt and earth and man. She could smell the dankness of the peat stacked in the hearth behind her.

The kiss was a savage counterpoint to the gentle way he was cupping her face. His teeth nipped the corners of her lips, and then he soothed the tiny hurt with a swipe of his tongue before diving in again. Cece slid her hands to his hips and pulled him closer, so they were melded together through their clothing. His skin was hot to the touch, like he'd absorbed the fire crackling behind them. She ran her fingers back and forth, tenderly brushing the rough scars. She wanted to set her lips against every single one of them. She wanted to hunt down whoever had carved his body like this and give them a taste of their own medicine.

His tongue stroked hers, his hand bunching in her skirt to raise it. She didn't protest, only circled her hips against his hardness, trying to soothe the ache from the kiss. Trying to find relief like what she'd seen in his face when she'd bared her knees and he'd spilled into his hand. He finally worked one hand beneath her skirt and gripped her thigh, curling it around his waist. She looped her arms around his neck to steady herself against the need. Now she was the one hanging on as if her life depended on it.

She whimpered when he rocked against her. He was bigger everywhere than her husband had been. She knew nature had made them to fit one another, but she'd seen the way he was made. That part of him even now sliding against the fabric of her drawers, making her gasp, was like one of the posts they used to secure boats. Solid and heavy and thick. Like an oak.

The wetness gathered there, and he dropped his hand from her face, sliding it down the front of her chemise, a fleet brush with the backs of his knuckles across the hardness of her nipples that made her whimper again.

His mouth dropped to her cheek, peppered kisses along her jawline. "It's your turn, Little Wren," he growled into the shell of her ear.

Those callused, rough, warrior hands knew what they were about. His thumb slid to the button at the juncture of her sex and flicked it.

She moaned, her legs suddenly too shaky to hold her. Like she was a block of ice melting into a puddle beneath the summer sun.

He did it again as he slipped two fingers inside her. His wicked thumb stroked and circled as those fingers slid in and out. He dropped his face to her neck and nudged aside her collar. "Your body wants this. Come for me, leannan," he commanded before he sank his teeth into her shoulder.

She couldn't help herself. She clenched her jaw against the spiraling violence of her release.

Her abandonment was the trigger to his and he groaned and shuddered. She felt the trickle of his release against her thigh as he surged against her and his arms tensed around her body.

The world was so fuzzy her head was light. Standing on her own when she was this dazed was impossible. She slipped from the edge of the table and fell forward.

He caught and lifted her. When he settled into the massive chair before the fire, she snuggled into him.

His chin nuzzled the top of her head as she pressed a kiss to his chest.

Chapter Twenty

Mal

Letter dated December 23, 1853.

Dearest Husband, All seven of us traipsed into the forest today in the hopes we'd find a suitable log for Yule. We didn't find a log, but we did end up in a snowball fight against some lads from the village. They thought to catch the Wainwright women unawares, launching missiles from between the safety of the buildings. We took up our own defense and pelted them so fast and furiously they were pleading for mercy.

I found that I have quite the arm and quite the aim.

MAL NEVER WANTED TO move. The scent of them, mingled together, teased his nostrils. He circled the satiny skin just beneath her elbow, felt the smooth, dark silk of her hair when he laid his cheek atop her head.

"I never meant for this to happen, Little Wren. But I'll not apologize. Because I'm not sorry. Even if I can never let it happen again."

She lifted her head from his shoulder. "You deny yourself too much. There is no harm in this."

No harm? Only the permanent wounds she'd inflict on his heart.

"This was a lapse in judgment. Because I cannot in good conscience lay the blame at your feet, I'll ascribe it to the sense of cheer you seem determined to spread in your wake. I haven't celebrated the season since I left here when I was barely more than a lad. Not truly."

He felt the curve of her smile against his chest. "So you wouldn't have bought the ham?"

"No. Nor the other fripperies you insisted on. I make my appearance at the village fete, but that is all."

"Do you dance at the fete or do you simply brood and nurse your whisky in the corner?"

"Moira would claim I do nothing but brood and nurse my whisky in the corner."

She twisted her body so she could face him and lifted her head. "What if I want to dance with you?"

"I don't dance, Little Wren. My knee is too unsteady for that. We'd either wind up on the floor or crash into another couple."

"Then I shall sit in the corner beside you. I may drink the rum punch instead of the whisky, though."

"You will do no such thing. You have spent most of your youth in widow's weeds and I'll not have you acting like you're still confined to them. You'll dance to your heart's content."

"What if I don't care to dance with anyone but you, Malcolm Lockhart? What if I think sipping rum punch at your side for the entirety of the evening sounds wonderful?"

"What if there's no rum punch to sip? What then Cece Wainwright Thompson?"

"There's always rum punch at a village fete."

"If there's rum punch, you can sip it beside me while you rest your feet. But I want to see you kick up your heels, leannan."

"You're going to insist I take to the floor for a reel, aren't you?"

She sounded quite put out. Her irritation amused him, and he brushed his thumb over her lips before pecking them. "Aye, I'm going to insist I'll not have you making sacrifices for me."

Her brow wrinkled. "'Tis not a sacrifice."

"If you say so, Little Wren."

She tipped her head back into his chest. "I do. I also say you need to bring some holiday cheer to this cottage."

He tightened his arms around her again. "Cheer doesn't chase away all the shadows, but I'm willing to entertain some of your schemes. What do you suggest?"

What if rum punch and Yule logs were the recipe for holding his demons at bay?

"A Yule log for starters. And a tree from your wood."

"A Yule log? For making wishes or to ensure good fortune? And why would I consent to honoring the German tradition popularized by the Hanovers when I am a Scot through and through?"

"The Yule can be for both things. Though I'm not certain what I would wish for, if anything. And you should consent to the German tradition as you call it because it will make you feel more festive."

Mal's bark of laughter echoed through the room. "I'm not festive, nor will I ever be. I'll look for a suitable log once the snow eases, but I'll not entertain the tomfoolery of a tree."

"I'll convince you," she murmured between two jaw-cracking yawns.

He shook his head at her misplaced confidence in her own persuasive abilities. Before he could correct her, she snuffled against him, fast asleep.

She hadn't slept in the loft last night. He'd laid her down in his bed, because he was loath to wake her. He'd been the one to climb the ladder and collapse onto the straw ticking.

The relentless thumping against the front door woke him. It felt like there was an anvil sitting in the middle of his chest and his body was covered in the sheen of a cold sweat. When he opened his eyes he half expected to see nothing but smoke and fog.

He threw the plaid around his waist and jolted downstairs. When he swung the door open, Duncan pushed his way in. He was covered in snow, even his beard. Since it was even longer than Mal's had been, he looked like Saint Nick. His eyes gleamed and his cheeks were rosy in the light of the dying fire.

Mal didn't know what had prompted this visit. Duncan was forever trying to move him from his routine.

Mal crouched before the fire, stoking the flames. "What brings you here so early and in such foul weather?" He asked as he added a brick of peat.

"I heard rumors, mate. That you had a bonny house-guest. I know you don't entertain, so I came to see the truth for myself. Where is she?" Duncan asked as he stripped the gloves from his hands and unwound his scarf.

"She's sleeping. At least she was until you fair beat down the door." Mal suspected she hadn't been sleeping well in the loft and he wanted to let her catch up on her rest in his bed. He was going to insist she take it from now on.

Duncan smiled slyly. "Mayhap I was hoping to disturb the two of you. Is she sleeping in your bed?"

Mal shot him an annoyed look. "Aye. Without me. I slept there." He jerked his thumb in the direction of the loft.

"Skinner's lass, Maggie, said you were the most solicitous she's ever seen you in the market yesterday. She said your glower was less fearsome than usual and ye were carryin' her packages."

Mal rose to his feet and braced an arm on the mantle. "There's no reason to gloat. She has no plans to remain in Scotland. She has a life and a family in England."

"Well, love has a way of changin' one's plans. It's clear from your expression how you feel, Mal. Have you asked her how she feels?"

"No," Mal tersely answered. "And I'm not going to. What decent woman in her right mind wants to be bound to a dour, scarred sheep farmer who lives in the back of beyond?"

Duncan's expression sobered. "Mal, ye know I was only ribbin' ye about yer scars, right? The single lasses in the village don't care a whit aboot yer scars."

"They should. They're the ones who are going to be rubbing liniment into my decrepit limbs."

"Decrepit? Ye're not yet forty, mate. We're the same age, and I've no intention of settlin' down anytime soon."

Mal sighed and turned to face him. "It has nothing to do with age. She's Henry's widow, Duncan."

"Not the one that wrote all those letters ye told me aboot?"

"The very same."

Mal hadn't told Duncan about his own role in the exchange of correspondence between Cece and her husband, but he had told him about what those letters meant over a bottle of whisky or two. He'd confessed that he credited his sound mind and safe return to her letters. They'd been what kept he and his fellow soldiers going with their hefty dose of reality and humor.

"Does she ken what those letters meant to ye?"

"She kens a little. I'll not burden her with the full confession."

"Why did she seek ye out?"

"I sent back the letters she wrote him. I'd kept them since his death because I couldn't bear to part with them."

"What changed yer mind?"

"I couldn't keep them, Duncan. They weren't meant for me. And she deserved to have them returned to her." Mal's admission was anguished.

Duncan's face filled with sympathy as he wagged his head back and forth. "'Tis a foin' pickle ye find yerself in, cousin. Surely ye knew that if she was half as tenacious as she appeared to be in those letters 'twas only a matter of time before she sought ye out."

"What am I to do? Tell me how I'll send her on her way now that I truly know her." Not only did he truly know her, he knew she was the other half of his heart.

"Ye'll have to convince her to stay. Do whatever she asks. No matter how much ye think ye'll despise it."

"She asked me to find her one of those infernal trees. Like the ones the royals have made all the fash over."

"She wants a Tannenbaum, does she?" Duncan's tone was disbelieving. "She knows how ye feel about the season?"

"She knows I don't celebrate it, but I didn't tell her why. She thinks it's because I'd rather drink whisky than dance." Mal turned toward the fire again. "A Tannenbaum? Is that what they're calling it?"

"Aye. And ye've a whole wood full o' Scotch Pine to oblige her with. Make the lass happy, man."

"She wants me to dance with her as well. And procure a suitable Yule log. And mingle instead of drinking my whisky in the corner."

Duncan's eyes crinkled as he guffawed. "The minglin' part is somethin' I've been trying to get ye to do since ye returned. Maybe ye'll listen this time." He braced his elbows on his knees and narrowed his gaze. "Make the lass happy, Mal. That's what ye need to do. Maybe then ye'll finally be happy too and stop stompin' around like a gloomy giant git. I know this season has brought you nothing but sorrow and loss – but what if she's the one to change that?"

Mal crossed his arms and glared at his friend. "I stomp around like a gloomy giant git because someone needs to worry about the state of the wool market and keep the head on their shoulders when things get out of hand."

Duncan sighed. "Mal, I love ye like a brother, but ye can be dense. Am I not yer man o' business? The wool markets are fine and the ledger's finally in the black. We've secured contracts with three of the tweed manufactories and we've plenty of food and drink. It's finally time to congratulate yerself on all that ye've accomplished."

"Aye. We've finally succeeded where everyone thought we would fail. They all said sharing the profits of our labor like this was addled. And it's working and I should be over the moon. But what happens when I'm no longer needed? When the aching muscles and headaches that plague me become too much? What then?" It was a rhetorical question Mal already knew the answer to. He knew what would happen. He'd be old and alone with only his memories and regrets.

"What happens then, cousin, is that ye finally get yer well-deserved rest. Ye've earned it. And ye should have someone to share it with. Make the lass happy, Mal. So ye can convince her to stay."

Chapter Twenty-One

Cece

Letter dated January 2, 1854.

Dearest Little Wren, Your recounting of the holiday festivities at Heathsted cheered us all. They
provided us with an extra helping of hardtack
I think the stores could scarcely sustain if the
grim expression of the quartermaster was any
indication. Most days we get by on thin gruel.
One of the Scot's friends who served with one
of the sawbones told him to find a water source
other than the river. He said it was so polluted

by the privies the army placed all along it we'd become sick. He trudged into the mountains and found a spring. We fill our canteens from it every few days, and he has a big canvas bag lined with the bladder of something he traded for. He carries it on his back.

CECE HADN'T MEANT TO eavesdrop. But the words of Mal's friend rang in her ears. Make her happy. Make yourself happy.

She smiled as she envisioned his reaction to being called a gloomy giant git.

Was this part of some divine plan? Was she sent here not to find answers, but to find her destiny? Was this man the next chapter in her life? Were they meant to bring each other the solace they'd been looking for?

She wondered what her sisters would say. They'd probably accuse her of being rash and impulsive and swayed by romantic notions that would only bring her to ruin. He'd yet to ruin her. She knew he probably thought himself too honorable to do it fully. But she was a widow and she should hold herself to a different standard.

Arie hadn't confessed much about her courtship with Thad, but Cece knew her sister had finally decided to seize the things from life that had been stolen from her. To seek her bliss. Perhaps it was time Cece did the same.

She raised her hand to her lips. They still tingled from his kiss. She wondered if she'd slept alone in his bed.

She arched her back and stretched her toes toward the ceiling. His bed was much more comfortable than hers. Maybe she should have let him give it to her instead of insisting on the loft.

The floor was so cold beneath her bare feet she almost shrieked. Until she remembered she wanted to hear more, undetected. She rummaged through the chest at the edge of the bed until she found a pair of huge socks. She slipped them over her legs and threw the blanket at the foot of the bed around her shoulder.

Cece crept to the door and eased it open. She took a moment to watch the two of them, unobserved. Mal's arm was braced on the mantle and his expression was closed and faraway.

His friend's tone was animated, and he was making sweeping gestures with his hands. She crept closer.

"Mal, ye've seen enough sorrow. I never understood why ye left for India in the first place. Or why you enlisted as a foot soldier in Her Majesty's Army. I don't know what ye were runnin' from or what ye thought ye would find. But this is yer chance to start again. To replace all those memories with something better."

"There's no replacing them, Duncan." Mal said bitterly.

"Then don't. But at least consider that ye deserve more and stop punishin' yerself with yer whisky and yer brood-in'. Tell the lass why the season brings ye sorrow. Ask her to help ye overcome it and find reasons to celebrate."

"I'm not punishing myself. I've seen and done things you can't comprehend. Things that scarred me, and not just on the outside."

Duncan shook his head and Cece bet he'd rolled his eyes as well. "Ye're never going to heal if ye keep all the scars to yerself, Mal."

The man's words resonated. Cece had scars too. She felt like she'd spent her entire life being buffeted about. Never certain of anything. She'd let those wounds bleed a little in front of someone she shouldn't feel this instant kinship with. Now she understood why she'd done it. Because he had wounds too and wouldn't judge her for the way she dealt with hers.

She took a deep breath and cleared her throat. Mal turned first, and she couldn't make out his expression. Would things go back to the way they were? What had last night meant to him, if anything?

"Duncan, meet my houseguest, Mrs. Thompson. Mrs. Thompson, this is Mr. McTavish."

The other man stood and made his way over to her. When she extended her hand, he raised it to his lips. His eyes twinkled mischievously, and she liked him immediately. His easy humor was the inverse of her host's stoicism. "The rumors weren't merely rumors. Ye're a bonny lass, Mrs. Thompson. And ye're wearin' my cousin's socks."

"You may call me Cece." She held her hand out as regally as she could, like a queen demanding obeisance. Duncan obliged her, and stepped close enough to take her hand in his and kiss the back of it.

"You may not." Mal contradicted from his place across the room. "Do not encourage him, Mrs. Thompson."

"I'm not encouraging him Mr. Lockhart."

"I think you are encouraging me." Duncan said in amusement. "You asked me to call you by your first name. He's still calling you Mrs. Thompson."

Cece smiled. "That's because he chooses to do so. Most of the time. I've asked him to call me Cece and he refuses. When I call him Mal he gets this funny look on his face, like the one he's wearing now."

Duncan dropped her hand, backed away and sketched a bow. "I know that look all too well. It's his impatient one. He's going to insist some manner of livestock needs more fodder. Which is my cue." He turned to face Mal. "Follow my advice, friend. The effort is most certainly worth the reward."

He wrapped a woolen scarf around his neck and pulled a battered knit cap over his ears. "I bid you adieu, fair maiden," he called over his shoulder as he disappeared through the door.

It felt like a summer storm had just disrupted the fragile peace between she and her host. There was a charge in the air.

"Your friend cares for you."

"Duncan is my cousin as well as my friend, and he may care for me, but he's incapable of minding his own business. The whole purpose of his visit was to see if the rumors about my houseguest were true."

"There are rumors about me?"

Mal shrugged. "Apparently. No doubt stoked by Moira."

Moira probably had stoked the rumors. She'd seemed inordinately pleased when Cece told her she was staying in his cottage. "Does the knowledge of those rumors annoy you, laird?"

He dropped his arm and walked toward her. He stopped a few lengths away and cleared his throat.

Cece held up her hand to forestall whatever apology he was going to make. "Don't."

He clenched his jaw. "I must. I took advantage of your trust yesterday."

Cece shook her head. "Is that what you've chosen to call it? Taking advantage of me? Some would say I took advantage of you. That I've been doing so since I landed on your doorstep."

"We should let our emotions cool. They got the better of us last night."

"Fine, Mr. Lockhart. I shall let my emotions cool and try to forget that kiss. And the fact you had your fingers inside my body."

"Cece…" he growled in warning.

One of her hands went to her hips. She could feel the fury boiling to the surface. "So you'd like me to forget the sight of you stroking your big cock? And the sight of you using my petticoat to clean yourself after you lost control?"

"It shouldn't happen again."

Her fury was quenched almost as rapidly as it had ignited. "You said shouldn't Laird, not can't or couldn't."

"I won't be one of your adventures, woman. I should have kept my thoughts and my hands to myself."

"Who said anything about this being an adventure? Why can't it simply be the natural progression of two lonely, mature adults finding comfort during a blizzard?"

"Blast woman, why must ye be so bluidy stubborn?"

He'd cursed and his brogue had snuck in. She'd unbalanced him. "I'm not being stubborn. I'm simply being mindful and purposeful about what I want. And I want you, Malcolm Lockhart. Do with it what you will."

She sketched a curtsey and clambered up the ladder.

Cece fumed as she splashed the cold water from the ewer into the basin by the mattress. She dipped the cloth in and patted her face and neck, scrubbed beneath her arms and all the places he'd touched her last night, and steeled herself to go about the day not thinking about it.

It was Monday, which meant Moira and the other women would be carding the wool. Cece wanted to learn and she needed to put space between herself and her host.

She donned her warmest dress, a dark gray wool, and her thick red stockings.

—◦—

The carding shed was at the end of the lane, and when Cece entered it, all the chatter came to a halt. Moira stood to welcome her.

"'Tis glad I am ye made it, lass." She said as she enveloped Cece in a hug.

"I needed a distraction." Cece explained.

Moira cackled. "The laird's drivin' ye mad."

Yes, he was. In more ways than one. "Aye."

"I'd give me eyeteeth to have 'im drive me mad," a blond at the head of the carding table confessed.

"Och, hush Sadie." Moira chastised her.

"Mayhap ye can tell us, miss, are other parts of him as big as his feet?"

This question came from a redhead who shot Cece an impish grin.

Cece flushed to the roots of her hair. "I wouldn't know," she managed to stammer in response.

The girl grinned even wider. "Och, but ye know somethin'. Care to share yer thoughts, miss?"

"Grace, mind yer tongue. Mrs. Thompson will never keep us company again if you lot don't leave off." Moira surveyed the room with a stern look, her hands on her hips.

"I'm accustomed to teasing from my six sisters," Cece assured her. "I just didn't expect to encounter such pointed questions."

"We're only bammin' ye miss," the redhead grinned again. "The laird never dances an' we've never heard o' him keepin' company with a woman. We're just curious."

Cece sank into the empty seat beside the head of the table. "The laird and I are not keeping company."

Moira shook her head. "Ye may not be yet lass, but any fool can see 'tis only a matter o' time wi' the way he looks at ye."

"The way he looks at me? Like I'm a burr stuck to the wool of his cloak?"

"That's not how he looks at ye. He looks at ye like a man starvin' for a morsel o' yer affection."

"Do ye think he's sweet on her, Moira?" The blonde at Moira's side asked.

"Aye, Sadie. I do."

"He's not sweet on me. He'd barely look at me this morning."

Moira chuckled. "Och, lass, that's a sure sign he's sweet on ye. And doesnae ken what tae do wi' his feelins'."

Sadie, Grace and the rest of the women nodded in agreement.

"Moira's right, miss. If a man willnae look at ye it means ye're all he can think aboot." Grace said.

By his own admission, Cece knew what her letters had meant to him. But surely it was mere infatuation he felt. And lust of course. She'd been here barely a fortnight. "I believe your laird is accustomed to getting his own way in everything, and I'm not known for my malleability. I'm sure he finds me confounding, not intriguing. As I've said, I believe I'm more like an irritating burr in the heel of his boot or a bee in his bonnet than a woman he's interested in."

Moira grinned. "I'd wager ye on the truth o' that, but I haven't the coin. Now, let's get ye started." She handed Cece a clump of fleece.

"It's softer than I expected."

"Aye, it's already been washed, this is the combin' process," she explained as she drew the right card over the left one. "Our lass Grace is the fastest, she can make nearly thirty rolags or rovings in an hour."

Cece furrowed her brow. "What are rolags and rovings?"

"The small bundles o' combed wool are rolags, and the larger ones are rovings. When we've finished I'll show ye how to dye and spin."

The smell was the first thing she noticed when she crossed the threshold. The odor was even more pungent when she expelled the sharpness of winter from her lungs. A perfectly symmetrical evergreen was propped in a bucket beside the door. She almost blurted out she'd overheard that portion of his conversation with his cousin and confessed she wanted to know why he chose to indulge her when he never celebrated the season.

"I thought I'd wait to set it up properly. So you could tell me where you want it."

He strolled into view, his hands clasped behind his back and his gaze expectant.

Cece turned away to hang her shawl and scarf by the door, momentarily flustered. Was this merely a sign of good will or was her taciturn host indeed sweet on her as all the women had told her he was? He'd gone to no small amount of trouble to procure the tree. An ax nearly as wide as the trunk was propped beside it.

She turned around and approached it to get a better measure. "It needs to be the first thing someone walking in the door will notice. It's meant as a sign of welcome."

"Then we shouldn't move it far from its current station."

Cece tipped her head and tapped her foot. "I think it would be better suited nearer the sitting area. Isn't that where your guests usually settle in?"

"Aye. But what if the tree encourages them to wear out their welcome?"

She giggled at his beleaguered expression. "Like your cousin, Duncan? His visit this morning seemed to exasperate you."

Mal tossed her a wry grin. "Duncan is overly fond of exasperating me. He thinks it is his mission in life. A calling, if you will."

His grin was punctuated by the bracket of a dimple in his right cheek. She hadn't noticed it when he'd smiled before, because of his stubble and the dim light in his study.

The stubble was gone, and she knew he'd shaved again while she'd been away. She swallowed her disappointment. She'd quite liked the way his whiskers had scratched against her skin when he'd kissed her last night.

"My sisters were put on this earth with that very same calling, laird, so I can empathize with your plight."

He crossed his arms and legs and feet as he leaned against the wall across from her. "Out of curiosity, Mrs. Thompson, how does one go about decorating this tree?"

"They're usually festooned with ribbons and candles."

He quirked a brow. "Candles? We can't spare the tallow for that and 'twould be dangerous in a cottage with a thatched roof."

"I wasn't suggesting we use them. My sister Arie didn't even use them at the party she hosted at the manor last year. But we could tie the branches with random bits of cloth and other odd bits."

"I don't have any of those things here, Mrs. Thompson. But I'm sure if you ask the carding circle for contributions they'll pool their resources."

"I'll ask them tomorrow."

Cece was settling into the pace of life in this backwater corner of Scotland so easily it felt like she'd always been here. She took tea with Moira nearly every afternoon, and after her carding lesson this morning she'd agreed to teach Sadie and Grace tatting and fancy embroidery.

"Grace and Sadie have asked for tatting and embroidery lessons," she informed him.

He went still as a statue, his expression unreadable. "You're making quite the mark on Lockhart Farm, aren't you Cece Wainwright Thompson?"

There hadn't been censure in the question, but she could tell he didn't like the thought of her making a place for herself. She sniffed, so he'd think she was affronted. "I'm not used to idle hands, Mr. Lockhart, and you've found other ways to occupy yourself since the shearing that don't include giving me husbandry lessons."

He gave her one of the infuriatingly inscrutable looks she was becoming accustomed to and said, "I haven't been doing much husbandry, Mrs. Thompson. The weather has prevented it, and the sheep are hardy enough to fend for themselves. I've been occupied repairing stone fences and helping the smith forge and temper new blades for the plow so all will be ready in the spring."

He'd abandoned the fence repairs for at least one day. The proof of it was leaning against the wall. Because of something she'd said. He'd indulged her whim and she wondered why.

"What made you decide to find a tree when you were so set against it? That bit about Germans was a ridiculous excuse."

He shuffled and ducked his head. As if he was avoiding the question.

"Mr. Lockhart, care to elaborate on your sudden change of heart?" She prodded.

"I remembered one of your letters," he mumbled.

He remembered what she'd written in one of her letters? That's what had prompted this about face?

"Which one?" She couldn't recall writing about Christmas trees in any of them. But perhaps her memory was faulty.

"There was one we received right before the start of the season. You talked about traipsing into the wood with your sisters to find a log. There was also mention of a snowball fight."

Cece laughed aloud. "That was the most wonderful day. Especially the snowball fight. My sisters and I proved quite proficient at both creating our missiles and launching them."

"You seemed extraordinarily proud of your accomplishments on the field of battle. Especially your newly discovered and honed aim."

She sighed wistfully. "Yes, I would have liked to see if it extended to rounders or cricket."

"I was the leading batsman for my regiment in India."

Given the delicious breadth of his shoulders, Cece wasn't surprised. "Are you boasting or proposing we pit our skills against each other?"

He straightened. "Perhaps a bit of both. Although I don't know when we would have the opportunity. You are returning to Cumbria when the weather clears."

"The weather's much clearer now than it was the night I arrived," Cece challenged.

"They can't keep the snow from drifting onto the tracks. All the train departures have been cancelled as a safety measure."

"Are winters always this harsh in this corner of Scotland?"

"They're harsher here than on the coast because the wind sweeps down from the mountains. You should have done your research before you set out on your journey, Mrs. Thompson."

"I don't need your admonishment, Mr. Lockhart. My sister Jess is going to be particularly upset at my absence. I promised to help her make the pageant costumes for her students."

"Surely they can all get on without you."

"Getting along without me isn't the point. I've always spent the holidays with my sisters. And since Arie and Fran married I've gained even more family members. Especially nieces. I was looking forward to the celebrations."

He grimaced. "I wasn't making light of your absence. I apologize if I seemed to be poking fun at your spate of melancholia."

"The tree will help with my melancholia. As will the Yule log. We are obtaining one of those as well?" She hopefully asked.

"I had planned on it, yes. For the luck." He pushed his hands through his hair. "And because it will make it seem more like home to you," he mumbled.

"When I tell Moira about the tree, she'll insist I persuade you to gather boughs or some such."

When he sighed, it sounded like a heaving bellows. It was a sigh of exasperation. Cece had already deduced that little happened in Dunkirk that wasn't stirred by Moira's hands or words. Cece knew Moira worried about the man standing in front of her, and would use every tool at her disposal to lure him into celebrating the holiday with his tenants.

Chapter Twenty-Two

Mal

Letter dated November 27, 1853.

Dearest Husband, When you wrote that you and your friends feared you wouldn't have enough layers of clothing for winter, my sisters and I started a knitting circle. We're bound and determined to ensure every single one of you has a sturdy cap, warm mittens and stockings at the very least. You mentioned your friend the Scot is quite large. Perhaps you could send his measurements along? We wouldn't want to make

him something that would barely fit over his thumb.

AFTER THE NIGHT MAL had carried her to his room and laid her on his bed, there'd been no battle about who would sleep on it and who would sleep in the loft. His cat had taken up permanent residence with her as well.

Mal hoped Cece knew he wouldn't allow her to reclaim her original quarters. When the snow had tapered off he'd clambered onto the roof of the cottage behind his to assess the damage. The extensive repairs it required would have to wait until the spring thaw. He'd patched the hole with a piece of canvas from one of the old fishing skiffs, and resigned himself to her presence in his home for the foreseeable future.

He was feeding one of the lambs whose mother had turned away from it, when Moira found him.

"Laird, ye know 'tis Mother Nature's way of culling the weakest among us. Every year ye try to save them and it breaks yer heart when ye can't."

Mal gazed down at the lamb that was drinking goats' milk from an old kid glove. "I have to try, Moira. He went to the trouble of kicking his way into this world. The least I can do is give him a fighting chance."

"Ye want everyone to think yer the thorn, but yer not. Yer the petals, Malcolm Lockhart."

Mal felt the heat in his cheeks. Now he was clean-shaven, he couldn't hide it. "Ye're addled, Moira."

"Ye're blushin', laird. Ye ken I'm right."

"I'm neither a thorn, nor a petal, Moira. Just a man."

She snickered. "Aye. A man with a hankerin' fer his guest. Ye're bollocks at hidin' how she fascinates ye."

He let the protest die on his lips. He couldn't fool her. "She's leaving soon Moira. Unless someone spends their youth here and knows what to expect, there's nothing to entice them into staying."

She crossed her arms and tilted her head to scrutinize him. "She looks at ye too. And when ye come up in the cardin' circle, the lass blushes just as yer doin' now. A pair o' fools the two o' ye. And most of the families in this community have moved here from elsewhere. Because of you. Laird. Why can she not do the same?"

"Don't bandy my name about the carding circle, Moira. And she can't do the same because she has a life and a close-knit family in Cumbria."

She threw her hands in the air. "Ye're the laird. Yer name's bound to come up on occasion. And the good book tells us to cleave to our spouse above all others. If she decided to stay, that's what would happen. Ye'd become her family."

"I wish the lot of you would stop calling me that. There hasn't been a laird at Dunkirk since the Rising. And no one mentioned wedlock."

"Ye're the laird in everythin' but title, and we all ken it. Even yer new lass. And ye can't deny it. I've never seen ye so taken with a woman. Whether ye've admitted it to yerself or not, ye've thought about wedlock." Her gaze grew speculative. "She told us ye got her a tree. This morning the other lasses brought her a basket full o' bits and bobs to decorate it with."

To his consternation, Mal blushed again. "She spoke of the season often in her letters. I wanted to make her feel at home."

"If ye're so keen to celebrate, ye can go find boughs for the ceilidh on Christmas Eve."

"I have work to do, Moira. I don't have time to go scouting through the woods for greenery."

"Ye'll make time. And ye'll take the lass with ye." She held out her arms. "Hand over the wee thing. Ye've a tree tae garnish."

He knew it was no use arguing with her, so he passed over the lamb. He'd purposefully stayed away, just as he'd done every evening since *that* happened. He waited until dark, rushed through his dinner, mumbled a good night, and climbed into the loft. And laid there thinking about her.

When he let himself into the cottage, his obsession was sitting at the table with an inkpot, a plume and a piece of stationery. When she'd said she needed to write her sisters and advise them she wouldn't be home for the holidays, he'd bought her a sheaf of paper.

His empty boots thumped to the floor and she looked up. When her gaze landed on his stockinged feet, she grinned.

"This is the earliest you've darkened the doorway in at least five days, Malcolm Lockhart. You can help me compose this letter to my sisters. They expected me home almost a week ago."

Mal snorted. "You don't need my help. You're quite adept at letter writing. If you're struggling with an explanation, set it aside."

"Easy for you to say! If I don't send word soon, the whole lot of them are likely to show up on your doorstep – out of their minds with worry."

He marveled that she had so many people in her life that desperate to ensure her well-being. It had always been only he and his parents. And then he and his grandfather. He'd been an only child, cosseted and fussed over until he'd lost them both. His grandfather wasn't one to cosset or fuss, and even when Mal didn't even reach his waist, he had him spending the day laboring on the farm. He'd insisted on two things. That Mal know every hill and dale and stream on their holding, and that he learn math and reading from the village priest.

The old man had been devastated, and then resentful, when Mal signed up with the East India Company, and though he'd been stationed there for years, he knew his grandfather hadn't expected him to write and trusted in God and country to bring him home safely.

He'd never been a letter writer. Until her. It had been like all the things he'd been storing behind a dam broke through the surface. Years of internal monologues and random observations and philosophical musings.

"The things you need to say will come to you if you stop dwelling on them. Meanwhile, let's garb your tree. Moira said you have a basketful of frippery."

She pushed the chair away from the table and stood, rubbing her hands in the small of her back as she stretched on her toes. "I know how much you detest frippery, so I'm honored."

When she stooped to lift the basket, Mal put his hands in his pockets and tried not to look at the luscious curve of her bottom. He stared at the ceiling, and then pursed his lips in a tuneless whistle.

The basket was overflowing with red yarn and bits of tweed and plaid. She wordlessly handed it to him for inspection. "So we're going to tie these to the branches?"

"Yes. It will cheer up your starkly furnished abode," she primly informed him.

He started whistling again and she gave him a quizzical look. "Is that pathetic pipe of air meant to be a whistle?"

Mal flushed. For the third – or was it the fourth?- time that day. "I could never quite manage a proper whistle."

"Set the basket down. This is more important. Everyone should know how to properly whistle."

He set the basket back on the floor.

"Now show me how you hold your tongue when you whistle."

Mal felt like a right eejit, but did as she said.

She leaned over to peer into his mouth. Then she shook her head, as if she was ashamed on his behalf. "That's why your attempt was so pathetic. You have to place your tongue on the roof of your mouth, just behind your two front teeth, or it won't work."

He wedged his tongue against the roof of his mouth, feeling even more self-conscious.

She shook her head again. "No, not like that. Like this." She puckered her lips and exhaled.

The sound was so loud it nearly pierced his ear drums. "That's worse than a terrible fiddle player," he muttered.

"You can modulate the volume. How loud it is depends on how hard you blow. I was just demonstrating."

Mal did as she instructed. Nothing happened.

"You need to practice. What if you need to catch someone's attention and there's no other way for them to hear you?"

"If I promise to practice, can we decorate the tree?"

Anything was better than feeling like a boy in breeches on the first day of lessons.

"Yes. But you have to share when you master it."

He gave her a curt nod of agreement, eager to abandon the subject altogether.

<hr>

She hummed a carol beneath her breath, but otherwise they worked in silence. Mal was too embarrassed to practice whistling in front of her and his friends had once told him his singing voice sounded like a cross between a croaking bullfrog and a braying donkey.

"I think we've finished," she finally said when it was beribboned to her satisfaction.

"Is this where it's staying, Mrs. Thompson?" Mal doubted it, but held his breath and hoped she'd say yes. Being this close to her, when it was dark outside and the cottage was quiet was almost too much for him to bear.

"No, Mr. Lockhart. We need to place it somewhere it will show to its best advantage. I'll need you to tote it about the room for me so I can decide where that is."

He carried it to the seating area because he remembered she'd said it should welcome guests.

"A bit to the left," she directed.

He maneuvered it to the side.

"No, that's not it. A smidge more to the right."

"A smidge? What's a smidge?" Mal sharply asked.

"About this much." She spread her thumb and forefinger apart about two inches.

"No one will notice a difference of that much," he complained.

She rolled her eyes. "Fine. Just there will do."

He steadied it in the metal pail. He'd brought in some rocks to help hold it upright, and he was confident it was going nowhere unless Shep or Sal tried to tackle it to the floor.

"Perhaps you should invest in one of the metal stands they now sell."

"Why would I do that? This is a one-time occurrence ye ken?"

"You would do that for next year's tree. Because now you've set up an expectation for your visitors."

"My visitors are infrequent and this seems a lot of bother," Mal grumbled.

"Your visitors will be more frequent now you're demonstrating your hospitality."

He wondered if she knew the thought of people crowding into his personal spaces made Mal's stomach turn.

"Wonderful. More meddling and chicanery to disturb my solitude." His response was rife with sarcasm.

"You need more of those things, Malcolm Lockhart. But I know you have to be eased into the water like a baby duckling." She fluttered her hands in his direction. "Go outside and smoke your pipe. You look like you're on the brink of jumping out of your skin at the mere thought."

He sketched a bow. "I'm going to do that. I bid you adieu for the evening, Mrs. Thompson."

Chapter Twenty-Three

Cece

Letter dated October 19, 1853.

Dearest Little Wren, I miss Sunday morning sermons. That's something I never thought to say. But Sunday morning sermons give one the chance to contemplate. I was too busy fidgeting as a lad to appreciate the rarity of that . Contemplation is hard to find here. It's too noisy and crowded. And all the possibilities are too close for comfort. Life. Death. Love and Hatred.

Courage and fear. We stand on the cusp of them all.

A S HE TAPPED HIS pipe against his thigh and strode out the door, Cece mused on how little, and how well, she knew her host. His bow had been slightly mocking. And he was back to putting distance between them by calling her Mrs. Thompson. She'd responded in kind.

He'd shared the occasional confidence with her. He'd shown her how his body reacted to her presence. He'd comforted her when she'd cried.

But she didn't know him.

She knew his pipe tobacco smelled faintly of dark cherries. She knew his shaving soap smelled of lavender and bergamot. She knew when he kissed you it made your world tilt on its axis and your knees go weak.

But she didn't know him.

She wanted to know him beyond his touch and taste and scent. She wanted those things too. But she wanted his broken dreams and regrets and fears. She wanted to hold him close and forgive him for all the things she knew he couldn't forgive himself for. She wanted to teach him how to do that and how to properly whistle.

She sat back down at the table to tell her closest sister what she'd decided.

Dear Emily,

I'm finally leaping in with both feet. Just as you've been telling me I should do since Henry's funeral. It finally feels natural to wear something besides the black that was my constant companion. You were right. I was hiding behind it. I see that now. It wasn't a cocoon, it was a prison. I'm writing to you first because I think you'll understand why I've decided not to return home for the holidays.

It would feel like I was stepping back into the cocoon. I need to leap from the ledge instead. There is a clarity of purpose here that I could never find in Cumbria. I've learnt how to shear a sheep and how to card wool. I'm giving embroidery and tatting lessons.

And I've met someone. I don't know how to describe what's between us, I just know it's something I want to pursue.

You may share as much, or as little, of this letter with Vin, Jess and Gert as you wish. Give them my love and tell Jess I know whatever pageantry she has planned will be a smashing success.

All my love, Cece

She folded the letter, slid it into the envelope and took a deep breath as she scrawled the address across the front.

The decision she'd just made hadn't been an easy one. The holiday season in the Wainwright house was filled with laughter and joy. One never felt alone or forgotten. The punch flowed freely, there were plenty of tarts, and now there was a whole host of people to coerce into a game of blind man's bluff or snapdragon.

As much as Cece wanted to experience those things again, she wanted to experience this more. She wanted to kiss this stoic Scot beneath the mistletoe. She wanted to coax him into a waltz, whether he was sure of his gait or not.

Before she could question the wisdom of her decision, she looped the shawl over her head and slipped outside.

He wasn't hard to find. He was leaning against the door-jamb, his pipe dangling from his hand. The smell of the cherry smoke still lingered in the air. She leaned next to him, her shoulders almost touching his upper arm.

A sough of air passed through his lips, and she realized he was practicing his whistle.

He turned to her with a sardonic grin. "Come to torment me about my whistling, lass?"

"No. Though I do find your need to do it in private amusing. I've reached a decision I need to share with you."

His face hardened, as if he were bracing himself for an unwelcome revelation. "Out with it."

"I've decided to stay here – at least through the holidays. Perhaps longer."

His brow creased in obvious confusion. "You don't have obligations you need to return to? You gave me the impression your sisters needed you to assist with the festivities."

"No, they'll be fine. There is nothing that cannot wait. Nothing that binds me there besides their love. And distance won't fade or alter that."

"Why did you change your mind?"

She looked down at her boots and then tipped her head toward the stars. "I'm at a loss to explain it fully. I simply know I crave more time here. I'm immersed in the ebb and flow of things in a way I wasn't at home in Cumbria. A way that escaped me." She sighed. "Here, no one but you knows me as the tragic widow who stayed in her weeds far longer than was stylish. I'm not a kitten here. I'm more like a lioness – and I haven't felt like a lioness since I was a girl."

"I knew you were a lioness from the first letter."

Cece's hand went to her mouth. She remembered it well. "I spent an entire page ranting about the need for a more efficient way to distribute food to those in the parish who needed it."

His mouth quirked in a faint smile. "As I said, a lioness. When I thought back on your letter, it sparked the idea for this farm. A place where we share what we sow and reap. Where everyone of us has a roof over our head and food on our table. Where all hands contribute equally in the way best suited to their talents."

"My letter inspired you to establish a utopian community?"

"We're not exactly utopian. There's no collective religious tenet that binds us and I still retain ownership of the farm. But in all other ways, yes. Your letter germinated the seed. I thought about what you said – that no one who does an honest day's labor should go hungry."

"I can't believe my words led to what you've built here."

"The way Henry spoke of you, I knew you were remarkable. We were all lonely and we did what soldiers do. Those of us that had sweethearts talked about them – because then we felt less lonely. He talked about your hair and your eyes and your figure, and yes, I imagined you. But when he read your letters, I could hear you too. Even though I didn't know you, it felt like I knew you, and you were always the voice in my head when I was deciding between right and wrong, north or south."

"North or south?"

"A cryptic reference to heaven or hell, Wren."

"You're the only person who's ever called me that name aloud."

She felt the slight movement of his shoulders brushing against her arm as he shrugged. She wished she could see his expression.

"It fits you."

"I've always thought of wrens as shabby, nondescript little birds. No matter how much my husband tried to gild the lily."

He was shaking his head, a fierce expression on his face, before she'd even finished her sentence. "Wrens are not shabby. You are not shabby. Wrens are the best of everything a man fights to protect. Just as you are."

Cece self-consciously shrugged. "I don't think I'm the reason Henry was fighting."

He stepped forward and captured her chin. "The thought of you, the glimpse of home you gave us in those letters... you're the reason all of us fought."

"Surely there were other soldiers with wives and sweethearts."

"None with the devotion to write every week. We needed those letters like God needs the devil. Reminding us that no matter what we did or what we saw, we were still just men. Full of the frailty and strength of our kind."

"I'm glad my letters kept you tethered, Mal."

He closed his eyes. As if her letters had been the only thing keeping him tethered. But she was more than her letters and he seemed to appreciate all those parts of her as well. No matter how much she aggravated him.

The sum of everything he was boggled her mind. He was a puzzle- like the columns of numbers that criss-crossed the pages of his ledger.

"Do you have any mementos you can share with me?"

He let go of her chin and turned toward the stars again. "This is what I love most about winter. How near the stars are."

"They're no closer than they are in any season."

He shot her a sideways grin. "I know that, Mrs. Thompson. But that doesn't change the fact they look like they could fall on our heads at any moment. They were the one constant. Your husband used to say that he could look up at them and know you were looking up at them too. He said it made him feel like you were lying right there beside him."

He was avoiding her question and Cece decided to prod him again. "Do you have any other stories?"

"Your husband gave me the bible I keep on my desk."

"Will you show it to me?"

"Yes, because I'll have no peace from you until I do now you know of its existence."

He clasped her hand and tugged her into the house behind him.

Chapter Twenty-Four

Mal

Letter dated March 8, 1854.

Dearest Husband, I think a marriage should be a happy occasion. Your youngest sister Gladys was not the picture of happiness at her wedding today. I think she may have purposefully kicked her new husband in the shins when he picked her up in the middle of a reel. Your other sister, Priscilla, told me the groom is one of your father's colleagues and it was all arranged. Perhaps that explains Gladys's misgivings.

S HE FINGERED THE WORN binding of the bible, her face full of wonder. "Our marriage is recorded in this. His father clearly disapproved of our hasty union, but insisted no one would join us in holy matrimony but him. He's an Oxford don."

"Henry said one of the reasons he joined the army was his father. I think he was trying to earn his approbation."

Her gaze flickered to his. "They didn't have an easy relationship."

"I think our relationships with our guardians are fraught until we have children of our own. My grandfather and I were constantly at odds as well once I surpassed him in height."

"Perhaps because you were big and grumpy."

Mal chuckled. "He was grumpy too. I'm certain I modeled my behavior on his example."

"Will you answer another question?"

He crossed his arms and raised a brow. "It depends on the question."

"What were you thinking about when you crowded me against the shelving last week?"

"My thoughts would scandalize you, Mrs. Thompson."

"My sisters can tell bawdy jokes with the best of them, and Emily is fond of frequenting the tavern to glean information."

"Why does your sister use the tavern to glean information?"

"She's an amateur investigator. Last month she secured her first paying customer."

"Taverns are indeed a fount of ill-gotten gossip," he wryly observed.

"They are. And she shares everything she hears with us. Which is why I won't be scandalized. So stop avoiding the question."

"I crowded you into the shelves, Mrs. Thompson, because my only other recourse was to tumble you onto this desk and swive you six ways to Sunday."

"Perhaps I wouldn't have complained."

"You're so sure of what you want, Little Wren."

She'd dug beneath his skin with her questions and her empathy. Just as she had when he'd caught her sneaking one of the strawberries. She had that same reckless, devil-may-care gleam in her eye.

"I am sure of what I want. And I see no reason to be coy. You threatened to hold me just there," she pointed toward his desk. "And show me why one should never antagonize a man who is hanging on by a thread."

She walked forward and burrowed the tip of her nail into the hollow between his pectoral muscles. He held his breath as she rose to her toes and the point of contact slid lower. "I want to do more than loosen that thread, I want to snip it in half," she whispered into his ear as she squeezed his cock.

She'd said the word snip as she'd grabbed his cock. She made him daft, because he wasn't apprehensive, he was aroused. Her antics should have the opposite effect on his body. The little Valkyrie's determination should frighten him.

He wrapped his hand around hers and decided to show her the kind of grip he liked. "You should know by now, Little Wren, that I'm not the kind of man you can lead around with your apron strings. I won't let my cock guide my actions."

"Then why is my hand on it?"

"Your hand is on my cock because it's time for another lesson."

Her pulse fluttered with excitement beneath his grasp, and her eyes were glittering like amethysts against the pink of her cheeks. "What kind of lesson?" She breathlessly asked.

"The kind where little wrens who venture from their nests learn the consequences of playing with fire."

"I'm both very studious and contrite."

She might be studious. At least when it was a topic that piqued her interest. But she wasn't contrite in the least. She knew exactly what she was about. He stepped around her and brushed everything aside. The papers went fluttering to the floor and the ledger landed with a thump near his foot. He'd put the inkpot in the drawer last night, or he'd be contending with it as well. "Lay flat on my desk."

She hopped eagerly onto the sturdy scratched surface and laid back.

When she started working the material bunched at her hips, pulling it upward, he shook his head – denying her.

"No. Let go of your skirts. That's why you came looking for me and I grow weary of this game. Undressing you is my duty tonight and part of your lesson."

She exhaled gustily, and her eyes gleamed even brighter as she obeyed him. Her willingness to do so sent a bolt of lightning straight to his cock.

He dropped to his haunches and took over the task she'd abandoned.

Her stockings were sturdy red wool today without a hint of lace, but when he removed her boot, they still molded the curve of her calf and ankle. They stopped just above the sweet indentation of her knee and he lifted her left leg to his shoulder.

Mal slid his nose along every inch of skin he bared. He knew she was wet for him, because he could smell the tang of her arousal. He wanted to bury his face just there and feel the bead of her sex pulse against his tongue. It had been years since he'd had the chance to lavish his attention on a woman, to feel her legs tremble around his neck, to hold her steady as her body bowed in release.

He pulled his kilt up and tucked it into his belt so he could stroke himself in time to his ministrations. He quickly realized what a terrible idea that was because he was surrounded by her scent and wouldn't last if he took himself in hand. And he wanted to last.

The removal of her second stocking wasn't as subtle an exploration. He removed it with his teeth, yanking it down with the force of his impatience and desire before he tossed it behind him.

He braced both hands on her upper thighs to spread her wider. "Now you may hold your skirts, Little Wren. I want you to watch."

"What are you going to do to me?"

"I'm teaching you a lesson, remember? I'm going to show you how strawberries should be consumed. With tongue and teeth and care."

He gave her a feral grin when her knee twitched beside his ear and lifted her other leg to nestle it on the opposite shoulder. "I don't think you're prepared for this lesson, Mrs. Thompson. You may want to lock your ankles behind my head."

He closed his eyes and rubbed his cheek against the satiny skin of her inner thigh. It felt like the softest lambswool, or the silky petals of a hothouse flower. He circled the bud of her sex with his tongue and her hands clutched his head, tangling in his hair as she moaned.

Her knees were pressing against his ears like a steel trap, and her locked ankles drummed into the space between his shoulder blades when he licked her again. This time it was a long, luxurious stroke that spread her arousal over her folds. Her thighs quivered again, and salty sweetness filled his mouth. Mal growled against her before lifting his head.

"It's not just the savoring, wren, it's the plucking."

He pinched her clitoris between his thumb and forefinger as he cupped her in the palm of his hand.

"More, please," she raggedly begged.

"Patience," he admonished. He dropped his mouth to her inner thigh again, sucking the skin between his teeth to leave a ruby red mark on her creamy skin.

She was a bountiful feast, the curve of her ripe bottom in his hands as he tilted her closer to his mouth like the halves of a juicy apple, the slick hotness of her cunny like a dripping strawberry gushing against his tongue.

"Laird, I –I -I -didn't know it could feel like this…" she wailed, her hips lifting, her head thrashing. Her hands were curled against his scalp like claws as she pulled him against her even more tightly.

He felt her come because she drenched his tongue. He slowed his assault, until he was nipping her softly, using his tongue like he was wielding a paintbrush.

Her grip on his head loosened and she fell back.

"I didn't know," she whispered.

Her irises were blown wide, like the faces of men he'd seen in battle after they escaped enemy fire. She looked flushed and ravaged and utterly lost. He was full of selfish satisfaction that he'd been the one to show her. That he'd been the one to treat her without mercy.

"Now you do." He rose, his knees stiff from being locked in position so long. His body felt every bit of its thirty-nine years.

He pulled his shirt over his head and dropped his kilt. He wanted her to truly see him before she decided to take him into her body. He knew his scars wouldn't be as harsh under the flickering shadows of the hearth, and he welcomed the grace the lack of light offered. It meant that although the way life marked him would be revealed, some of his dignity would be spared. He wasn't yet prepared to face her pity.

There was no revulsion or pity in her face when he stretched his arms wide and slowly turned to ensure she saw the whole of him, and he breathed a sigh of relief. "This is all of me, Little Wren. Scarred and broken. It all belongs to you if you want it."

He waited for her response, his entire body tense, cold sweat pooling at his nape. His hands had even gone clammy where he braced them on his hips.

She bit her lip, her eyes drifting over every inch of him. Her gaze didn't linger on his scars. Instead, it lingered on his cock, like a physical stroke. When he lifted his hand to oblige her, she murmured, "Yes. My turn to watch."

She righted herself and rolled her skirts and petticoat to her waist. She held them in place in the crook of the arm she braced behind her, and moved her other hand to her center.

They moaned in unison when she sank her fingers into her channel.

"Not like this, lass. I want to be deep inside you."

She removed her hand and crooked her fingers.

He closed the space between them and seized her wrist so he could lap up the rivulet of arousal sliding toward her elbow.

He stepped between her legs and pushed them up until her feet were flat and her knees were just below her ears. She was luscious and open.

"Watch your body swallow my cock, Mrs. Thompson." He cupped her nape to hold her gaze immobile.

She licked her lips and tilted herself more firmly into his embrace. "Do your worst, Mr. Lockhart."

Her saucy reply made the blood pool in his groin. "Good lass," he praised as he thrust forward and sank all the way in.

He pulled out, one excruciating inch at a time, her core clenching him tighter than his fist ever had. His aching balls were tucked up against her as he thrust forward again, hanging on with the barest frisson of control.

Frigging himself raw to thoughts of her could never compare to this. She reached around his waist, trailing her fingers over the rugged map of his scars before she dug her nails into the curve of his arse to tug him closer.

"Swive me hard, Mr. Lockhart," she taunted. "Swive me like a good lad."

"Not a lad," he gritted as he drummed his hips against the edge of the table.

Her hips met his own with the same faltering, falling cadence. "No, not a lad," she gasped in agreement.

"I've dreamt of this for far too long, I'm sorry to cut our interlude short." He dropped his head and set his teeth against her shoulder. Just as he had after the strawberries.

She shuddered and broke in his arms and his answering roar was muffled in the silk of her skin.

Mal knew he'd done something he couldn't take back. This was why he'd been afraid to let her in.

She dropped her legs and leaned back on her elbows. Her skirts were still hiked around her waist and her hair was tousled. Her cheeks and chin were rosy from the scratch of his beard.

"If you open your mouth and call me Mrs. Thompson again, I'll skewer you with the fire poker I saw in the corner."

"From this point on, we'll be Cece and Mal."

He scooped up his discarded shirt and handed it to her. "What's this for?"

"I want you to use it to clean up, just as you bade me do that first time."

"As long as I'm doing it for you as much as for myself."

"Aye." He pushed his hair from his forehead and hesitated. He wasn't sure how he was supposed to broach the subject of the consequences of their recklessness.

She must have sensed his unease, because she raised a brow. "Yes, laird?"

"If there are consequences, I'll not send you away."

She tossed him his shirt and stood. "Vin insists all of us carry tincture of pennyroyal. It's not foolproof, but there's less chance of a babe. If there is a babe, I won't let you send me away. It's likely I won't let you send me away regardless of what happens."

He wrapped his arm around her waist. "Does that mean I'm the one sleeping in the bed with you tonight instead of the purring beast?"

She giggled and tapped his chest. "I think you're a purring beast too."

Her chin landed just under his heart when he picked her up.

***

He was gone when she woke the next morning, but the pillow beside her head was dented, and the space beside her was still warm from the heat of his body. He hadn't been awake long.

She yawned and stretched, closing her eyes on a smile that threatened to permanently carve itself into her cheeks.

"I made you tea, leannan, and now I'm questioning the wisdom of brewing it. If you stay abed, I can demonstrate just how much I've wanted you."

Her eyes snapped open. He was lingering in the doorway as he was wont to do. As if afraid of breaching a space that wouldn't welcome him.

"I have a lesson with Grace and Claire this morning. They are determined to finish embellishing the gifts they've made."

He swiftly crossed the room and set the tea on the sidetable. "I'd have a morning kiss before you go, Mrs. Thompson."

He gave her a teasing smile and she knew he was using the formality to emphasize how much their relationship had changed. "I'd like one as well, Mr. Lockhart."

He dropped onto the bed and crawled up her body, bracketing her between his mountainous thighs. She could feel the pulse of his arousal against her core, like a scorching caress through the cotton sheet wound around her body. He pulled her wrists above her head, holding them in place as he peppered kisses along her jawline.

His mouth nipped at her collarbone and the tender slice of skin just behind her ear and she moaned. "More kissing like this and there will be no lessons."

"Just a reminder to end the lesson well in advance of the evening meal."

"I can hazard a guess as to the menu you have planned, laird."

"You are the menu, Cece." His eyes darkened before he swooped in for one final kiss. His tongue traced the contours of her lips and teeth before stroking inside her mouth to tangle with her own. His weight pressed against her, his hips rocking gently as he made certain his kiss would fill her thoughts. When he pulled away and handed her the tea, it was no longer steaming.

Cece gulped it down despite the tepid temperature and rose from the warmth of the bed. She dipped a rag in the basin of water on the table and swabbed her body before pulling on her undergarments and dress.

He leaned against the doorway, watching her, arms and ankles crossed. When she'd finished, she sauntered toward him and popped up to deliver a kiss. He scooped her against him, his lips on hers a hard, quick press.

❖

Cece walked into the carding shed with a grin she couldn't contain. Grace and Claire were already waiting for her, and Moira was seated at the table as well.

Moira cackled gleefully when she saw the expression on Cece's face. "The laird made his move, I see."

She flushed. Was the tumbling about she felt inside so evident? The evening shadow of his whiskers had scraped against her face and neck, perhaps that was what gave away her secrets. "We are on a first name basis," Cece primly informed her.

"Then the two of you can be responsible for gathering the boughs to decorate the hall for our holiday ceilidh. You have four days, since we're holding it on Christmas Eve."

"Why nominate us?"

"Because this year, I suspect the laird will be doing more than nursing his whisky in the corner. Because of you."

Cece flushed again. "Moira, it's just passion between two people who are lonely."

Moira grins. "Lass, the laird could have his pick of anyone in Dunkirk. I thought he was determined to be alone forever. But now I know he was waiting for you."

"I saw the way he was looking at you in the market." Grace interjected.

"His eyes never left ye and he was carryin' yer packages like it was his solemn duty to be at yer beck and call." Sadie giggled.

The observations of the three women were both subtle and pointed as bullets.

Chapter Twenty-Five

Mal

Letter Dated December 10, 1862.

Dear Sisters, I hope this letter finds you well.
I don't think I've satisfied my yearning for adventure. Scotland has been more diverting than
I expected. I've learned to shear a sheep and
card wool. I was gifted a new pair of boots from
a cobbler I'm certain came straight from that
fairytale about the elves. Especially since the
only payment he asked in return was an ogre
taming. The ogre isn't really an ogre. His name

is Malcolm Lockhart and he served with Henry. I'm still looking for answers. I trust all of you to carry on without me. Vin, let Alaric's daughters win at snapdragon. Or any other game you play with them. Jess, don't be shy about asking for help with all the holiday plans. All my love, Cece.

SHE HAD STEW WAITING for him when he entered the cottage. The cozy sight of her ensconced by the fire with a cat draped over her lap and her hands twisted up in a bit of mossy green yarn, nearly brought tears of gratitude to his eyes.

"I posted a letter to my sisters this morning. I know you think the weather may lift in time for me to go home for the holidays, but I'd rather spend them here. With you."

Her soft confession undid him again. "I don't know much about the season and there's much you'll have to teach me. It has never been a time of joy in the Lockhart household."

She laid the yarn in the basket beside the rocking chair and set the cat on the floor. She pointedly ignored its drowsy, baleful glare as she made her way to him.

When her hands crept to the ends of his scarf and she began unwinding it, Mal closed his hands around her hips.

He'd felt the phantom outline of them all day long, and those daydreams were no comparison to the lush reality.

"I'll enjoy teaching you, Laird," she promised and rose on her toes to plant a kiss on the corner of his mouth.

"I meant it, Cece. This season has always reminded me of the losses I've suffered. My parents drowned beneath the ice when they snuck away with their skates."

Her hand flew to her mouth. "Mal, that's terrible," she said and covered his hand with hers.

"My mother was my grandfather's only child, and his wife died in childbirth. I've never had the comfort of being surrounded by a large family during the holiday season."

Her eyes filled with sympathy. "I'm beginning to realize why my letters affected you so profoundly. Though large families can be as much a burden as a joy, I will never again take my meddling sisters for granted."

"I've learned to take nothing for granted," he told her as he wrapped his arms around her and clasped her against his chest. He brushed a kiss over the crown of her head and let the scent of violets and honey wrap around him and seep into his bones.

She lifted her head and pressed a chaste kiss on his cheek. "Come. Have some soup. I've brought water in for a hot bath to soothe you, and I have some liniment that won't make my eyes water when I apply it to your scars."

Mal groaned in appreciation. "I wrenched my shoulder setting one of the posts today, and I've a new gash across one of my right knuckles. Will you tend me, Mrs. Thompson?" He asked with a wicked grin.

She stepped back and lifted his hand to her lips, feathering soft kisses over the cut. As if taking care of him and soothing his hurts was her aim in life. "I will gladly tend you, Mr. Lockhart. Your supper will stay warm – would you like your hot bath first?"

"Only if you join me."

She laughed and shook her head. "You are not a man of reasonable proportions, Mal. And though I'm not complaining, the tub isn't big enough for both of us. Not if we don't want all the water displaced onto the floor."

"If we're careful, and I promise to behave, we'll not spill a drop."

"What if I don't want you to behave?" She asked beneath lowered lashes as she slid her hand into the space between his collar and shoulder, stroking his skin.

"You are temptation incarnate, Wren. You make me forget the weariness I feel, or the fact my boots feel like lead weights on my feet."

"Discard your clothes, Laird, and I'll prepare your bath." She turned away slowly. As if she was exceedingly reluctant to do so.

Mal loosened the laces of his shirt and yanked it over his head. His fingers were on the buttons of the trousers he'd worn to protect against the chill when he noticed her lifting the bucket. She grunted as she did it, and though he knew she was perfectly capable of lifting the full pail and pouring it into the tub, he balked at the thought of how her muscles would twinge afterward.

He strode forward and placed his hand over hers. "Let me."

Her eyes flared with irritation, and he chucked her beneath the chin.

"I'm not undermining your strength or capability, lass. I can pour the water while you warm the bath sheet and retrieve my soap."

She must have sensed his implacability, because she allowed him to lift the bucket from her grasp. "Fine," she muttered.

He smiled at her obstinacy and swatted her rump with his free hand as she turned away to do as he'd asked. The indignant look she threw him made him grin even harder, and his hearty laugh spilled between them.

Her gaze softened when she heard it.

He watched the sway of her hips as she walked away, and the raised brow she cast over her shoulder at his immovable stance finally stirred him to finish the task.

He emptied the six buckets of steaming water into the tub and swiftly stripped. She still hadn't seen the extent of his scars, and he wanted the water to hide the worst of them from her eagle-eyed perusal. The gnarled flesh of his left leg was more like the bark of a tree than skin. When she turned back around, he was stretched out, his head against the rim as the steam soothed his aches and pains.

Her touch on his nape startled him. "I promise to behave," he murmured.

She giggled against his shoulder. "You were nearly asleep, just now, Laird. You're in no condition for further exercise."

"Making love is not exercise," he protested.

"Hush and let me tend you as I promised." She rubbed gentle circles over his back and shoulders, her hands kneading the tight muscles as she stroked the cloth across his skin.

It felt as if his bones were melting.

The nip of her teeth on his earlobe startled him. "My ministrations sent you straight to sleep, Laird. Come, and I'll rub liniment into your back."

"I'm fine," Mal drowsily insisted. He wasn't ready for her to see all the dips and hollows the fire had carved into his body. "I know we've shared much, but will you turn while I wrap myself in the sheet? I can see myself to bed."

"I know you find it hard to believe, Malcolm Lockhart, but you don't need to hide from me."

He gulped. She said that now. But what would she say when she saw the full canvas of his scars? "Please," he rumbled.

She sighed in exasperation. "You're the most stubborn man I've ever met. Fine. My back will be toward you when you exit your bath."

She kept her word. Her arms were crossed and her back remained ramrod straight while he dried off and wrapped the warmed towel around his body, hiding the worst of it.

"Are you finished?"

"Yes, Wren, I'm finished." He wrapped her in his arms, so her back rested against his chest. "Thank you for understanding."

She sighed again. "You're welcome, Laird. But don't think the reprieve will last long. Are you certain you don't need the liniment?"

"Aye, I'm certain." Mal knew the liniment would ensure he fell asleep sooner, but the fear she'd reject him was like a claw in his gut. "Will you sleep beside me tonight?"

The darkness in the bedroom would envelop them once the candles were guttered.

<hr>

The next morning dawned bright and clear, and Mal decided it was the perfect opportunity to gather the greenery Moira had requested.

He always rose before Cece. When he hadn't been able to lie still any longer, he'd dropped a kiss to her forehead and left the bed to stoke the fire and make his coffee and her morning tea.

When she finally stumbled from the cocoon of their shared bed, wrapped in a blanket and blinking the sleep from her eyes, he gathered her in a hug.

"Good morning, Little Wren."

She kissed the space just below his shoulder, and he felt the sting of her lips through the wool of his shirt. "Good morning, Laird," she replied on the end of a yawn.

"Moira brought over warm bannocks and I'll pour your tea."

"That sounds lovely," she said as she gave him a soft smile.

By the time they were bundled and out of the door, it was past noon. The day was still bright and clear, but the weather hovered on the brink between drizzle and flurries. The roads would be more passable but covered in a treacherously thin layer of ice. Mal thanked his stars that Jed was steady and surefooted. He'd safely transport the two of them and a cart stuffed full of greenery.

Jed was usually the calmest steed Mal knew, so when the squawking cardinal emerged from the hedge, he didn't expect the steadiest plow horse in the world to take off at a lumbering gallop. Cece had been standing in the cart so she could stack the boughs as Mal trimmed them from the tree. She toppled to the floor as the contraption drifted perilously close to the frozen stream.

Mal ran, desperate. Jed was spooked, but the horse wasn't as spry or energetic as he'd once been. Mal hoped the mad dash was short-lived and he'd be able to overtake them. He cursed the weakness in his left leg as he fell further and further behind.

He watched in horror as the cart tipped onto one wheel and Cece slid out. She tumbled down the hill, and then she was skating across the ice as it cracked around her like a thunderclap. Mal fell to his knees and careened after her. He reached for her hand just as she sank into the dark water.

Mal panicked, but he didn't hesitate. He stripped and dove in after her. Her outline was dim in the dark water, barely visible, and he stretched toward her falling body. Her skirts were pulling her to the bottom. He finally managed to grab a handful of the material and used it to haul her against him, praying it wouldn't rip. He kicked his way to the top and tossed her near the bank with all his strength.

His body felt like it was on the verge of collapse, his left leg protesting the brutal treatment. He bent his head to the ice to catch his breath, bracing his elbows before he used his upper body to lift through the opening.

She'd only been in the water a handful of minutes, but Mal had seen what happened to men with even less exposure to the elements in the midst of a Russian winter.

He grabbed his discarded plaid and made his way to her. She'd rolled to the side, and was coughing the water up from her lungs. Her teeth were chattering and her fair skin was already showing a hint of blue.

After all the ruckus, Jed had come to a stop, the broken harness hanging from his withers. He was calmly chewing through a branch.

Mal scooped Cece into his arms and wrapped his plaid around them both. He hoisted himself onto Jed's back, the left side of his body protesting the sudden movement. He'd lost his patch in the water, and the light pricked his bad eye like a thousand daggers. He closed it and clucked softly to their mount.

Jed ambled forward until Mal dug in his heels. He set off in a rollicking, bone-jarring canter and Mal wrapped his fist around the harness and the horse's mane. Cece was quiet in his arms, her breath rattling in her chest as she shivered.

Mal started shouting as soon as they reached the edge of the village. "Someone get the physician! My wife's been hurt!"

It was midday, and people stumbled from their cottages, gawking as he passed. He mordantly thought he made a more fearsome spectacle than the Lady Godiva would have parading through the streets wrapped in nothing more than her long hair.

Moira's husband was the one who finally took charge of the situation. He came barreling out of the tavern, his hat askew. "Laird," he called.

"Yes, Farley?" Mal gritted through his clenched jaw. He didn't have time to waste.

"The doc's at the Buchanan house. Here. Wrap this around the two of you. Your wife needs more warmth than your sorry plaid. And you're not decent, man."

As the man drew near, Mal realized he was carrying a wool blanket. "Thank you." Mal wrapped them both in the extra layer.

"I saw ye out the window and grabbed it. Go, they'll not turn you away."

Mal and Dr. O'Rourke had a tenuous relationship. The man was forever telling him to go easier on his leg. Mal was always telling him to stow his warnings because he could rest when he died. Of course the doctor then told him he was hastening his way to an early grave because of his lack of care.

⸺◆⸺

"Ye've gone an' done it now, lad." Moira's voice broke into his dreams. She sounded smug.

He yawned and stretched. He felt like he'd been in a brawl. "I've done what, Moira?"

"Handfasted yerself to the lass."

Mal frowned. When had that happened? They'd made love and even now he could taste her on the back of his tongue, but there'd been no exchange of vows.

"We're not handfasted," he protested. He wouldn't coerce her into staying into Scotland. She'd said he couldn't send her away, but she'd been sated with passion.

Moira's eyes narrowed and she poked a bony finger into his shoulder.

"Ye rode through the middle of town, naked as the day ye were born. Her too. Shoutin' fer the doc and yellin' that yer wife was hurt."

"She fell in the stream and I jumped in after her."

"Of course ye did. And landed in a mess afterward."

He threw the covers aside and planted his feet on the floor. He grimaced when his head started spinning. "How bad is it?"

"There's nothing to worry about, mate." Duncan's booming voice preceded him.

Mal sighed. "Are you here to gloat?"

"No gloating. Just congratulating myself on my powers of observation. I knew she wasn't just innocently sleeping in your bed."

"She was until last night," Mal grumbled.

"Ye've both been asleep for two days. We started planning yer church wedding as soon as her fever broke."

Mal grabbed the fourposter and stood. "Has she recovered?"

Moira and Duncan stepped forward and pressed him back down. Mal felt as weak as a newborn kitten. If he had all his faculties, they wouldn't have been able to maneuver him so easily.

"She's on the mend, lad," Moira assured him.

"She's healing." Duncan smirked. "And verra surprised to find out she's a bride."

Mal clasped his head in his hands. "What did she say?"

"According to Grace, not much."

Grace and Duncan had a very tumultuous relationship. Apparently Grace had relented and he was in her confidences again.

"She must have said something."

"She asked Grace what it meant when you handfasted with someone, and how you knew you'd done it."

Moira's gaze sharpened. "How did Grace answer the lass?"

"Grace told her that handfasting could be for a year or forever. She told her it was up the couple and you'd know if you did it because you exchanged promises."

"I need to see her."

What if his idiocy had trapped her here when she wanted to go home?

"Ye're not leavin' this bed, laird." Moira shook her finger and glared.

Mal fell back against the pillows with a groan. When Moira played nursemaid she was like a wolfhound guarding a keep. He wouldn't be able to evade her until nightfall.

<hr>

Cece's mind was restless. And she was tired of gruel and broth. She felt fine and she wanted bread and cheese. And something to quench her thirst besides water.

She tugged the quilt over her shoulders and eased to her feet. She tiptoed to the door, testing every board on the way.

When she opened the door, he was standing there, his hand raised as if he'd been on the verge of knocking. He stumbled back, into the opposite wall.

He had a blanket secured around his shoulders too. His long bare feet peeked out from beneath it and she mused at how bravely beautiful they were – just like the rest of him.

"I don't know why I called you my wife."

She crossed the hall and propped her shoulders beside his. "You don't?"

He swallowed. "It's not that I don't want it. But I'll not let my idiocy trap you so far away from your family."

She slid her hand around his clenched fist. "Look at me."

He swallowed again, but met her gaze. His eyes were full of anguish. Because he thought he was causing her pain.

That was all the confirmation Cece needed. "For once, Malcolm Lockhart, you were letting your heart speak louder than your head."

"This isn't something you want."

"There's a part of me that wants it. I wouldn't have risked lying with you, otherwise. I was looking for something when I set off for Scotland three weeks ago. I think I know what it was."

He inhaled, and she thought he might have bitten the inside of his cheek. "Not me."

She squeezed his hand. "Yes, you."

"So we're allowing Moira and the rest of your carding circle to plan our wedding?"

"We are."

"If we stay handfast, you can return to Cumbria when this turns out to be something you don't want. "

She lifted her hand to his jaw and he closed his eyes as he leaned into her touch. "Why don't you believe you're worthy of my decision?"

"I've done things, Cece," he rasped.

"Those things are behind you, Mal."

Maybe she'd come to Scotland to heal this man. To convince him he was enough. That he was more than the sum of the broken parts he saw when he looked in the mirror. Her sisters had been at her first wedding – this one would be just her and him and the community that had adopted her.

"February will mark my fortieth year. I have gray in my beard. My muscles ache – and not just when there's bad weather coming."

His persistence made her laugh. "You're not going to change my mind, Mr. Lockhart. I'm looking forward to becoming Mrs. Lockhart. Especially if it means I can distract you when you're at your desk."

He pulled her into his side and nuzzled her hair. "Don't forget I gave you the chance to renege."

She laid the flat of her hand against his pounding heart. "And don't you forget that I scoffed at your request, Laird."

Chapter Twenty-Six

Mal

Letter Dated December 17th, 1862.

Dearest Sisters, When you receive this missive, I will no longer be known as the Widow Thompson. I am to be married three days hence, on Christmas Eve in front of the entire hamlet. This was not the outcome I anticipated when I boarded the train three weeks ago, and I know my actions may seem rash and ill-advised. And likely out of character. I don't know if I have the words to explain the confusion I'm feeling.

I freely admit it is tempered by slight resignation to my fate. But that is not all I am feeling. This outcome seemed inevitable from the moment my future husband opened the door. Yes, I am marrying the ogre who isn't truly an ogre. Though I don't know if I would call this happiness, my heart is filled with the hope of new beginnings. A hope that has escaped me for longer than I care to remember. I will become Mrs. Malcolm Lockhart, my fate tied to this remote farm populated by more sheep than people. I will become the wife of a man who is both respected and loved from afar. A man who is still more mystery than not. But I cannot ignore the flare of longing between us or my growing irrational urge to soothe all his hurts and heal him of the tragedies that have weathered his soul. Please know that I am content with the consequences of my adventure, and hopeful for my future. All My Love, Cece.

MAL WAS CAUTIOUSLY HAPPY. Though he'd be marrying in haste, it was the culmination of all the longing he'd carried pent up for a decade. He was afraid to trust what he was being given, though. Gift horses and all that. Life had a way of yanking things away from him. Especially people he loved.

And he loved his new wife. He'd loved her for so long, he didn't even know what it felt like not to love her. He knew now that most of that loving had been for the dream of her, not the reality. He'd built an image of her in his head based on her letters, and while she was just as wry and beautiful and tenacious as her words had portrayed her, she was many other things too.

Her heart was wide and warm, her smile at the ready for everyone she met. She effortlessly coaxed even the most obdurate souls into laughter. Even him. Moira had given him a hug when she'd left the side of the physician. "I'm happy for ye, lad. I knew this lass was the one because she made ye smile."

Duncan slipped into the chamber and handed him a thistle pin. "I'd be honored if ye'd pin it to the Lockhart plaid."

Mal took it from him, turning it over in his palm and holding it up to the evening light streaming in through the window. " 'Twas your father's. And our great-grand-father's before that." Mal remembered seeing it on the stooped old man's shoulder before he passed.

"Aye. And I want ye tae have it. Ye're the laird in all but title, cousin. Ye take care of every creature here, and ye deserve the love of this lass to help you carry your burdens."

Mal gulped against the sting of tears in his throat. He knew his cousin loved and respected him, despite his teasing, but they were both men who'd been to war after all. They weren't fond of demonstrating how they felt – it was just assumed. "I thank ye, cousin," Mal said as he pulled Duncan into a rough hug.

"She does love ye," Duncan insisted as he drew away.

Mal ruefully shook his head. "She wants me, as I want her. But that's only earthly desire and we're both held in its thrall. The first time I touched her it was just our loneliness awakened."

"She wasnae compelled to consent to this union. She has strong feelings for ye. She defends ye, and her eyes follow ye."

Mal placed his hand on his cousin's shoulder. "You needn't pacify me, cousin. I know there is an imbalance of feeling going into this marriage. My future wife may not love me yet, but I will win her affections."

Duncan laid his hand atop Mal's. "I've no doubt ye will, cousin. And 'twill not be a monumental undertaking. I assure ye, the lass is already there. Trust me, cousin, when the two of ye come together again ye'll appreciate the waiting."

Chapter Twenty-Seven

Cece

Letter dated December 27th, 1862.

Dearest Sister, Your letter caught all of us by surprise. There was no indication in your correspondence that you held any affection for your host beyond a fascination with his long limbs and what you called his "crinkly nest of a beard." You've continually referred to him as a curmudgeon of few words. The antithesis to the sister I know and love. We all wonder at the haste of your wedding. I say this with the utmost delica-

cy but want to be sure you understand we would never turn you away for what you perceive to be an impropriety or indiscretion. You are seldom rash or impulsive. We can only recall one other time you were overcome by such strong passion it outweighed your common sense. You have borne the consequences of that rash decision as a young widow, and none of us wish to see you in such a situation again. This is your home, and it will always be your home, and we hope you were not compelled to marry this virtual stranger. With enduring affection, Emily.

CECE HAD BEEN CRAVING his touch since he'd bade her lay flat with the edge of the desk digging into her hips. Since his raw confession in the hallway. They'd been besieged with company, and Moira had forbidden Cece from seeing him without what she called an appropriate chaperone. This usually meant her. Moira had informed her that when a Scot openly called a woman his wife in front of witnesses and there'd been no churching, it was assumed they were handfasted and had pledged their troth. Cece had even attempted to sneak from her room after midnight – in the hope he'd have the same thought. When she'd opened her door, Moira had been propped against the opposite wall. She'd simply shaken her head and wagged her finger with a gleam in her eyes.

"Now Cecily, I'll not have this churching tainted by the whiff of impropriety," Moira officiously stated.

"If we are already handfasted, isn't that as good as married under the law?" Cece asked.

"Lass, the laird must maintain certain standing in the community. He is the moral compass for Dunkirk, and your union must have the blessing of the priest."

Moira's expression was filled with infernal glee, and Cece knew it meant protest was futile. "I just want a word with my future husband. Since I'll not have my family here to celebrate our nuptials."

Moira wagged her finger, as she was inordinately fond of doing. "A word with both meself and Duncan present is permissible. But no private words. I've seen the way he looks at ye."

Cece caught the edge of hunger in his eyes sometimes before he hurriedly glanced away, but was there more in his gaze? "What do you see in his eyes when he looks at me?"

Moira laid her hand against Cece's cheek. "I see a man who can't move or breathe for the want of ye."

"Truly?"

"Aye. As if ye're bread and water and his slice of heaven all wrapped into one."

Cece blushed. "There is carnal attraction between us, but I don't think our bonds extend beyond that."

"The two of ye could light a fire in every hearth in this house from your glances alone. Attraction like that always means ye have a deeper connection. Even if ye're denyin' it."

———◆◇◆———

When they finally had the chance to speak, Mal tugged her into an alcove beneath the stairs.

"I've missed your lips, leannan." He growled as he pinned her to the wall.

She could feel every delicious inch of him against her and circled her hips to push him over the edge.

His kiss was furious and ferocious, all banked longing and heat. The alcove was dusty and full of crates. Cece valiantly held in her sneeze – until she couldn't bear it. She placed her hand in the center of his formidable chest and turned her head, burying her nose against her shoulder.

When she sneezed violently at least six times in a row, he laughed.

"Everyone is conspiring to keep us apart," his tone was full of frustration. "The minute I manage to spirit you away, the only place I can find safe from immediate discovery is this dusty alcove."

"Moira and Duncan probably knew it wouldn't do for a tryst and that's why they aren't dogging our steps."

"You're likely correct," he darkly agreed. "Duncan watches my every move. Like a bloody wolfhound."

"Moira is the same."

Mal tightened his grip and simply held her. "He had the temerity to tell me I would appreciate the delayed gratification."

"Moira hasn't been quite as blunt, but she did say the separation is for our own good."

"They're wrong. You're going to be sore come Christmas morning, Wren."

"Why will I be sore, laird?" Cece asked him through lowered lashes as she propped her chin in her hand.

"Because I'm going to have you at my mercy, bent over every empty surface in that damned cottage."

"When you say you'll have me at your mercy..." Cece ran the tip of her nail over the skin bared just above the collar of his shirt.

"The mercy of my hands," he said as he slipped one broad hand into the tight bodice and nudged the tip of her breast to a sharp point. "The mercy of my teeth," he said as he bent and nipped her left earlobe. "The mercy of my tongue," he said as he drew it up the side of her neck before kissing her again. "And lucky for you, leannan, I am without mercy," he finally groaned into her mouth.

Cece inched her feet further apart, so she could feel the ridge of his arousal through the layers of their clothes. Her chemise chafed her beaded nipples as he pressed closer, and she wished it was the shadow of his beard. "I'm completely without mercy, too, laird," she reminded him as she lifted her hips and her hand slipped under his kilt.

He was hot and silky and groaned when she gripped the base of his cock.

"I like the way you wear your kilt, laird," she murmured. "Bare beneath and always ready for my touch."

"We only have a handful of minutes, minx. If you're going to make me lose control, then do it," he grunted as he thrust into the clasp of her hand.

"I'm going to wait until Christmas Eve. Until after we exchange our vows. After all, Moira and Duncan have been telling us that anticipation makes the reward all the sweeter," she teased.

He closed his hand over hers. "I'm praying for another blizzard, Wren. I want the reward to last for days."

When they exited the alcove, he tugged her to a stop, his hand cradling her face.

"What is it, laird?" His gaze was unreadable and sent butterflies tumbling through her stomach.

"I don't regret or resent any of it. Not your unexpected arrival. Not the way you make me long for more of the world. Not the way you pushed me to show my face and those who would judge me be damned. Not calling you my wife in front of the village and where my fear of losing you brought us."

Cece leaned up and kissed his scarred cheek. "I don't regret or resent any of it either," she assured him.

Their fingers tangled together briefly before they made for their chambers at the opposite ends of the house.

⸺◆⸺

Grace, Sadie and Moira had dressed Cece in a plain linen gown decorated with lace at the collar, hem and sleeves. An arisaid in the traditional plaid of the Lockhart clan was draped over her shoulder and belted at her waist. When she'd said, "I'm not Scots, and therefore not entitled to wear this," they'd just shaken their heads and assured her it would please the laird beyond measure if she wore it.

When she halted at the top of the aisle, he was all she saw. He'd tamed his mane of reddish blond hair into a queue, and he faced her full-on. The scars on the left side of his face were shadowed, but visible, and his patch made him look like a pirate bent on ravaging her. His plaid was pinned over his shoulder and fell in folds to his knees.

Moira was seated at the organ and began thumping out a tune Cece didn't recognize. She could see the glow of all the upturned faces as she glided toward her future husband and mused that she felt a bit like a princess. Soon after their mother had died, Arie had told her a fairytale about a maiden who'd made the heart of a beast come alive again.

Cece imagined she knew exactly what the maiden had been thinking as she walked toward her destiny.

That the man who waited for her had scars that made him vulnerable. That he guarded his heart out of fear, and it was a privilege to see it bared.

Though this life wasn't what she'd expected when she stepped off the platform at Galashiels, she felt the rightness of it. When she came to a stop in front of the man who would be her husband, twisting her hands in the folds of the plaid belted at her waist, his eye glittered with unshed tears. He took a visible breath and threw back his shoulders. As if he was bracing himself for what was about to befall him.

Cece knew it wasn't reluctance. She wondered if it was fear that she would renege, or that he was caught up in a dream of his own making.

He pulled a ring from the pocket of his plaid and let it rest on his open palm. " 'Twas my mother's and I never thought to place it on a woman's hand," he softly told her.

The priest cleared his throat, impatient to begin. "Mrs. Thompson, place your hand atop Mr. Lockhart's."

Cece obeyed, and Duncan stepped forward with a strip of tartan. He handed it to Malcolm.

"As the two of you say these words, you'll wind the bit of cloth about your wrists, to symbolize the binding of your hearts before God. Mr. Lockhart, you'll make your pledge first. Repeat after me. Blood of my blood, bone of my bone, I pledge my heart and body to yours."

Mal cleared his throat and slipped the cloth around her wrist. His eye was gleaming and Cece felt the tremble in his touch. "I, Malcolm Ignatius Lockhart, vow that you, Cecily Wainwright Thompson, are blood of my blood and bone of my bone. I pledge my heart and body to yours, that we might be one and with my body I thee worship. I pledge to be your protector, to be your shelter against wind and rain. I pledge to honor you above all others."

When he'd finished the words, he let his hand rest beneath her own and she could feel the steady throb of his pulse. He looked strong and sure and committed to this course that neither of them had anticipated.

"Mrs. Thompson, if you'll say your vows," the priest prompted her.

With my body, I thee worship. All the other words of the vow were muted to Cece's ears. She would worship him with her body as well. Show him she'd never seen his scars when she looked at him. Only the man, never a monster. A man whose emotions ran so deep they were like a buried seam of coal far below the surface. Ready to flare and burn and keep whoever ignited them warm for a lifetime.

Cece had asked the women in the carding circle if there were traditional vows that were exchanged in their village and they had all contributed bits and pieces of what they'd heard and remembered. She had woven them together until they conveyed exactly what she wanted them to. She inhaled and stared directly into Mal's face. His craggy features were already unbearably dear to her. "I, Cecily Elise Wainwright Thompson, vow that you, Malcolm Ignatius Lockhart are blood of my blood and bone of my bone. I pledge my heart and body to yours, that we might be one. I pledge to be your wayfarer's rest and hearth and home. To bring you peace and light when your soul is troubled."

When Mal's hand reached for hers and he pulled her to the center of the floor, with the skirl of bagpipes and a lively fiddle surrounding them, Cece's heart skipped a beat. She belonged to him now. He belonged to her. They hadn't said the words to each other, but as he spun her in a tight circle, she thought she saw them reflected in his eyes. He looked at her as if she were some miraculous creature.

She wondered what anyone watching her would see when she looked at him. Would they see a woman who saw the man beneath the scars? Would they see a woman swept up in crosswinds she couldn't name or control?

"You're steadier on your feet than many partners I've had."

"I appreciate your loyalty, wife, but doubt your perception of my abilities."

Cece pinched his waist. "I'll not hear anyone speak ill of my husband or his abilities. Including the man himself."

He chuckled warmly and tugged her closer. "I long to show you the full extent of my abilities, Little Wren."

Cece stepped into the turn. "They say there is nothing new under the sun, Mr. Lockhart. Surely you have already demonstrated your rather encyclopedic knowledge."

"We have only just scratched the surface, leannan."

He stroked his thumb from the corner of her eye to the crest of her cheek. She gulped at the heat that flared in his gaze when he let his touch rest against the pulse in the side of her throat.

"We were all a little in love with you, you know. We knew we could depend on the regularity of your correspondence, steady as the constellations we saw in the night sky half a world away."

She felt the spike of her pulse beneath his thumb. "Even you?"

"Especially me, lass," he murmured and dropped a kiss to her forehead.

"Is that why you were so boorish when I arrived?"

"Yes, minx. When I returned your letters, I thought I was finally ridding myself of your ghost."

"My ghost?" She asked in confusion.

"Aye. Your ghost. The one that haunted me from the moment your husband shared your first missive. You belong to me now, Wren," he growled into the shell of her ear as he clasped her even closer. They were simply swaying, her skirts tangling around his bare legs.

"As you belong to me, Laird."

Chapter Twenty-Eight

Mal

Letter dated December 23, 1819, from Walter Lockhart to Eileen Lockhart, on the date of their first wedding anniversary. (found by Mal in his grandfather's desk after his passing)

Dearest Eileen, Beloved Wife, A thousand lifetimes wouldn't be enough to spend with you. But I cherish each morning I rise from our bed with your kiss on my lips and your song in my heart.

MAL'S HEART LEAPT AT the thread of possession in her reply.

"Let's leave them to their whisky and dancing, Wife."

She dipped her head, feigning shyness. He wasn't fooled. He felt the tremble of her hand in his and her breath quickened. He felt it in the rise and fall of her chest against his own. He turned and tugged her behind him.

"Come."

Mal caught the bright gleam of her eyes. Like heather in full bloom.

The crowd jostled them as he made a path, Duncan and the other men slapping his back and filling their ears with bawdy jokes and whistles. When they reached the door, he twisted and swung her into his arms. She snuggled against him – just as she had the morning after she'd crashed into his cottage.

She tilted her face and placed a kiss just beneath his jawline, and then at the hollow of his throat. He wondered if she could feel the way his pulse thundered beneath his skin, like a runaway horse.

When he reached the door to the cottage, he pushed it open and kicked it shut behind him.

Cece wriggled her way out of his arms and slid down his body. "You may properly kiss your wife now, Malcolm Lockhart."

"You are mine, now, Cece Wainwright Thompson Lockhart. You are everything I've dreamt of and I'm never letting you go," Mal told her and pressed her against the sturdy timber door. The faint glow of the moon filtered through the fanlight above their heads, throwing her upturned face and bowed mouth into sharp relief. He lifted a strand of hair that had fallen from her upswept style to his nose and inhaled. She smelled of lilies and linen and the sheen of perspiration that had dampened her nape while they danced.

When he took her lips, a storm broke over the two of them.

"Bedroom," she murmured. He hefted her into his arms again and acceded to her wishes. When they reached it, he lowered her to the floor. She pushed him onto the bed with a gentle nudge and he went willingly, the flurried movement making his kilt rise to the tops of his thighs. Her irises gleamed like the lights in the midnight sky.

When Mal was a boy on the Isle of Lewis, he and his parents spent hours watching them flicker across the horizon.

The look in her eyes made him feel almost exactly as he had then. Like he was on the cusp of something beyond his understanding. Something so wonderful and painfully beautiful it made his chest ache.

He couldn't speak past the sudden lump in his throat, mesmerized by the angle of her body as she leaned over him and pushed the folds of the kilt inexorably, excruciatingly up, up, up. His cock hardened and swelled with each measured press of her palms.

When she'd bared him, she sat back on her heels. He felt the pinprick of her gaze and moved his hand to cover the mass of scar tissue that snaked from his left hip down to his knee.

Her eyes blazed angrily and she pushed his hand away. "You never have to hide from me. Your scars are a part of you."

"But they are unsightly. The first time we made love they were cloaked in shadow and the extent of the damage wasn't as discernible as it is here in a well-lit room."

Her expression was both fierce and disbelieving. "You are so idiotic sometimes, husband. Your scars make you more real and interesting than some unmarred prince. The things you have seen and experienced have given you your character, and it is only fitting they have left a visible trace on the terrain of your body."

She bent forward, and he felt so raw he closed his eyes. He never removed the patch and she had no idea what lay beneath it.

Her hands wove through his hair as she slipped it from the queue, and gently lifted the patch away from his eye. He refused to look at her, afraid to reveal the disgusting opaque color of his left iris. Afraid she would shy away or gasp and cover her mouth in horror. When he felt the flutter of her lashes against his cheek as she kissed the corner of his drooping eyelid, he couldn't bear it.

"Stop," Mal hoarsely pleaded.

"No." She replied with a voice full of iron that slid like a whisper over his scars. "Show me."

"If I show you, you'll think me an ogre in truth."

She smiled against his cheek. "I already know you're an ogre, Laird. But now you're my ogre."

"We were surrounded by fire at Balaclava, and I was told my injuries were horrific. That it was a miracle I survived them since they went virtually untended in the Russian prison. The only person here who's seen it up close is Duncan, and even then it was a single time."

When she gently brushed his hair from his forehead, he knew she wasn't giving him a choice. She was too persistent and stubborn by half.

"Show me," she repeated.

Mal clenched his fists and slowly opened his eyes.

He focused on her with his right eye, and immediately recognized the pity in her expression. He closed his eyes again to shield himself from it, his throat working to hold back the howl of disappointment. "I knew you'd be disgusted by it. That you'd pity me," he croaked.

The hand that had been stroking his forehead stilled before she slid it to his clenched jaw. "I don't pity you, my love. I'm humbled by your fortitude and the things you've survived. You are a warrior, and your sacrifice is honorable."

She slid her hand into his hair once more, and lowered her body over him, until her nose was buried in the crook of his shoulder. "Let me in, Husband. Let me see you. Let me heal your invisible wounds."

Mal couldn't pretend immunity. The howl emerged, but it was subdued and full of relief instead of pain.

She feathered kisses across his brow, down the slope of his nose, and over the scars webbing his left cheek and disappearing into his hairline.

Every brush of her lips was a tiny benediction. She wielded them like tiny darts full of warmth, flitting them over the mottled skin of his throat and shoulder, rubbing them gently over the scars that laced his ribs and stomach.

She slid down his torso, her kisses anointing the divots carved into his hip and the ridges along his outer thigh. When she reached the ugly mass of tissue that circled his knee, her breath grew harsh. When she raised her eyes to his, they were wet with tears. The landed on his skin, lashing it with her sorrow. "The things you've borne..." She raggedly whispered.

"They brought you here to me, to this moment. All the pain was worth the glory of you."

"I am a simple country lass," she protested through the veil of her tears as she propped her chin on his chest.

He snorted. "You've never been a simple country lass, Wren. You've always been more. At least to me. An endless universe of discovery with pragmatism and a poet's heart."

She rose to her knees. "You're far more than a simple Scotsman, as well, Husband."

He looped a tendril of hair over her ear, his fingers trailing across her cheek. "You're the only one who's ever bothered to see beyond my armor and my scars, Wife."

"I see all of you," she fiercely said. "I see all of you and I want nothing more than to build my life here with you," she repeated as she stroked his cock into place and sank down.

The feel of her was exquisite. She arched her back as her hips rose and fell against him, her hand kneading the knotted muscles of his thigh behind her. She laced a hand over his clenched fist and smoothed the tension away. When his fingers were no longer curled, she lifted them to her breast. He obliged, and her nipple hardened into a decisive point against the roughness of his callouses. Her head fell back when he raised himself enough to replace his hand with his tongue and teeth.

Her thighs tensed around his, and her body bowed impossibly further. Her skin was covered in a fine sheen, like the cascade of moonlight over rippling water. "Come for me, wife," he growled around her breast.

He felt the tremble of her thighs again, and she moaned. He lifted his hands to her hips so he could control her movements. He maneuvered her up and down, slamming himself into her wet heat. Harder and deeper. She started keening again, her hands scrabbling over his chest before she found purchase and latched on. Tomorrow he'd bear the brands of crescent moons – evidence of her passion and his. She wailed into the empty room, and he felt her clench and ripple around him as she came. His shout drowned out her keening as he emptied into her womb.

She fell on top of him with a beatific smile as he lay there stunned. "Good night, Husband," she murmured as she kissed the scar tissue above his heart.

He curled his arm around her waist and kissed her forehead. "Good night, wife."

As she drifted off to sleep, Mal lay there. Completely flummoxed by the gifts he'd been given.

Hours later, he woke with his heart in his throat. He'd heard the incessant drip of water that had nearly driven him mad in his cell, and then he'd felt himself falling. His brow was clammy and his grip on his new bride's waist was so tight he was afraid he'd left bruises.

She snuffled quietly, like an adorable kitten, and thrust her nose into his armpit while she curled her leg around his hip.

He knew then that she would heal him. Just as she'd said she would do. That the way she cared for him, even if it wasn't quite love, was enough to chase away the shadows and the nightmares. To make him feel more whole than he had in a very long time.

After a week of wedded bliss, Mal was firmly convinced his wife was a marvel. At the moment, she was haggling with the wool merchant like she'd been born to do it. He'd let her take over the negotiations when the man refused to budge on his price and Cece kept whispering suggestions in his ear.

"Sir, you have freely admitted this wool is superior to any other in this area. You haven't hidden your admiration of its fine texture or light heft and openly confessed it would be as suited for swaddling clothes as it would a hunting tartan. Why are you quibbling over a fair price?"

"I quibble, Madam, because I can. Your husband will tell you I do not lightly take on new consignments. Though the reputation of Lockhart Farm precedes your offering, the nature of your enterprise is somewhat suspect."

Cece braced her hands on her hips and leveled a glare at him fit to make any man wriggle. "The nature of our enterprise, sir? What do you mean by that?"

"I mean the sharing of profits. It is reminiscent of John Locke and his treatise."

"Sir, you are being ridiculous. You cannot judge a man for his convictions when they do not align with your own. Especially when those convictions have done you no harm."

"They haven't done me any harm," the man grudgingly admitted.

"Then your conscience must dictate you treat fairly with us."

"I bet your husband thinks you're a right harridan," he grumbled as he held out his hand. Cece accepted his concession and shook it.

When they'd wrapped up the negotiations, Mal stepped into the man's space. "Don't ever call her a harridan again. Or anything else. If I hear of you referring to her as anything other than Mistress Lockhart, you will rue the day you lost control of your tongue."

The man gulped and lurched backward. "My abject apologies, Master Lockhart," he blubbered.

His wife's eyes gleamed like amethysts at his defense, and he wanted to pull her into the alley and kiss her until she saw stars. He offered his hand instead, and when she took it, all was right with the world.

The ride home was quiet and filled with the tension of their wanting. As soon as they were inside the cottage he caged her against the door.

"I want your hands on me, Wife."

Her gaze smoldered as she threw him a saucy grin. "I'm only too happy to oblige, husband. But I've been dreaming of another tryst on your desk."

She reached under his kilt, and he felt the slide of her knuckles against the sensitive skin of his inner thigh before her grip curled unerringly around his thickening member.

She gave him a deliberate squeeze that made the blood rush to his head and pool in his cock, hardening it beneath her possessive grasp.

Mal thrilled at her enthusiastic response but feared he'd spill his seed too soon if he didn't slow their pace.

He covered her hand and forced it to his thigh.

Her mewl of disappointment made him smile. "You unman me, Wren. Let me bring you pleasure atop my desk first."

He grasped her hand in his and she followed him into his sanctuary, her merry laughter surrounding them both.

As soon as they stood in front of his desk, Mal tipped her backward and she wrapped her legs around his waist. She'd insisted on using a mix of linseed and lemon oil on the shelves and furniture, and the tart scent wafted around them. She braced her hands behind her and used her ankles to propel him forward, until he was seated at the juncture of her thighs.

He pushed her petticoat and skirt up her thighs, his hands tingling with the knowledge he now had of the satiny feel of her, and how wet he knew she was. He'd impatiently swiped his hand over the desk, but some of the papers were still in place, and crackled beneath her as she laid back.

She set her hand on one and picked it up to toss it to the floor with the rest, but when her eyes landed on it, she squinted in confusion. "Husband, what is this? It looks like a copy of a letter I wrote to Henry, but in the same handwriting he used in his letters to me. Why do you have this in your possession? Is this your handwriting?"

Mal's heart sank to his stomach and his gut clenched in fear. He'd forgotten to put the copy he'd made of her final letter in its hiding place when he'd finished reading it the night before. He cleared his throat, his whole body taut with dread. "Yes. It's my handwriting."

Her face darkened in anger and she crushed the paper into a ball before hurling it at him. "It appears you've been keeping secrets."

Malcolm wanted to take back his decision to tup his wife in this room.

There was hurt in her eyes and he didn't know how to repair it. He wanted to turn the clock back a quarter of an hour. To when he'd caged her against the cottage door and shown her the full extent of his insatiable hunger. Before she'd scooted back on his desk and her hand had fallen to the letter he'd carelessly left there when he'd been unable to sleep last night. The letter in his handwriting that he was certain she knew as well as her own.

She scrambled away from him, and angrily brushed the tears from her cheeks. "I should have followed my instincts when you called me Little Wren. You claimed you were echoing his sentiments, that you understood why he called me that. But it was you, all along. Sitting in a tent half a world away and pouring your heart out to me."

Her hand flew to her mouth as she choked down a ragged sob.

Mal stepped forward and raised his hand. He hoped she would take it. Because he couldn't bear it if his idiocy and secrets finally pushed her away.

"What's done cannot be undone. We are on this journey together, leannan."

"You've been lying to me from the moment we met. What am I to do with that information?"

Malcolm's face hardened in the face of her despair. What was he to do with it? How could he fix it? "You could be happy with it. That you're married to a man who worships the ground you walk upon."

Her gaze sharpened. "Does he? Wouldn't a man who feels that way have thought twice about deceiving me in such a vile manner?"

"I never intended to deceive you. I could never find the right moment to tell you."

"I was sure of one thing, Mal. That Henry loved me. How many of those letters did he author? Were you merely the transcriber? Or were the thoughts yours instead of his? The poetry and philosophy always made me wonder because it was so unlike him. But I chalked it up to our hasty marriage and concluded I simply hadn't the opportunity to plumb those depths."

"We all loved you. Not just Henry."

"All of you? Some more than others I'll warrant. Those letters nurtured the love I felt on our wedding day into something even more steadfast and true. Something I knew would withstand the test of time. Something I had faith in. Your deception undermined every decision I made about my life. It undermined my grief. As much as I suspected Henry hadn't penned the letters himself, finding out you are the one who composed them, and kept that secret from me, breaks my heart anew."

Chapter Twenty-Nine

Cece

Letter dated January 1, 1863.

Dear Husband, I had no choice but to leave your side. Though I've always suspected Henry didn't write my letters, finding out you were my correspondent somehow makes the betrayal all the more painful. There were so many times you could have told me and chose not to. I feel foolish, as if I've been victimized by the biggest con in all of Christendom. Because as I look back, I see all the signs. You had a copy of my

favorite book. You can recall every single word I wrote – nearly a decade later. You're well-read and perfectly capable of debating philosophy with an Oxford don – and winning. A part of me understands why you were compelled to hold your truths close. Another part of me feels as though you've shattered my trust in the most abominable way possible. My family is all still gathered for the holidays, and I need their advice and comfort. Please allow me this space and time to figure out what our path forward will be. I know that even now I could carry our babe, and I don't know what to do with that momentous uncertainty. Your Confounded, Conflicted, Chastised Wife.

CECE FELT AS IF everything she believed to be true had been torn asunder. This husband had been the one to write the letters that had made her widowhood bearable. This man had been the one whose words brought a smile to her face and made her feel cherished and appreciated.

Not Henry.

Mal had told her about Henry's difficulty reading and writing and she'd felt ashamed. She'd wanted her husband to appreciate poetry and stories as much as she did and when he brushed off her love of them, she resented it.

She felt guilty for the way the words he hadn't written made her feel. Because those words had only made her fall deeper in love with him. And he hadn't written them.

She'd packed up her things, blinded by tears, and banged on Moira's door in the early hours just before dawn.

Moira had flung the door open, and upon seeing her sorry state, wrapped her in a hug. "Och, lass," she'd soothed. "I don't know what he's done to upset ye so, but I'm assumin' the act is egregious enough that ye need space."

Cece could only shake her head and wipe her nose on her sleeve, her eyes red-rimmed and her chest aching from the violence of her sobs.

"I'll fetch Farley to take ye to the train station."

"I left him a note, but we both know how stubborn he can be. Make sure he knows I am not yet open to persuasion."

"I'll make sure he doesn't immediately run after you."

When Cece had confessed her stomach's aversion to traveling, Moira had packed her a bundle of ginger cookies and a flask of chamomile tea. She'd spent the entire train ride nibbling the cookies and sipping the tea and morosely gazing out the window.

When she'd knocked on the door, Vin had flung it open. Her sister had obviously been expecting someone else, because her brow creased in confusion, and she gasped.

"Why are you here instead of Scotland? Your letter telling us of your marriage sounded hopeful, if not eager."

"What does one do when everything they believe has been turned upside down and inside out? When the seams around your dignity have come unraveled and it hurts to accept the clarity the unraveling reveals?"

Arie had crowded behind Vin, and at Cece's forlorn confession she thrust her way forward. "Come, little sister." She wrapped her arm around Cece and handed her battered valise to her other dumbfounded sibling.

"Take her valise, Vin, and put it in your room. She'll need the comfort of her sisters."

As Cece settled into the familiar comfort of the worn paisley chair, Arie knelt before her and stroked her brow. "I could hear how scared you were beneath the words you wrote. But I also heard your jubilation. Just because we fall in love quickly doesn't mean it isn't true."

"It didn't feel like I was hurtling into something unknown or putting myself in the path of someone I barely knew. I must have sensed, on some level, that he was my correspondent, not Henry."

"So his deception is why you've returned home after barely a week of marriage. You can at least take comfort in the fact that the sentiments were Henry's – even if the words weren't."

"Arie, I don't know that they were Henry's sentiments. My husband was plain-speaking and had no patience for my love of poetry. He called it nothing more than balderdash once, and our quarrel lasted for two days before he apologized and begged my forgiveness."

"But he did beg your forgiveness. Because he loved you."

"My new husband claims he loves me too. That he's loved me for years."

"Isn't falling in love with someone sight unseen, through their letters, the purest form of love?" Arie sounded wistful. "There's a level of intimacy and self-awareness in our letters sometimes because it's easier to empty your thoughts onto a blank sheet of paper."

"But he fell in love with a version of me that was the young wife of a soldier. A girl full of fancy and gaiety. A girl who sang the loudest and laughed the most. Not the woman I am now."

Arie threw her arm around Cece's neck. "The woman you are now is that girl. All grown and shaped by the world that tried to break her. We all see your strength of spirit, Little Sister."

"I miss him, Arie. But he broke the fragile trust between us. Rendered it meaningless and foolish."

"It's quite apparent to me that all his actions sprang from a sense of self-preservation. He was afraid of losing you."

"If our relationship was based on a lie, he never had me. It was only an illusion."

"What you felt for him, the undercurrent all of us saw woven through your letters, that was no illusion. You should take time here to think about your marriage, but do not take too long. We must seize our happiness when we find it."

Fran was breathless as she leaned against the doorway. As if she'd run full tilt when she heard of Cece's return. "I knew that bastard had taken advantage of her," she pronounced to the room at large. "What's he done to her, Arie?"

"He's betrayed her trust and made her both look like a fool and doubt the truth of what she feels. Just the usual blunders men are wont to make because they seem to believe we're made of glass instead of steel," Arie explained.

Fran snorted. Vin came pelting into the room. "What are you snorting at, Frannie? What's her idiot husband done?"

"I think he's broken her heart," Fran surmised.

"I'll prepare a vile concoction for you to douse his tea, Little Sister," Vin fiercely promised.

Cece shook her head and smiled wanly at the three of them. "You can't do that. It's my own fault. All of the signs were there. I can't believe I didn't see them."

"All the signs of what?" Fran carefully asked.

Cece sighed. "He wrote the letters. I think Henry dictated the first few, but after that he gave Mal free rein to compose them in their entirety. All those lovely words were his – not my dead husband's."

"What are you going to do?" Fran's query was sympathetic. She'd endured a betrayal of similar magnitude. She'd thought the man who was now her husband had perished on the battlefield and returned home with a broken heart. Only to find him working at the same hospital over five years later when she accepted a teaching position at St. Thomas Hospital.

"I don't know what to do," Cece sobbed as she buried her face in her hands.

"You love him." Vin announced.

"Obviously she loves him. I've never seen her this outwardly distraught. She was like an icy statue when Henry died," Emily observed as she stepped into the room.

"That's unkind, Em," Arie chastised. "We all handle grief differently."

"What do you need from us, Cece? Do you truly want us to hunt him down and pour one of Vin's vile poisons down his throat? Or do you want us to dispatch Thaddeus and Mac for a thorough drubbing?" Fran prodded.

Cece's laugh was watery and garbled from her tears. "They'd likely receive the drubbing. He's as tall and broad as the biggest oak in the forest. And though he's a gentle giant rather than the ogre he thinks himself to be, I doubt he'd willingly submit himself to more pain than he's already endured."

"He was a soldier too. In more ways than one. Perhaps more of one than Henry ever was or ascribed to be." Arie's appraisal was full of certainty.

"He was. And he's been fighting his whole life for a place to belong. He built one and I felt like I belonged there too. By his side. Even more than I feel like I belong here."

Arie patted her hand. "You don't need to apologize. I know you've been floundering a bit. I think all of us sensed it."

"Please tell me what you think I should do," Cece pleaded.

"We can't do that, Little Sister," Fran said apologetically. "You need to figure it out for yourself."

"Fran's right," Emily agreed. "All we can do is be your soft place to land."

"Do you think he'll follow you here?" Arie probed.

Cece nodded solemnly. "I departed just before dawn – before he was awake because I knew he would have tried to persuade me to stay. I left him a note, but he'll want to hear everything face to face."

"If he does, should we welcome him, throttle him or send him away?" Fran asked.

"I vote for throttling," Vin said darkly.

"Throttling isn't the answer. It would hurt me as much as it would him. If he shows up, I'll speak to him."

Chapter Thirty

Mal

Letter dated Jan. 5, 1863.

Dearest Little Wren, There are so many things
I want to tell you. So many things I need to
say. Things you likely don't want to hear. I don't
know how many different ways there are for
a man to express his remorse or tender his
apology, but I will grovel on my knees for the
rest of my life if you'll but let me. I am sorry
my idiocy caused you pain. I am sorry I made
you doubt yourself. I never could have predict-

ed that outcome and my heart aches that you would question your own instincts and discernment. From the moment I first heard your words, you've filled my soul with light and I hope you can find the grace to forgive me for my secrets. I kept them to protect myself. If you only knew how ridiculous that notion was from the very beginning – because I never stood a chance. I fell for you when I was muddy and lonely and far from home. I've been calling you mine since that first moment– even though you weren't mine to claim until now. I'm coming to you, because I can't bear the distance between us. I refuse to accept my obstinacy has lost you forever. My heart is yours – it always has been. Your Devoted, Dejected, Desperate Husband

"I'M HERE FOR MY wife."

The two men glared at him with crossed arms.

"What makes you think she'll go with you?" The taller of the men asked. He was nearly Mal's height, though not as broad of shoulder.

"And what makes you think we'll allow her to go?" The other one challenged.

Mal hadn't left Scotland since he'd returned from war. His wife was the only woman he would ever brave ridicule for, and he needed to see her. To apologize again on his knees or prostrate himself at her feet if necessary. "She is a grown woman. Who are you to speak for her or keep us apart?"

"I am Thaddeus St. Simon." The older of the two men informed him. He had an air of quiet authority, and Mal suspected he'd served in the army as well.

"And I am Cormac Byrne," the tall man told him with a piercing gaze. "And we are her brothers by marriage. She is welcome to find shelter with either of us and our wives. Or remain here in this cottage."

"You deceived her and hurt her, and we're not inclined to let you make amends."

Mal sighed in frustration and threw his hands in the air. "We are wed. For better or for worse. Whatever has happened between us is between us. And us alone."

The one called Byrne glared at him. "You took advantage of her."

St. Simon cocked his head and tapped his finger against his chin. "He's right, Mac. We *should* stay out of it."

"Fran told me this morning it was my duty to protect her," Byrne retorted.

"Arie told me the same thing. But she also said she trusts my ability to judge his character."

Mal crossed his arms and widened his stance. "I take care of those I belong to."

St. Simon strode forward at this pronouncement and thrust out his hand. "If you'd said she belongs to you instead of the other way around I would have sent you on your way. But you just showed me you love her. Whether she knows it or not. You'll find a way to make her see it and believe it."

Byrne rolled his eyes and shrugged. "If this is a disaster, I'm blaming you."

He offered his hand as well. After Mal had heartily shaken both men's hands, with a slight grip to hint at his determination, and the fact he was clearly capable of crushing the bones beneath their skin, he gave them a curt bow.

"I am Malcolm Lockhart, formerly of Her Majesty's Fourth Dragoons."

St. Simon's gaze was suddenly full of respect. "Your company fought valiantly at Balaclava."

"We did what we could to survive."

The other man shook his head in agreement. "Aye. I've oft told my wife it is only by the grace of God and sheer luck I survived the whims of our idiotic leadership."

Byrne snorted. "Leadership whose whims meant I had to perform entirely preventable surgery."

St. Simon picked up the decanter full of amber liquid and raised it in their direction. "I think this calls for a truce. We'll not get in the way of a fellow soldier, and we know the Wainwright women, though bloody cantankerous, are worth the fight."

Mal took the tumbler from his hand and held it to the light. "Not as appealing as a Scots' brew at first sight, but 'twill do the trick."

Byrne raised a brow. " 'Tis in fact an Irish brew and will knock you on your arse, Scotsman."

The man had let the lilt of his native speech slip into the warning and Mal knew it was a challenge. "I accept."

Whisky had a way of breaking down all the walls between men and cementing their friendship. He knew Duncan would approve of his approach to wooing Cece's family.

———◦◦◦———

When Cece returned from the school, where'd she'd been helping Jess put things to rights after the pageant, Fran and Arie ambushed her in the hallway.

"Mac and Thad have cornered your husband in the study. They'll ply him with Mac's foul draught and issue warnings on your behalf," Fran warned.

"They needn't bare their teeth on my account," Cece protested. "I am perfectly capable of standing up to my husband."

Fran laughed. "Trust me, sister. They look forward to thumping their chests in an exhibition of masculine affront. It is not a hardship. I warrant the night will end with all of them well into their cups and the best of friends by morning, despite their aching heads."

Arie laughed as well. "I'll make certain I have tonic available at breakfast. Thaddeus always complains that it tastes like pig swill and then thanks me for sparing him an aching head."

Later that night, certain the men were all in an alcohol induced stupor, Cece snuck down the stairs. She wasn't precisely avoiding her husband, but she didn't think she was quite ready for the confrontation that was sure to ensue.

She'd raised herself to the tips of her toes to reach the fresh scones Arie had set on the top shelf when strong arms encircled her waist.

The pine forest, brisk air scent of him filled the room and she had to bite her lip to quell the urge to take a deep breath and inhale it, so it could rest in her lungs.

"You could grow wildflowers in the darkest parts of my soul."

His confession was hoarse and ragged.

She closed her eyes and bit her lip again, so she wouldn't turn around. He deserved to suffer for his betrayal. He didn't deserve the forgiveness she'd already secretly granted him.

"I require more groveling, Husband. Especially since I singlehandedly convinced Vin not to throttle or poison you."

"I thought Gertrude was the bloodthirsty one, not Lavinia. Isn't Gertrude the one that scribbles away at those awful penny dreadfuls?"

The blasted man remembered every single detail she'd included in her letters. The more the scent of him seeped into her and the more solid his arms felt, the harder it became to hold her body rigidly away from him. *It's too early, he doesn't deserve your acquiescence*, she reminded herself.

"I already told you in my letter, Wife. I'll grovel on my knees for the rest of my life if you'll but let me."

She sniffed – even as she wanted to melt against him. "I received no such letter, husband."

"I took the train. I've likely arrived ahead of it."

"What else did your letter say?" She needed a recounting. So she could weigh her options.

"It said that you brought light to my world," his thumb stroked a slow circle just above her navel. "It said that the last thing I ever wanted to do was make you doubt yourself or your instincts and discernment."

"Then tell me again why you did it."

"It will make me sound like a terrible friend and a man without honor," he warned as he began rubbing her hip beneath the shawl she'd flung around her shoulders.

"Tell me Mal. You must tell me if you want me to understand. If you desire my forgiveness."

"I didn't tell you because I've always thought of you as mine. Not his. Never his. I was his friend. We watched each other's backs. I loved him as a friend. And the whole time, I wanted his wife for my own. Before we ever met. Long before you showed up on my doorstep. It's why I finally sent the letters back, Wren."

"I still don't understand, Mal. Why did you send them back?"

"You want me to lay everything bare. You'll leave no stone unturned."

"If you want my forgiveness, I deserve to know the whole truth."

She felt him shudder against her back. "The nickname was my idea. Henry was always describing you to us, and one day I said you sounded like a little brown wren. He latched onto it and told me I had to include it in the letter. He said he couldn't wait to hear your sharp reply to that letter."

"I was never his Little Wren, not really." The blunt truth of his admission should have felt like an icy dagger. She was surprised to realize it felt more like the last shadow of her black garb had been cast aside.

"You were always mine. I sent the letters back because there was a kernel of hope, even though my grandfather cautioned me against ever feeling it, that returning the letters would encourage you to seek me out. That somehow those letters would be the catalyst that finally brought you to me."

"Were you shocked when your ploy bore fruit?"

"I was humbled. And shocked. And grateful. And scared witless. I didn't know how to convince you to be mine. How to make you fall in love with me. I was worried my words would give me away, so I tried to build a wall to keep you out."

Cece snorted. "If you wanted to keep me out, you shouldn't have kept staring at me like you wanted to bend me over the first available surface."

He laughed dryly. "I didn't have a choice. Especially after I caught you spying. Before that, I thought I was imagining your interest, building castles out of air. After that, I began to believe you might see past my scars."

She couldn't hold back the words even if he'd see them as a concession. "I've always seen past your scars."

"Please come home with me, wife. Let me grovel for the rest of our lives."

"What do I receive in exchange for my forgiveness? What can you promise me?"

He pressed her against the edge of the cupboard, and she knew beyond the shadow of a doubt he'd probably worn his kilt to torment her.

"I can promise to love you. To worship you. To help you fill our house with bairns and laughter."

"You love me?"

"How can you doubt it, woman? I love you more than I've ever loved anything or anyone. I need you to breathe and think and exist."

Cece bit her lip and gathered her courage again. There'd be no going back. "I love you too," she finally confessed. "I love how you're nothing but the softest lambswool beneath your gruff exterior. I love the way you bear everyone's burdens on your shoulders without complaint. When you lay one at my feet it feels like the greatest privilege on earth. I love your tears and your poet's heart. Just as you love mine."

She felt the bob of his throat against the side of her neck. "Does this mean you forgive me?"

At her imperceptible nod, he spun her around and lifted her into his arms. He whirled her about, his jade green eye glimmering with relief and happiness.

"There aren't enough bedrooms here for comfortable tupping wife. Please catch the train home with me in the morning."

Cece wanted a thorough tupping. And she wanted all the other things he'd promised as well.

⸻ ◆ ⸻

The next morning, her husband hefted her onto one of Thaddeus's coach horses and they waved farewell to a beaming throng of people. Arie and Fran had both pressed tins of ginger biscuits in their hands, and Thaddeus and Mac had promised to bring their families to Scotland soon for a visit.

The man who was no longer an ogre and the woman who'd always been a wren didn't have to wait until they reached their cottage for the reunion they'd been craving. The train car was inexplicably, blessedly empty save for the two of them, and Cece Wainwright learned there were more effective and deliciously distracting methods to deal with her queasiness than ginger biscuits.

Afterward, once they'd straightened their garments and smoothed down each other's tousled hair, she brought her husband's hand to her lips. "When I was a girl, I wished on a Yule log for a husband who would read me poetry in bed and make me tea. My Christmas wish finally came true."

"Awww, Wife," he simply murmured in return.

She could tell his heart was full, and she knew the words would spill out eventually.

Epilogue

Late Spring, 1863

MAL'S HEART WAS FULL. His home was full. So full they were both overflowing.

The stone walls of the cottage reverberated with laughter and running feet – his new nieces were whirlwinds unto themselves. Thaddeus and Cormac had held true to their promises. They'd brought their entire families to the farm on Dunkirk Lane.

This morning, he'd introduced all of them to the new lambs.

"Papa, can we please take one of them home with us?" Callie asked.

Thaddeus's twin daughters, Rissa and Callie, had developed an obsessive kinship with one of the lambs Mal was bottle-feeding.

"The lamb belongs with its brothers and sisters, girls," Arie admonished.

"Claire and Clem are home with Aunt Vinnie and Aunt Jessie right now. So why do lambs always have to be with their brothers and sisters?"

Mal grinned. His new nieces were experts at confounding what appeared to be the unassailably logical explanations. He dropped to his haunches and swept his hand over the lamb's glossy coat. "Would you like me to bring him to you once he's been weaned?"

Thaddeus threw him an exasperated look. He already had a sizeable herd of sheep. "Daughters, why can you not adopt a lamb from the herd we already have?"

"Because Papa, our lambs aren't as adorable as Sugarfoot." Rissa explained.

"Sugarfoot?" Cormac repeated in amusement. "Not exactly a name to instill fear in the hearts of other rams."

He yelped after his observation, and Mal saw his sister-in-law Fran had a pinch of fabric near his ribs clenched between her fingers. She was vigorously shaking her head.

Mal rose from his crouch, his limbs creaking, when his wife strolled into the circle of chairs they'd set up that morning in her wildflower garden. His wren had told him that confession, that she planted wildflowers in the darkest parts of his soul, was what had been the linchpin to earning her forgiveness. He'd insisted on giving her a sanctuary and this is what she'd wanted – because it reminded her of their love story and their resilience.

He held out his arm and she slipped beneath it, resting her head in the crook of his shoulder.

"Hello, Husband," she murmured and rose to kiss his cheek.

He squeezed her hip, pressing her closer to his side. "Hello, Wife."

"I have some news for you."

"Just for me?"

She flushed. "For everyone, if you don't mind sharing your joy."

Mal knew his wife wanted bairns. It was one of the reasons she'd so deeply mourned the death of her first husband, because she hadn't borne any children to keep his memory alive. They'd been enthusiastic in their love-making the last five months, and he held his breath.

Cece clapped her hands to secure everyone's attention. When they all turned toward her, she curled her hand into Mal's free one. "We have some news."

Fran and Arie both straightened in their chairs, so they looked like eager spaniels, ready to pounce.

"The brood of children here will soon have a new addition. If I've calculated correctly, our babe will be born in October."

Mal picked her up, twirling her about, his hands steady on her hips. She looped her arms around his neck and tossed her head in joyous laughter.

He set her back down and kissed the tip of her nose. "You are the light of my life," he solemnly told her and swiped the tears from his uncovered eye. Even though she'd reassured him his damaged eye was a part of him, and she loved him so much she could never be repulsed by anything that was a part of him, he kept it covered. The good doctor had advised him that leaving it uncovered and susceptible to light exposure had the potential to intensify his headaches. The doctor had said optic nerve damage to that extent was always irreversible. Mal didn't mind leaving it on. He liked it when his wife insisted on playing captive of the dread pirate lord.

Arie and Fran crowded them as soon as he set her down, enveloping her in their own embrace, and Thaddeus and Cormac thumped Mal between the shoulder blades, their own eyes misty.

This was the family he'd always wanted, and Mal could hardly believe that clinging to her letters and then returning them to her in a fit of melancholy had brought him more happiness than it felt like his heart could hold.

Note to Readers

The things I researched for Cece and Mal's story were extensive. Some of the most interesting things were how and why The Charge of the Light Brigade happened, how tweed was created, commercialized, marketed and distributed, how Crimean War widows and wounded veterans were treated in the aftermath of the conflict, sheep farming in all its glory and communal living models. I perform both primary and secondary source research, and am a huge fan and proponent of using my library's access to scholarly journals and interlibrary loans as well as sources I find on the web.

The Battle of Balaclava was immortalized in Tennyson's poem, *The Charge of the Light Brigade*. The ill-fated charge lasted a handful of minutes and was made famous because of the coverage of the war by the newspapers of the time. Around 260 men of the Light Brigade's 673 were killed or wounded, and 475 horses were lost. Total British casualties were around 615. At least 45 British soldiers were captured – all due to miscommunication between commanding officers. The British National Army Museum offers a succinctly brutal account of the officer ineptitude that led to the tragedy.

The tweed industry became a huge enterprise in the Scottish Lowlands in the early eighteenth century, and the town of Galashiels, where Cece departs the train, was one of its hubs. At its height, there were more than two dozen tweed manufactories. The way mid-19th century wool was gathered, carded, dyed and spun was changing rapidly and there were dozens of steps to bring it to market. Galashiels was especially notable for producing "Border Blue" textiles and checked patterns (what we would call houndstooth designs today). If you'd like to read more about the Scottish wool industry, there are some incredible resources, including a fascinating web accessible overview on Wilderness Scotland.

Until the Crimean War, there was truly no such thing in England as a widow's pension. In the wake of the Crimean War, the Patriotic Fund was established, overseen by Prince Albert. There were many restrictions on the disbursement of these funds, however, and they were not a long-term solution. The funds were insufficient to support a woman left with children to manage as well. Similarly, the provision for soldiers who served less than five years, and were discharged because of the end of the conflict or because of wounds, was egregiously, woefully inadequate.

The history of sheep farming in Scotland is fascinating. Especially in the Lowlands. There is a history of displacement of traditional farming that has been captured in much Highland literature, but not many stories have addressed the changes the introduction of large-scale wool production brought to the Lowlands. One of the most significant changes was the introduction of non-native breeds. The black-faced, or "dun" sheep was likely developed on the Anglo-Scottish border before the thirteenth century. There are monastery records from that time of the collection and export of its wool to mainland Europe. This breed has several strains but the traits they share are what make them ideal for the brushy hillsides and rugged terrain of the Scottish hills. Efforts to displace it completely with breeds such as the Cheviot were met with climactic challenges. In 1989 their wool accounted for nearly 40% of the total wool production of Scotland and one twelfth the wool production of the United Kingdom.

Communal living was at the height of the experimental stage in the mid-nineteenth century. Communities such as the Shakers embraced the idea of sharing resources and were proponents of self-sufficiency and industriousness.

Acknowledgements

First and always – to my husband Anthony. Who lets me read aloud all the scenes I should have used Barbie and Ken dolls to choreograph. He's not shy about letting me know if he thinks what I'm describing is anatomically or acrobatically challenging or impossible. He also makes sure the coffee pot is brimming with much needed fuel and the wine carafe is present when I buckle down to write those Barbie and Ken scenes. Without his cinnamon roll caretaking heart, finding the time to write would be especially challenging.

To my beta readers – *Charlotte, Jen, Iesha, Tracy and Whitney.* Your insight and encouragement and enthusiasm kept me motivated during the writing of Cece & Mal's story!

To the *Historical Romance Collab Group* chat members on Instagram – this group of readers and writers has been a lifeline of wisdom and support! Thank you to Gloria for setting it up and giving so many historical romance writers a place to commiserate, collaborate and convene.

To all the members of my historical romance ARC Team, *Cravats and Crinolines*, for taking a chance on my words and my stories- even if the genre was new to them.

A special shoutout to five readers that literally dropped everything when they received the ARC of this book and read it in less than 24hours – *Heather, Iesha, Maria, Raeann and Whitney.*

About the author

Andrea has been reading historical romance since she purloined her aunt's copy of Ashes in the Wind in 1985. She's endlessly fascinated by the minutiae of history, and loves to delve into obscure topics in the name of research. She loves to write about ordinary men and women who experience the extraordinary experience of falling in love.

Cece Wainwright's Christmas Wish is the third book in the Wainwright Sisters series. You can read *When Araminta Greaves Traded Her Dignity for Bliss* and *How Frances Wainwright Learned to Love* on Amazon or Kobo, or purchase paperback copies from all major retail platforms.

You can also join Andrea's historical romance Facebook group, Cravats and Crinolines, by searching for the public profile, or subscribe to her newsletter via her website at andreajenelleromance.com

Andrea also writes steamy, small town contemporary romance (The Willow Creek series), urban fantasy romance (The Sons & Daughters of Lir series), and has several audiobooks available from Audible and iTunes.

If you'd like to borrow any of the Willow Creek or Sons & Daughters of Lir books from your local library, let your librarian know the books can be stocked via Hoopla or Overdrive (Libby).